To Paris with Love:

A Family Business Novel

To Paris with Love:
A Family Business Novel

Carl Weber
and Eric Pete

www.urbanbooks.net

Urban Books, LLC
97 N18th Street
Wyandanch, NY 11798

ISBN 13: 978-1-60162-571-7
ISBN 10: 1-60162-571-5

First Hardcover Printing December 2013
Printed in the United States of America

10 9 8 7 6 5 4 3 2 1

Distributed by Kensington Publishing Corp.
Submit Wholesale Orders to:
Kensington Publishing Corp.
C/O Penguin Group (USA) Inc.
Attention: Order Processing
405 Murray Hill Parkway
East Rutherford, NJ 07073-2316
Phone: 1-800-526-0275
Fax: 1-800-227-9604

Acknowledgments

I just want to thank my family, both old and new (crazy, huh?), as well as friends and readers for all their support over this decade in the business. I am appreciative and humbled by the love I've felt from all of you and am so glad you've found a place in your heart for my stories.

Also, special thanks to my co-author Carl Weber for his insight and advice on this journey that is *The Family Business* as well into the industry as a whole. You're at the top of your game, bro.

Portia Cannon, what can I say? Having a tireless champion like you in my corner is invaluable. A toast to these creations blessing the big screen soon.

I'll show some brevity as I have words to type, sentences to construct and ideas to form, so see you next time. Hope Paris n company have your mouths hanging open by the time you finish.

More to come, people. More to come.

Can't stop. Won't stop. Believe that.

-Eric

@IAmEricPete

Acknowledgments

I would like to acknowledge all of my great fans for supporting *The Family Business* series, I hope you are all looking forward to the TV show.

Dedication

This book is dedicated to the Dumpson family
for many years of love, friendship and support.

Prologue

Now

After almost nine hours in the air, the pilot announced that we would be descending into Nice Cote d'Azur Airport. One of the benefits of first-class international air travel is that I had slept the entire plane ride in comfort. My seat unfolded into a bed where I stretched out and dozed like a baby. Coming to Europe to celebrate my girl's wedding meant spending all my time partying. The next time I expected a full night's sleep was the day I would be boarding a flight back to New York. Hell, being off Daddy's radar for the first time in over a year meant I could finally go back to being me, Paris "The Rich Bitch" Duncan. I loved my son Jordan more than anything in the world but damn if I didn't feel like I was freed from a Turkish prison. The little rug rat barely gave me any breathing space. I couldn't begin to tell you how good it was to be free from him and his shitty diapers for two weeks. I intended to use every single minute.

I pulled out my compact and reapplied eyeliner and lip gloss. Damn, I looked fine if I did say so myself. Of course all I had to do was glance to my left where the chubby older man was staring at my lip gloss as if he wished it were a part of his anatomy. I gave him a little extra show when I stood up. As soon as I entered the airport baggage area, a voice stopped me in my tracks.

"Bitch!" she screamed at me, all blond hair, Louis accessories, and badass Lanvin dress.

"Who you callin' a bitch!" I hollered back, flaunting in my Chloe top, J Brand Jeans, Balenciaga shoes, and Céline bag. I dropped my bags as we raced into each other's arms, screaming and shouting, hugging on each other for dear life. Irena Sokolov was my girl from back at Chi's Finishing School. She came from one of the richest Russian families and the fact that she looked like a *Sports Illustrated* swimsuit model didn't hurt her popularity. But she was down and we had each other's back from day one. I really wasn't one to hang with women but she was as close to a girlfriend as I had after my brother Rio.

"Girl, I missed you," Irena shouted.

"All day long," I answered her.

A fully attired chauffeur stepped up, waiting for our love fest to break. "Ma'am, your luggage," he addressed me.

"My luggage looks like this." I picked up the burgundy carry-on I'd brought with me.

"Yes, ma'am," he answered before heading to the baggage carousel.

"Don't tell me that's the Bottega Veneta alligator?" Irena didn't bother to hide her envy.

"Yes." I smiled, happy she knew that I still knew how to hold it down.

"It was so limited that, by the time I tried to buy a set, it was sold out."

"Girl, we gonna have to get our shop on." We high-fived each other, laughing like two devilish children. Suddenly I felt my entire body tense up, and my jaw dropped open in complete shock as I spotted the one person I never expected to see again. "Oh, shit."

"What?" Irena put a hand on my arm, following my line of vision until she too locked on the beautiful Persian woman. "Who is that?"

"That, my Russian friend, is the bitch who stole my life." I spat the words out, anxious to remove the vile taste they left in my mouth.

"What are you talking about?" Irena's accent became heavier. "Who is she?"

"Her name is Nadja and she's the one who made Paris Duncan into the cold-hearted bitch I am today." I seethed as I watched her head into the ladies' room. Nadja had cost me everything and the fact that she was able to walk around breathing seemed like the ultimate betrayal.

"She's beautiful, I know that."

"Don't let her good looks and her sunny disposition fool you. That chick is as cold-hearted as a Siberian winter."

"What do you mean by that?" I could hear Irena on edge waiting for the real story.

"If it wasn't for her, my life would be completely different right now. It's because of her that I may never ever be capable of loving again." I sighed, the harsh reality of what had gone down between Nadja and me exhausted me and, if I was being honest, it still hurt. My girl must have seen it in my eyes because she led me over to a set of chairs.

"Your bags aren't even on the conveyor belt yet. So you got to tell me what the hell you're talking about."

"All right, but you betta promise to keep my secret."

"I am Russian. I was born to keep secrets," Irena answered as she waited for my story to begin.

Paris

1

My first three years at school taught me more about life than I could ever begin to learn in the outside world. I had sopped up those lessons like a hungry bitch going in on a plate of biscuits and gravy. And now with graduation right around the corner, I would be the student awarded the grand prize for most accomplished. That's if I got to graduate because bitches like this one kept challenging my last nerves.

I tightened my grip around her neck, pulling her into a headlock. She whipped around and flipped me over her head onto the ground. In seconds I was up on my feet, crouching like a caged animal ready to strike again. Her hand shot out, coming down on my shoulder. The pain shot through me but there was no way I'd let her be the first one to finally take me down. I had an uncontested track record of wins. I kicked her in the solar plexus and kneed her in the jaw, causing three of her teeth to fall to the ground. I grabbed her in a bear hold, bending her arm behind her back until her short gasping breaths grew almost inaudible, making her drop the weapon at my feet. Still holding on to her I slid my hand to the floor and retrieved the Glock 9.

"*Ggamdungi,*" she spat the words at me.

"*Shang nyun, Sheba-nom!*" I responded then jerked her arm harder, causing her to squirm in pain.

"Fuck you too, bitch!" She spat the words at me.

"Oh, so now you speak English? 'Cause I prefer to be called a beeyotch in English and not your slanty-eyed language!" I schooled her. Although my orders were not to cause physical harm, I wasn't feeling particularly generous. Last fool to use the N-word on me couldn't walk for a week and will probably never be able to impregnate a woman. I swiftly clocked her on the side of the head.

"*Paris!*" Yosef, my instructor, a former Israeli rebel fighter, grabbed me tightly from behind, his fingertips boring into my shoulder blades. The pain forced me to let go of Jae Kim, who fell in a heap on the ground and passed out. She probably fainted at the sight of her missing teeth.

A group of students gathered nearby, ecstatic to watch the spectacle.

"Knocked her the fuck out!"

I heard two palms slap together in a high five.

"Bam! Just like that."

"Damn! I told her not to mess with Paris," I heard one girl say as Jae Kim stirred near her bloody teeth.

"I wouldn't. Chick is fuckin' lethal," another added, then received a rousing round of agreement from the other girls.

It occurred to me that this would be a good time to practice passivity and restraint but my head and my badass attitude were out of alignment with my reality. *Fuck him, her, and the rest of these motherfuckers. I won this exercise fair and square.*

"I won!" I yelled out. There was no way they were going to mess up my record.

"Why do you do these things?" Yosef, the gorgeous six foot four inch, 240-pound Israeli instructor admonished me. He smacked me hard on the neck. "How many times do I have to speak to you about your inability to follow orders? Have you lost your fucking mind? Look what you've done."

I could hear the sound of my own heavy breathing as I tried to contain myself so that I could respond appropriately instead of what I really wanted to do, which was curse his ass out.

Yosef wasn't much older than us but he was the one person in the school who I truly respected. Not only was he built like a Mack truck but he was also capable of killing you with his bare hands without giving it much thought. I knew better than to piss him off too much because he could make your death look like an accident. It would take me years to know all of his secrets, but during our "private" lessons I made sure to get extra instruction, which somehow turned intimate over the past year. He wasn't the first man I'd ever slept with; however, he was the only one who put fear in my heart. As much as I pretended to hate, it I found it sexy as hell. Most men who acted all tough got the pussy and promptly turned into pussies. But not him; he kept sex and work separate and right at this moment he was all business, which basically meant I was fucked because I'd never seen him this upset.

"You need to gather your things and get to the headmistress office," he said as he led me through the tunnel that connected to the catacombs and back into the main building. It was the perfect place to flip this shit in my favor. I darted ahead of him, stopping and blocking his path.

"Yosef, she started it," I whined, flirting with him. He held up one finger, silencing me. Damn, even deep in the shit he made me get all moist and turned on. I leaned closer to him, brushing my lips against his neck.

"Please."

"Paris, you are such a hellion!" he snapped at me.

"Isn't that what you like about me?" I slid my hand over the outline of his penis. It quickly hardened under my touch. "Instead of sending me to the office wouldn't you prefer me putting my lips on this?" I rubbed his growing dick, motivating him to cave.

An hour later I found myself sitting in front of the headmistress, Madame Joan Marie, as she gave me her version of a come-to-Jesus talking-to. Yosef got the goods and still sold me out.

"Do you realize what you have done? Ms. Kim is from one of our most important families in South Korea. Imagine the conversation I will be having when her father arrives today.

Do you want to explain to him why his daughter needs extensive oral surgery?"

"No, Madame," I answered submissively.

"Young lady, you are among the best and brightest students to ever cross the threshold of our establishment," she continued in her thick French accent. "Rarely have I gleamed such raw potential in a person your age but you are also your own worst enemy. You act as if rules only apply to others. And no matter how many times I've talked, you continue to disobey orders and protocol and now you have proven to be a danger to others."

"Madame, I am so sorry for my behavior. It really was an accident," I lied, trying to sound as apologetic as possible so I could be on my way. I was ready for my vacation to begin.

"Mademoiselle Duncan, I believe that you believe that your apology is genuine. Then again, you always sound sincere after you've crossed a line. Unfortunately, the very next moment you rush headfirst into more conflict. I cannot allow you to continue to remain a hazard to the other students and to yourself."

She stood back, studying me. I tried to appear as vulnerable and defenseless as possible. If only this had been a man I'd have talked my way out of it already, but women didn't always get my charm. Finally she shook her head, resigned. "I must contact your father."

My bad attitude deflated and her words set off loud, scary bells in my head. *Danger! Danger!* "Nooooo!" The panic rang out in my voice. Anything but that. My father would have my head and that would only be the beginning of my demise. "I promise I will change. Please give me another chance to make you proud. To make my father proud. Please, Madame," I begged and pleaded. This time I meant every word because I had never been more desperate. If my dad knew that I was over here in Switzerland showing my ass and messing with his name it would be bad.

"You will have to change both your behavior and your attitude," she continued.

"I will. I promise."

"I sincerely hope that my decision to give you one more chance will not be wasted."

"No, Madame." I leaned up and gave her a quick squeeze, something you just didn't do with these Nordic types. She looked shocked. Shit, I would have dropped to my knees and had my first try at cunnilingus if it would have prevented her from calling my father.

"Good! Now we are done with this unpleasant conversation." She opened the door and led me into her outer office, where a group of students were gathered in front of the fire.

I joined her, partaking in the roaring flames, tapping my foot on the wooden floorboards beside my matching Louis Vuitton luggage. I threw on my designer sunglasses and quarter-length fur despite the heat being produced by the fireplace. Felt good to be out of my school uniform, so I bit my tongue and kept my impatience to myself while the jealous hoes who were my classmates looked on. They'd never be as fly as me and they knew it. Nor would they know how close I came to being a former student.

Psh . . . finishing school.

Luckily, my electives—while not my raison d'être, but my reason for being here—were da bomb dot com.

"Mademoiselle Duncan, you will be sure to enjoy yourself back home in the U.S., no?" Madame Joan Marie asked as she kissed me on both cheeks. Right before removing my sunglasses and placing them back in my hand. Of course, she meant the opposite of what she and her big-ass smile said. You had to look beyond that and into those tiny, cold eyes of hers. She wanted me to behave myself back home. Rein a bitch in 'n' shit.

"Oh, I will most definitely enjoy myself," I replied, meaning exactly what I motherfuckin' said. Couldn't wait to get out of here and back in the NYC, specifically Jamaica Queens where my family lived and ran things like motherfuckin' bosses. Yeah. To sleep in my own bed, eat some less bougie food, and see my fam would be all to the good.

Oh, yeah. And some good American dick, too. Don't get me wrong. These Euros could eat some pussy like nobody's business, but I missed the rhythm real niggas had back home when they were layin' it down.

But that could come later. For now, I really missed my family. And that was most important in this fucked-up world.

Family.

There was my daddy, Lavernius Duncan, who everybody called LC, head of Duncan Motors, the largest African American–owned car dealership chain in the tri-state area. My beloved moms, Chippy, had his back and was the rock of the family. Held it down for me and my four brothers: Junior, the big diesel one who was loveable as fuck; Vegas, the heart of the family whom I would die for; Orlando, the calculating one whom I would have to think about dying for; and Rio, my wild and crazy twin who I lived for. Oh, and my older sister London was part of the family too, but the less said about her the better. She and her lawyer husband, Harris, already thought their shit didn't stink, *but now that she was pregnant?* Fawk. Would never hear the end of it. Was almost enough to make me want to remain in Europe over break.

Almost.

Once I touched down back home, I'd just have to be civil. Steer clear of her, Harris, and the demon spawn in her gut.

Besides, it was only a month after all. Then back here to complete my schooling.

"Is your family sending a car for you, Mademoiselle Duncan? Or will you need transportation arranged?" Madame Joan Marie asked before she turned her attention to the next departing student, this Croatian bitch with bad skin. Madame Joan Marie liked everything to run with Swiss precision. And when it didn't, heads rolled.

The text I'd been waiting for came through on my phone, leading me to tune her ass out momentarily.

"No, Madame. My ride is here now," I said as I looked up at her, flashing my first genuine smile of the day.

"Very well, mademoiselle. Adieu," she commented as she took a slight bow and gracefully stepped aside. Funny that she never referred to me by my first name. Probably thought being named Paris, after a city, was *ghetto* or sumthin'. But not ghetto enough to refuse our money.

Had been counting down all week to this moment. So with a deep sigh of relief, I stepped, luggage in hand, toward the thick reinforced doors strong enough to survive a bomb blast. The inconspicuous school in this town, not far from the border with France, was on a lake bearing the same name. Until my parents sent me here to Neuchâtel, I only knew of this town for the Swiss chocolates they sold in America.

But my school was no Willy Wonka experience. No Oompa-Loompas around here. And creepy men in top hats and coats would get got.

Place was originally a hospital until, back in the late 1800s, it was converted into a school for the betterment and civility of young ladies like me whose parents had the money and desire to have them molded into so much more.

Leaving the toasty confines, I pulled my fur close to shield me from the cold rush of air on a sunny day. Just as the text said, a car horn to my right alerted me to the all-black Citroën C6 rolling in my direction down the slightly uneven Rue du Pommier. If I knew my daddy, he probably had it armored. I couldn't contain myself and waved frantically, dropping the poise and polish drummed into my head twenty-four seven over the past year. I hoped LC had made the trip across the ocean to surprise me. I couldn't wait to show him the new me I'd become and what I'd learned from my instructors.

Standing in the cold air I spotted Jae Kim being comforted by her fine-ass British hotty, who attended the male equivalent to our school in the next town. We exchanged bitter, hostile glares when I noticed him checking me out. Instead of continuing down the steps I stopped for a moment and a smile spread across my lips. When I finally approached them on the first landing of the steps I saw a look of confusion flutter across her face.

"Bye, Jae. Have a great spring break," I offered in my most conciliatory voice. "You heading back to Korea?"

"Don't you speak to me, you fucking bitch!" She glared then turned her back to me to punctuate her seriousness. But he shot me an apologetic smile. I stepped to him.

"If you didn't have such shitty taste in women I'd consider giving you some." I reached into my pocket and handed him a card with my phone number on it. "Just in case your taste improves," I finished, the sounds of them arguing followed me down the stairs.

When the sedan rolled to a stop in front of the school, I didn't wait for the driver to exit. Instead, I scrambled down the remaining brick steps and up to the car window where I tapped on it with my fingernails. Through the tint, I could make out a silhouette that had to be my daddy's.

As the passenger lowered the window, the driver exited and went about gathering my bags to place in the trunk.

"Hello, Paris," the voice said, taking me aback that it wasn't my daddy's.

"Orlando," I muttered dryly at the recognition of my brother, clad in a navy blue suit with shiny O.D. cufflinks that adorned his crisp white cuffs. "Where's Daddy?" I asked as he discarded a cigarette out the window while blowing smoke out his nose. Orlando was trying too hard to fit in with the cool and the chic out here. He had a woman seated on the side of him who looked to be Italian and probably didn't speak a lick of English. I guessed it was a high-priced whore whom he'd arranged to spend time with. I paid her no mind.

"Well, hello to you too," he replied with a grin certainly meant to piss me off.

"What do you want?" I asked my brother as the driver slammed the Citroën's trunk shut then opened Orlando's door for him. Bitch was getting cold and they wanted to play games. As Orlando exited, he allowed the driver to place his wool overcoat on him like he was a stone-cold pimp. The brunette stayed inside the car, never daring to look at me.

"C'mon, take a walk with me," Orlando said with a motion of his head.

The Citroën slowly trailed us in the distance as me and my brother strode along the lake on Quai Phillippe-Gaudet. As a little Smart car buzzed by, even I had to admire the postcard beauty of this town. But this was cutting into my free time and Orlando wouldn't come all the way here just to take a stroll with me.

"Why aren't we on a G5 by now?" I pressed Orlando who'd been much too quiet.

"Because you're not going back home."

"Huh?" I said, stopping dead in my tracks. "Oh, that's some serious bullshit!"

"At least not this time," he added, taking two more steps before looking back at me. "You know London's at the end of her pregnancy?" he said as both of us resumed walking, albeit much slower this time.

"Yeah. So?" I spat out, irritated at Orlando's mention of my older sister.

"Your sister's having some health issues, Paris. LC wants you to wait. Just stay away for a little while longer. Until the baby's delivered. Every time somebody mentions your name it's like her blood pressure spikes or something. You can see it in her eyes. Pop knows how y'all two are when you're together."

"London's still upset about that ex of hers? Damn. That didn't mean shit and I was younger back then. 'Sides, she should be thanking me for saving her from his lame ass."

"No. It's not just London's issue with you," he said, pausing to ensure our car was still trailing us. His disdain and disgust for that whole mess back when I'd visited London in college, especially my part in it, still showed. "Things are also unsettled over the stuff that went down with Vegas." He mentioned my second-favorite brother and the family peacekeeper. "Delicate times."

"And you're just swooping in to take over for the throne, ain't ya?"

"Your feelings for me aside, you need to shut the fuck up and listen," Orlando growled. "Instead of coming home this trip, we want you to stay in Europe. Got a resort for you in Spain. Five stars . . . just how you like. Sun and fun, so it's right up your alley. But try to stay low-key. We have enemies all over so we don't need you broadcasting who you are. Reservations are under 'Paris Wimberley.'"

"Spain, huh? And if I choose to go home instead?" I pushed, challenging my older brother. Fuck. I'd already planned my first twenty-four hours back home. Me and Rio were gonna get fucked up, go clubbin', then compare notes on the men we'd selected for the night. Thoughts of spring break were what got me through these last few months. But now?

"This was LC's decision. So he would be very disappointed in you," Orlando replied, meaning Daddy would go ape shit and cut off my funds. Or worse. "Any more smart aleck questions?" my brother added after gauging the look of fear on my face.

"Yeah."

"What now?" he said gruffly as he motioned our car over to pick us up.

"Can I get a new wardrobe?" I asked, batting my eyelashes.

Orlando frowned, consternation etched on his face as he no doubt wanted to object. "No! You've supported the rising stock prices for high-end designers long enough. Deal with it," he bellowed.

"Then you wouldn't mind me telling LC how you're spending your money on this trip . . . and at home. At least I have some material shit to show for my money. All you have are memories of nasty cum stains on some fake-ass titties bought by the last john," I said, setting his ass straight.

Niles

2

I had been gambling most of the night and although I was up I hadn't made a move. Yet. My biggest opponent at the table also happened to be the world's biggest asshole.

"What are you gonna do with that?" He slammed down his card, making a big show. His name was Jeffrey, another useless trustafarian. His father was a billionaire, which accounted for his snobby, elitist arrogance. I'd known him for a couple of years. Since I moved from London to Barcelona. "What? What you gonna do?" He slid a hand down the arm of his incredibly hot girlfriend. I'd seen her with him recently and couldn't figure out how he'd managed to land her. If I were a chick there wouldn't be enough money in the world to waste my time with him.

"Call." I nodded to the dealer. Tonight was one of those when I would have preferred to fly under the radar but I couldn't help but fuck with this arrogant prick.

"Why the hell you gonna call? You see my cards I got showing," he bragged, gesturing to the hand in front of him. The dealer laid down the perfect card for me. Lady Luck was definitely on my side. I revealed my hand: a flush.

"You fucking cheated!" He pushed up in my face. "What you gonna do?"

"I'm gonna take all your money and then I'm gonna take your girl upstairs and fuck the shit out of her!"

A look of shock colored her face a bright red.

"Whoa!" People reacted all around like cattle, one feeding off the next, all in awe like a group of kids on the schoolyard itching for a brawl.

"What the fuck you say?" Jeffrey reached into his waistband and pulled out a gun. The room swelled in a collective gasp. I shook my head slightly, amused at his misguided brazenness. This was not his best move. Instead of retreating I took a step toward him, pressing my chest against his weapon.

"You have any idea how many problems you gonna have if you shoot me?" I said. It was obvious that my words unbalanced him. I could see it on his face. This wasn't how he expected things to go down. "All of your daddy's money will be no match for the wrath that will rain down on you. Not to mention the lengthy prison sentence you're going to serve for shooting an unarmed man in a room full of witnesses. Something tells me you'd be a popular bitch in prison."

He swiveled as if noticing the crowd for the first time.

"*Put the gun down now!*" I demanded.

He wavered for a minute, trying to decide which was more important: his ego or his future. "You're not worth it," he snarled, lowering his gun.

I looked past him and addressed his woman. "You want to be with this loser, who is obviously all talk and no action?" I faced him again. "You pull out a piece then you should at least use it." Then I smiled at her. "Or do you wanna be with a real man?" I waited for our eyes to lock before I softly said, "I apologize for my earlier comment. I lied. I'm not going to fuck the shit out of you. I'm going to make sweet love to you like a real man." Her face spread into a smile and she took a step away from him, moving in my direction.

"What the fuck?" Jeffrey grabbed her arm possessively. She gave him an ice-cold stare and shook his hand off of her. I stepped in between them, ready to take him down.

"There is no need for that. I guess we all knew I was leaving with you," she said, placing her hand into mine. I removed my jacket, threw it on the card table, and filled it with the winning chips less the ones I handed the dealer. I then tied my jacket up like a satchel, making sure it held all my winnings.

"Ready?" I grabbed her hand again and walked toward the exit. We could hear Jeffrey in the background taking stabs to regain his dignity but it was way too late for that.

Rio

3

By the time my parents entered the back room at Peter Luger's, our family's favorite restaurant, I had already downed my first martini and was quickly moving through my second. I stood up to greet my 'rents; the liquid courage coursing through my veins helped me to look normal and not scared shitless. The old-school waiter rushed over and affectionately greeted LC and Chippy, having served them for decades.

"Champagne. Bring us your very best!" LC shouted, beaming down at me.

"Dad, it's okay. I'm already drinking vodka. Not good to mix alcohols."

"Honey, it's not every day you insist we have a private dinner." My moms beamed at me. This was clearly going to be a whole hell of a lot harder than I thought.

"Can I get another one of these?" I motioned to the waiter before downing my drink.

"Yes, son. This is a very big deal. When you got into Morehouse your mother and I were very proud of you, especially when you agreed that law school was your plan. Your mother and I couldn't help it so we checked your mail and saw that you got into every Ivy you chose plus a few Big Ten. Don't keep us waiting. Which one do you think you're going to choose?" LC, who normally kept his applause to a minimum when it came to his children's accomplishments, was damn near jumping out of his seat. An Ivy League law degree was simply as good as it got in his opinion. What parent didn't welcome the chance to brag to their friends about their offspring?

I steeled myself. There was really no point in delaying the unpleasant and inevitable. "Mom, Dad, we can talk about school next. First, there is something I really need to say to you," I started.

"Well, get on with it!" LC barked, anxious to get back to discussing my continuing education. "The more good news the better!"

"I'm gay!" I announced as if I were saying "ta-da!" I stared at the undisguised shocked expressions on their faces.

"What the hell? Oh, no, no, that's not possible!" my dad sputtered.

"Rio, you've always dated such nice girls," my mother chimed in.

"Like that pretty brown-skinned girl you brought home last summer? You two seemed close to me," he questioned.

"Erika is just a friend."

"Relationships that begin with friendship are often the best ones," my mom said, attempting to comfort my father.

"Look, I knew that this was going to be difficult for you but I can't help who I am." I spoke calmly even though I felt my voice shaking.

"This is bullshit! Whatever bored rich kid phase you're going through, get over it! No son of mine is becoming some man's little bitch." LC sneered at me.

The waiter couldn't have had worse timing as he chose that moment to present a rare and expensive bottle of celebratory bubbly. LC's cold stare convinced him to keep it moving. He grabbed the bottle and hurried away.

All my life my father had run roughshod over us children. He controlled all aspects of our lives. If our friends failed to measure up to his standards, he would let us know. If our hobbies weren't what he expected, he would make us stop. He even handpicked our respectable careers. Whatever we wanted to do or became second to what he expected and planned for us. Sure he made us think we had some say in it but when he pushed us in a general direction we all just went.

But my sexuality wasn't up to him and now that I had come out of the closet there was no way I would allow myself to be shoved back into the darkness in order to please the great LC Duncan. I was going to control this part of my life whether he liked it or not.

"Honey, this is upsetting to your father," my mother, ever the good cop, said sweetly as she leaned in close to me. It was her way of telling me to dial it back. "Son, this isn't a good time to have this conversation."

"Really? So that means that there is actually a good time?" I challenged her.

"How about that girl you went away with last spring break?" Dad questioned, sorting through his mental Rolodex for proof that I was absolutely straight like my brothers, Junior, Vegas, and Orlando.

"Alexandra was my beard. She liked girls and I liked guys so we were the perfect match. I could fly under the radar and so could she. Eventually she found a girlfriend and came out to her parents. Since her parents were so loving and supportive, she encouraged me to do the same." I dropped the words on the table like an avalanche. Undeniable. Heavy. I was hoping that my parents would get the hint and accept my declaration like Alexandra's parents. If they didn't, well, then I knew the damage would be permanent.

"This is the end of this conversation! We are not going to talk about it again. Ever!" my father finished, waving the waiter over. My mother patted my hand, her attempt at comforting me. He stared over at my mother.

"Did you know?" His voice bellowed through the room accusingly.

"I suspected," my mother admitted. She caught the look of shock on my face. I thought I'd had everybody fooled. Especially my parents.

"How could I not? When Paris got that Barbie Dreamhouse Rio cried until I told him that he could share it. He always hated getting dirty the way our other boys did and . . ." She turned to me. "You're still the only one that ever notices when I change my hairstyle."

"That doesn't mean anything!" My father's voice brought me back to this fucked-up reality in front of me. "You have coddled and babied him so much he's completely confused about what it means to be a man!" he accused my mother.

"LC!" Chippy's tone sounded like a warning bell.

"She didn't make me gay. I was born like this. I'm gay! G-a-y."

"No son of mine is going to be gay and that's final!" He stood up and motioned to the waiter. "Check!" he demanded from the confused server.

"Sir, your steak is being plated."

"I've lost my appetite." He shot a look across the table at me but I was too pissed and fortified with alcohol to back down from my father's wrath. "I'll have it wrapped to go." The waiter hurried away.

"This is 2010, Dad. It's okay to be gay!" I tried to reason with him.

"Not to me it isn't," my father snarled. He motioned to my mother to handle the check and bolted out the restaurant in a hurry.

"Baby, give him some time. Your father is from a different era." My mother tried to soothe my hurt feelings.

"Well, he better start living in this era. I am not going to pretend anymore because he's afraid of what his homophobic friends are going to think."

She stared at me. She really was one of the best mothers in the world but her Achilles heel had always been my father. We both knew that it would be a cold day in hell before he embraced my homosexuality. I decided right then and there it would have to be his problem. I had a life to live and, dammit, I was going to do just that.

Paris

4

"Señorita Wimberly?" the sophisticated and tanned man behind the counter asked as I checked in at the Hoteles Santos Las Arenas Balneario Resort. I didn't know if I was just paranoid but he sounded like even he didn't believe it was my last name. This incognito shit was messing with me, I didn't do low profile well. You know I came out my moms' va-jay-jay high profile.

I surveyed the lobby, which reminded me of a Roman palace with its many white marble columns.

"*Si*," I replied with a wink, wishing I knew more than my New York Spanglish from home. Or at least learned more from Roberto, the head of security at my school. But I was too busy giving him a mouthful of these titties in exchange for allowing me to occasionally sneak out to score some weed.

After Orlando dumped his floozy and agreed to take me shopping in the city for which I was named, it was a short flight with my new wardrobe on Air Europa from Charles de Gaulle into Valencia's Manises Airport. Just like Orlando's sorry ass to send me here on a commercial airline when nearby Majorca or Ibiza were more my kind of fun. But at least I had new clothes and was in a beautiful hotel on the coast. Besides, if I didn't find anything to get into here I could arrange the jaunt out to those islands in the Balearic Sea on my own.

But for now I was gonna be a good girl and stay low-key. For Daddy.

The bellman rolled my luggage onto the elevator for the trip up to my fourth-floor suite. Before the door fully closed, two others squeezed in. A tall, sexy motherfucker with high cheekbones, black wavy hair, and cream-colored skin was the main course. I couldn't tell if he was a local or something more exotic. Whatever the case, he carried on effortlessly in Spanish with some slutty, underdressed bitch. A lot of boobs and not much ass. She hung on his every word. I tried ignoring the good time they were having by admiring the tile beneath my feet. Oh, and my new shoes, too; Lanvin.

Still, I couldn't help myself and he caught me looking his way side-eye. Before I could turn away and play it off, he smiled at me.

Not wanting to give him the satisfaction, I rolled my eyes from behind my sunglasses. "Señor, your floor?" my bellman asked as we were already heading up.

"*Sí. Quatro,*" he agreed when he saw the button was already pushed.

Shit. We were on the same floor.

Here he was acting like his company was the greatest thing on Earth or sumthin'. Hoped they kept all that chattering down when they made it to their room.

"Hello. Are you American?" he asked me in perfect English. Not the shit I used, but the shit from like fuckin' England or sumthin'.

"*Sí.* I mean . . . yes," I replied as I fumbled along

"First time?"

"*Excuse you?*"

"First time to Valencia?" he asked for further clarification, making me feel more foolish.

"Yeah," I said, not giving much energy. "Somewhere new after Cannes, Monaco, and Zurich all the time," I was trying to floss with someone obviously more worldly than me. But a bitch wasn't a stranger to caviar, yachts, 'n' shit either.

The doors opened on our floor. Allowing his lady to exit first, he held the doors for the bellman and me.

"Oh. I see. Those are quite some nice locales," he said as I came oh-so-close before exiting the elevator. "Well, maybe I'll see you around then. The beaches here are wonderful."

"Yeah. I see," I commented with a backward glance. Damn. Had big feet, too. "Excuse me, *señorita,*" I purred as I walked right between the two of them. My bellman was more polite than me, rolling my luggage around them instead. Whatever shit she talked about me in Spanish, I couldn't care less.

As the door to my suite was opened for me, the smooth talker was entering his suite on the opposite end of the hallway. He caught me looking again and gave me a slight nod and a mischievous grin. It seemed cocky but I couldn't tell if it was the kind of cocky that I liked. This time, I just lowered my sunglasses for a second then put them back in place.

I was inside my room, the Mare Nostrum Suite, which, the bellman informed me, was Latin for "Our Sea" the name the Romans used for the Mediterranean, of which I had a perfect view right out my window. Seeing the style of the suite fit me, I silently thanked Orlando then slipped the bellman a fifty euro note.

"Will anyone else be joining you during your stay?" he asked, displaying his English. Like most of the staff, he still had his Spanish accent, but I could understand him perfectly.

"I haven't decided yet," I replied as I walked around, surveying the suite, including the terrace. "So . . . what is there for a girl to do around here?"

"Our amenities are the best. There is complimentary pampering for a lovely lady such as you, as well as our fine beaches," he recited from memory. "You will also enjoy the festival season in Valencia itself. Lots of history and culture all around us. And if you like the gambling, there is a casino about thirty kilometers away."

"Oh," I said, curious. "Are there some dangerous places around here? Where a *lovely lady such as me* could get in trouble?"

"Yes," he answered, his voice lowering as if scared to say so. As he began to tell me the list of those places, I began noting which might be of interest to me.

Pampering was good too, but a bitch might wanna get things poppin'.

Niles

5

"Hurry up, Niles," the woman whined in Spanish. I was deliberately taking my time with the key card as I wanted to get another look at the sister from the elevator, the sexy American. Caught her looking at me as I glanced over my shoulder, but only had time to throw a quick, awkward nod her way. After all, I couldn't risk losing the bird in the hand for the one in the bush. As my room door opened, the American sister responded with a smooth dip of her designer sunglasses followed by a dismissive shake of her head. Guess she wasn't feeling me although I found it rather hard to believe. Maybe I was just spoiled by European women Especially these at the business conference I was attending. Angelica slipped her arms around my waist, resting her head on my back as if asserting she was worthy of my undivided attention.

"Señorita," I said as I politely held open the door to my suite.

"Do you have something to drink?"

Turning on some soft music with the remote, I led Angelica to my bar, where I told her to help herself to whatever she fancied. Normally, I would've been a gentleman and helped Angelica with her drink but I'd been away from my room all day and had to tend to some business. I went out on the balcony and checked my messages

I was about to go back inside, but for a bit of movement out the corner of my eye. My friend from the elevator was on her balcony at the same time. I delayed for a bit, observing her as she checked out her accommodations while bickering with someone on her mobile. No doubt she was arguing with some boyfriend from back in the States. Call me intrigued, for I was. I hovered there, held in her thrall as I imagined her turning around any second and seeing me again. But then what? I was sure I could come up with something better than a nod this time. Maybe flex my muscles. Yeah. That's it. Acting like a horny schoolboy would be *sure* to dazzle someone such as her.

"Niiiiiiles!" came from inside my suite. Angelica summoning me back.

The American sister never turned my way. A quick change of direction and she was back out of view. Remembering my card was already full, I put aside foolish thoughts and followed the call of my name.

Angelica lay atop my bed. Whatever she'd poured herself was gone. Just a glass of ice remained on the nightstand. She was on her back with her bikini removed and legs spread wide, letting me see that the carpet did in fact match the drapes. She was a true redhead.

"You have a nice room," she commented as she pointed her toe at me then twirled it around as if it were a magic wand. God bless her. Strong and flexible legs were a good thing in life.

"One of the nicest in the hotel," I replied, stepping forward as I grasped her outstretched foot and kissed her ankle, holding it against my cheek. There was another suite on this floor equally as nice, but on the opposite end of the hallway.

"Your cock. Show it to me, *por favor,*" she begged as her hazel eyes flared devilishly.

I obliged her and pulled my trunks down, allowing them to fall around my ankles. I wasn't fully out of them before Angelica slid closer to the bed's edge. She sat there, taking me in her soft hands while marveling at it.

"*Bueno,*" she muttered softly with a smile just before she took me in her mouth. As her lips encircled my head, her demeanor turned less passive. She sucked wildly, her warm breath making my body tingle from head to toe as she convinced me there was nothing she'd rather be doing. I grasped the back of her head and held steady as she slobbered with wicked determination. When she stopped to catch her breath, I pushed her onto her back, startling her.

I grinned, ready for the main course as I snagged a condom from off the nightstand. I ripped the foil off the Magnum and quickly unfurled it onto my shaft.

"*Esto es lo que desea?* Is this what you want?" I asked with a low growl as I took her ankles in each hand and held her legs up to the sky. Angelica emphatically nodded as I entered her, her lovely gasps of pleasure escaping the deeper I slid. Finding our rhythm, I pressed her legs together and bent my knees slightly to hit her spot just right. Her ass quivered each time our bodies pressed together. Steadying herself, she rode up and down on my dick, going reverse-cowgirl and whipping her mane of long red hair about like some madwoman.

"*Sí! Sí! Sí!*" she cried as I pumped faster and more intensely, holding her legs ever tighter as I worked in and out. Sweet carnal music was played by our bodies, our instruments coming together to deliver the notes of passion. I gave Angelica my all, not a care for who heard us as I did my best to bring her ecstasy again and again.

Later, while my guest snored blissfully in my bed, I got up.

I was restless and my mind was somewhere else. I returned to my balcony a final time on the off chance that I might see her again.

Nadja

6

Just as I was about to step through the door for my meeting my phone buzzed. I knew Navid, my first assistant, was calling to give me an update on my pet project.

"Talk quickly," I pressed him, not wanting to be late.

"Lots of activity in Valencia," he said.

"More than normal?"

"Average. Nothing's sticking," he said in a cheerful voice.

"Good. Let me know if anything changes."

"Will do."

"And, Navid?"

"Yes?"

"Thanks. You're the only person I can trust with this." I sighed. From an early age I'd been taught not to trust people, especially when it came to work. I felt grateful that I had someone that had my back even if I paid handsomely for it.

After I got off the phone, I entered the dimly lit bar, noting all the stares and obvious signs of interest. With the exception of a scantily clad waitress every other customer was male. I spotted my party across the room and made my way over. A short, squat guy in an expensive suit turned from the bar and stepped in my path halfway to my destination.

"Beautiful girl, come and let me sit on your face." He waved a wad of currency in my face, hoping to entice me.

"Step out of my way," I snapped at this idiot. There wasn't enough cash in the world to force me to spend one moment alone with him.

"A golden shower will surely correct your bad attitude," he snapped, peeling off the American equivalent of several hundred dollar bills.

"Are you kidding?" I quipped as he attempted to shove the bills into my cleavage. I rewarded him with a swift uppercut to the jaw, sending him reeling backward.

"Oww, you fucking bitch!" he hollered in pain and shock as he came toward me.

"You're lucky that's all I did." I took another step toward my table when he grabbed me by the elbow. I shook my arm away from him.

"Don't you ever fucking put one slimy hand on me again or you will regret it."

"Do you know who the fuck I am?" he snarled, getting up in my face.

"Sure. I know who you are. You're Rasoul Habib, owner of the third-largest oil tanker in Saudi Arabia. You are married to Leila. And you have two mistresses, Yasmin and Zahra. If you continue fucking with me I will make sure they're all dead by sunrise." I stared him down until he went speechless. Then I stomped over to finally join my party, who had been watching the entire exchange with a slightly amused grin on his face. Rasoul moved past me and addressed the man I was meeting. It was clear that they knew each other.

"You gonna allow her to speak to me in such a disrespectful manner? To threaten me?" he questioned my party, who just shrugged his shoulders as if to say, "it's not my problem."

"She needs to be dealt with. No woman in this country talks to a man like that and lives." Rasoul glared at me, waiting for the wrath to befall me.

"She is not just a woman. She is my daughter, and unless you want those women murdered I suggest you step away from her." My father stared him down until he scooted back to the bar.

I slid into the booth, kissing him on each cheek. "Papa. It's ready. I need you to talk to him." I picked up my phone and dialed a familiar number.

"I'm sending you an e-mail. We want this taken care of by the end of business today." I hung up the phone and turned to my father. "Done!"

"Sometimes you are better than a son, Nadja, but you are not a man. You need protection in case anything ever happens to me. You must find a husband."

"I will not be defined by my marital status," I reminded him for the millionth time.

"That Western education I paid for has made you an independent woman but this is still the Middle East. We are far behind Westerners when it comes to women."

"You raised me this way!"

"I know. But it is not good. I've arranged for you to go home to your mother."

"No! Please!" I begged him.

"Do it for me. For your own protection you must find a suitor."

We stared at each other, my stubbornness inherited from him.

"Your mother needs you home on Friday. Some very nice young men are coming to meet you. This time your engagement must end in a marriage." I knew that he was only trying to protect me, but when it came to my relationships it was my turn to protect him. I couldn't tell him that the only man I would ever consent to marry would never be mine.

Paris

7

"All settled in?" My brother Rio phoned as I finished hanging the last of my clothes in the closet. His call was welcome, but he had to know I was pissed the fuck off at being banished. It was like my family was playing with me, but I knew Rio would come clean. He was my twin after all.

"Yeah," I replied with a long sigh. "You in on this too with Orlando? Messin' up my plans 'n' shit?"

"You ain't had no plans other than fuckin' and gettin' fucked up, beeyotch," Rio teased.

"True," I admitted with a devilish cackle, "but I still miss y'all."

"I miss you too," he said, seeming genuine. "I coulda used somebody around here."

"Then why don't you come out here, bro?" I shrieked. "You and I can blow up these clubs. And I know the music's right up your alley. All that electronic party shit."

"I'd love to be among those sweaty, hard bodies and pounding beats with you, sis. But . . ."

"But what?" I pushed, confused by his hesitation. Knowing Rio's tastes, he would have more than his share of men to choose from around here.

"I gotta stay around here. In case something pops off," he weakly offered.

"Boy, you know you ain't the one for that kind of drama. That's what Daddy got me for," I joked, semi-serious. "Is Daddy tryin' to shield me or somethin'? 'Cause I'm more than ready to—"

"You know they didn't let me in on shit," Rio blurted out, cutting me off. "All I know is that you need to stay yo' ass in Europe."

"Now you're sounding like Orlando."

"Pshh. Never," he scoffed. "This is what LC wants. And I ain't buckin' our father's wishes."

"Yeah, yeah," I sassed. "I'll go along with the program . . . for now. But if y'all niggas need me, I'll be on the first G5 out there to wreck shit. In my best pair of heels, too."

"And we know, Paris. That's why we love you."

"No, you love me because you ain't got a choice," I joked.

A knock at the door led me to end the conversation with Rio. Part of me hoped it was the fine, smooth English bloke from the elevator. Maybe realizing that he needed an upgrade from his old baggage to a fine piece of American ass such as *moi*.

Naw. Wasn't him. There I went being a silly bitch. Oh well, his loss.

"*Señorita*, you have a package," a man, different from the bellman who'd brought my bags up, said. A lot less friendly, too. Despite that, I signed for the designer gift box complete with a red bow, then tipped him handsomely. *Maybe the Englishman is smoother than I thought,* I pondered as I smiled and placed the square box on a table beside the computer monitor. There was a tiny note attached to it. It read:

> So proud of the progress you're making at school. Don't think for a minute by my keeping you away that you're not valuable to the family or to me as my daughter.
> Will see you soon.
> Daddy

"Aww." I sighed with a big, cheesy grin across my face as I hurriedly undid the bow and opened the box. I was definitely a daddy's girl. Inside was a silk Hermès scarf. I slid it carefully from the objects around which it was wrapped, and held it up to admire. Not too shabby, and I knew just the outfits with which to wear it.

But the expensive scarf was concealing the other true essentials in the box for a girl like me: a semi-automatic Ruger LCP compact .380 handgun and a carbon fiber stiletto knife. Analyzing the blade, I smiled. Light and subtle. Then, setting it aside, I took the gun in my hand. Checked its grip and its weight. I could hear my firearms instructor, the eternally pissed-off Israeli, hissing in my ear at the gun range as recently as last week.

"You shoot like a girl," he said, his Middle Eastern accent stronger than a cup of straight black coffee. I'd unloaded into the target downrange, planting six straight center mass.

I wasn't just the trust fund baby *slash* party chick *slash* "don'tcha wish your girlfriend was just like me" in exile. I was out here in Europe getting my education and preparing myself for a position within Duncan Motors.

Not just for pushing papers and looking all sexy. Y'see . . . the Duncans didn't just deal in cars. We dealt in a much more dangerous world than that. And it was my turn to be the family problem solver. Something my sister London was no longer capable of doing. And, bless her soft ass, no longer wanted.

Smart of Daddy to give me a little something for my protection, even if I was removed from the action back in the NYC and Queens.

But I should be out there, too.

I didn't need sheltering and protecting.

He would see.

They all would.

Too much random shit on my mind, I grabbed a towel from the bathroom and laid it out on the table. Took the small Ruger and began breaking it down just like I'd been taught. Ensuring my little gift wouldn't fail me in an emergency.

I reached for the room phone and dialed the hotel operator.

"This is *Señorita* Wimberly," I said upon their answering, as I held the bolt up to the light and squinted at it. "I'd like to schedule an in-room massage. But give me about an hour. I'm still getting settled in."

Rio

8

As soon as my parents ditched the restaurant I phoned Paris. I needed to hear her voice. It probably had to be that twin thing. I didn't want to ruin her good time by telling her about my conversation with the 'rents. She would have jumped on a plane and no doubt made things worse. For some reason they wanted her in Europe so I left things alone. I could have really used my running buddy tonight. There was no fucking way I was following my parents home. Instead, I hit the hottest gay club in Manhattan. The last thing I wanted was to pass my father on the staircase and have to pretend that shit was all copasetic.

Seven hours and two blowjobs later, I crawled into bed, exhausted, and fell fast asleep. I heard my door open a couple of times and assumed through the haze that it was my mother checking up on me, but I didn't stir. It wasn't like there was anything she could say to me that would lead to a different outcome. When I finally rose and opened my curtains the day was damn near over. Like a whoosh, all the nasty words came rushing back at me and instead of being cowered by my father like I'd been my entire life I got pissed the fuck off!

"Boy, what the fuck is you wearing?" Junior shouted at me as I stepped into the dining room. Everyone was already seated around the table having their pre-dinner cocktails. LC, Chippy, London, Harris, and Junior all looked up as I entered. Yeah, I decided that instead of shrinking from this I would take the opposite approach and become Rio Duncan, supergay. I'd rifled through Paris's closet and found a pair of fuchsia-colored satin stretch leggings that were cutting off my circulation, a tie-dyed tank top, and a multicolored boa. Beauty was pain especially 'cause I had shit to prove.

"Yeah, this ain't Halloween." London gawked at my outrageous ensemble. Her pregnancy had turned her into a hostile bitch on wheels so I ignored the intention of her comment.

"I thought I should dress for the occasion." I swept my hands in the air, being overtly dramatic. I was a caricature version of myself and hell-bent on enjoying it.

"What the hell you talking about?" Harris didn't bother to hide his distaste.

"Goddammit, Rio, I am serious about what I said to you last night!" my father screamed at the top of his lungs.

"So am I, Daddy!" I shouted so my voice matched his. Everybody reacted all at once. Not one of us had ever raised our voice at our father. Probably because we doubted he'd allow us to continue breathing after such a breach of ethics.

"Son, just let it go," my mother warned, trying to deter me, but I was Paris's twin. I was about to show them that we were more alike than they'd ever thought. They didn't think I'd heard all their snide comments over the years about her snatching the balls away from me in utero because I'd always been the calm, sensitive one and she, a hellion.

"Not a chance. Meet Rio Duncan, queen of the damned," I announced loudly. "We should all raise our glasses in a toast."

"Don't make me come over there!" my dad warned.

"What? You're going to punish me for not being straight? You gonna knock the black off me? No, I mean the gay out of me?" I challenged. "I don't think it's possible." I snapped my fingers multiple times in the air, giving the ultra-gay signal.

"I knew it!" London shouted. "Your faggot ass been gay a long time."

"Since I came out the womb," I offered.

"Holy shit!" Harris stared as if seeing me for the first time before turning apologetically to his boss, LC.

"Harris, worried it might run in the family? Bun in the oven and all?" I quipped.

"No . . . no. Uh. . . " Harris sputtered.

"Bro, I got your back. Anybody fuck with you, they fucking with me." Junior, ever the big brother, stepped up, showing his support.

My father and I glared at each other across the table. In all my years I had never acted disrespectfully toward my parents, but this was an entirely new ball game. And I wasn't gonna let him or nobody else tell me how to be.

"Well, you could start by telling your father that gay is not a choice I'm making just to piss him off. Unlike the other men in our family—and yes, I'm still all man—I am attracted to men and I will no longer hide my preference. So either put a hit out on me or deal with it, LC!" I screamed.

The room erupted in shouting and shock. My father came toward me, breathing fire and ready to snatch me up, but my mother blocked his path before he reached me. "I am never going to accept this. You want my respect then you need to be a man."

"I am a man, a gay man!" I shouted at him across the table. "And I'm not going to law school, either. The only reason I even took the LSAT was to please you. You wanted me to get a law degree from a top school. Well, guess what? I don't care what you want anymore. I'm never going to get your approval so I give up. I'm going to be happy and I'm going to be myself and that is gay, gay, gay, and gay!" I sang.

"I can't stand to look at you!" LC boomed as he stomped out of the room.

"Oooow!" London shouted. "Stop kicking me! This fighting is upsetting the baby!" She gave me the evil eye.

"I hate this place!" I rose and stormed upstairs and into my room. I leaned against the door, breathing heavy. After years of rehearsing my exit from heterosexuality, I hadn't expected things to escalate so quickly.

The tapping on my door interrupted me feeling sorry for myself. My mother stood on the threshold. I stepped out the way to let her into my room.

"Your father loves you. He does," she swore. I wasn't sure if she was trying to convince me or herself.

"Yeah, well, he has a damn hard time showing it."

"Don't do anything stupid," she begged me, and as much as I wanted to comfort her I couldn't. This wasn't about her or my father anymore. I just wanted to find myself, and one thing had become painfully obvious: I wasn't going to be able to do that here.

Paris

9

I stepped into the restaurant in my strappy five-inch Manolos and a fitted BCBG sundress and quickly surveyed the scene. All kinds of rich suits sporting Rolexes, Patek Philippes, and a Jaeger here and there whispered in at least four different languages as I walked by. From the way their voices went up in pitch, was like they'd seen Rihanna or sumthin'. I know we all looked alike to 'em, but damn. I couldn't sing, but I damn sure was finer. I had to admit that a sister could get used to the attention. There was something about being the rare piece of chocolate in a sea of vanilla. They clocked every move I made. Nothing like it.

"What's all of *this?*" I asked a passing member of the hotel staff as I motioned to all the people milling about.

"A business conference," the petite woman of olive complexion replied, amused. Her name was Adalia. "We host lots of them, señorita."

Then I noticed the name badges on most of them. And it wasn't just dudes. Cultured women in classy suits were on their shoe game while conversing with one another, handling their business too.

Lawd. I thought Orlando and Daddy set me up in a chill resort spot. Instead I was in the middle of an AARP convention. Yeah, I'd have to find my tribe and quick if my family expected me to stay here for two weeks. I had the hostess lead me to the best seat in the house with a clear view of the entrance. After ordering a real American breakfast I decided to check in with my other half.

"What's up?" Rio screamed out on the other end.

"Not a damn thing." I sighed.

"I wish I could say the same." He laughed, except it sounded like something got caught in his throat. Not his normal fabulous Rio-ness.

"You all right? 'Cause I would hurt a motherfucker that messed with my twin." When he didn't immediately throw out a response I continued, "Did you finally do the dirty deed?"

"No! Though I'm starting to think why the hell not?"

"'Cause we twins and I inherited the ho-ishness for the both of us," I joked. "I hate being here by myself," I whined. "At least if you were here we could get into all kinds of trouble. You know I work better with a road dog." I almost had to shout because of all the commotion on the other end of the line. "What's all that noise in the background?"

"Some bad foreign TV show. Girl, you just need to handle your business and get you some," Rio pressed me. "What about Mr. Big Feet?" he asked.

I almost wished I hadn't spilled about that last night but I was soooo lonely. As soon as he said the words those size thirteens-plus walked into the dining room. Damn, he was finer than I remembered. He was in a tailored tan linen suit and white shirt that showed off his dark tan. He waved to the hostess and I saw that it wasn't just his feet that were big. Brother had some massive hands that sent my mind racing in a dirty direction.

"You'll never believe who just walked into the restaurant." I lowered my voice to a whisper, trying to stop myself from bursting out in high-pitched laughter at my brother's squeal. Rio always stirred shit up.

"So you're not in your suite?" Rio asked.

"I wasn't gonna find no trouble holed up in there. There's some fancy dining room in this place with ocean views."

"You better go step to a brother and get you some. I want details on how big those feet really are," he kidded me.

"Your ass ain't hardly thinking about his feet." I laughed, watching the subject of our conversation. I turned before he spotted me staring at him. He was headed right in my direction.

"Mr. Big Feet is coming my way," I reported as he took a seat at the table directly next to me. I saw him checking me out. I even rewarded him with a little smile in return, then went back to my call. "Definitely interested!"

"Then hustle your ass over there. Dick first, name later!"

"A'ight, I'm gonna do it! Wish me luck!" I started to rise just as these two hyper blond hoes planted themselves down at his table. "Damn, two bitches just sat down with him," I groaned.

"Fuck those skanks. Paris Duncan don't let nothing and no one cock block her!" Rio pushed me.

"I gotta go. I wanna hear what the hell they're talking about." I hung up the phone, pretending to not be all up in his business.

"You were amazing last night," the blonde with the biggest rack purred.

"Yeah, you really know how to handle your business," her friend added, trying not to be outdone by the massive boobage.

"Thank you, ladies! Glad you enjoyed the show." He seemed to be flirting with them.

Show? I bet he showed them something. He looked up, caught my eye, and winked. *Oh, hell no. I'm not about to get stupid naked with his whoring ass.*

"Do you always get what you want?" Boobs Galore batted her eyes and bent back to give him the best display of her oversized assets. For some reason he chose to ignore her.

"Ladies, I have to prepare for my day." He waved a folder in their direction.

"I'd like to see you again." Her friend wasn't ready to just let him go.

"We'd like to see you again," they chimed in together.

"I'm around. Work now, play later, ladies." He tapped his folder.

"Oh, okay, see you later." They headed across the room to a table where they could have an unobstructed view of him.

He tilted his head in my direction and gave me this look like he was trying to apologize for the disturbance or some shit. *What the fuck?* I turned away and tried to concentrate on my food. According to what those tricks were saying he delivered.

Well, I didn't make a habit of getting into long lines for no man and I wasn't about to start. I had to get my ass up out of this old folks' spot and find me some good dick and potent weed and not necessarily in that order. I felt his eyes on me but I chose to ignore him. It would serve him right to know that not every pussy in the place had his name on it.

"Señorita," a familiar voice called out. I looked up in time to see Rio heading into the restaurant. I squealed, jumping up to greet my brother.

"Asshole!" I shouted at him.

"Bitch!" He gave as good as he got.

"Why didn't you tell me you were coming?"

"I wanted to surprise you. See what trouble we could get into together." He sat down, grabbing bacon off the plate.

"How did you convince the 'rents to let you fly all the way over here?" I asked, but Rio had already honed in on Mr. Big Feet and wasn't listening to a word I said.

"Damn, when you said fine, I thought you were talking about average, everyday fine. That over there is beyond supermodel fine." He swooned.

I snapped my fingers in his face to get his attention. I saw the look of curiosity on our neighbor's face. *Good. Let him worry that one female on this island had other options.* But of course Rio couldn't stop checking him out. You didn't need a gaydar to read his interest. So much for me trying to use the jealousy card.

"You did not answer me about the folks. They just let you join me?" I pressed.

"Technically I'm too damn old to run away so I didn't tell them."

"What? You hopped on a plane without saying anything to anyone? What the hell aren't you telling me?" While my parents didn't need to know our micro movements, international travel plans were always run by them. Something huge must have gone down for Rio to leave home without their knowledge. I stared him down, waiting for him to come clean.

"Well, I came screaming out of the closet and your pops freaked the fuck out," Rio announced.

I gasped. This was major. "Out? Like out out?"

"Like I'm gay and deal with it out." Rio sounded all bold.

I threw my arms around him. I'd never been more proud of my brother. "I can't believe you finally did it. That must have been so hard," I consoled him.

"Yeah, it was, until your father started acting like I didn't have any rights to my own sexuality. Like I needed his permission, which he wasn't about to give me." Rio shook his head.

"Oh, he'll get over it. Once you get that Ivy League law degree he'll be parading you out for all his friends." I laughed 'til I saw the look on his face. "What? Rio?"

"Yeah, that's not going to happen either."

"You ditched law school? OMG, Dad must have flipped the fuck out."

"You think? That was his dream, along with the one about me being interested in pussy!" Rio didn't notice his voice had risen.

Our neighbor had an amused smile on his face. I wanted to tell him to mind his own damn business but he got a look on his face and rushed out like he had something urgent to take care of. *Probably running to meet some highbrow Euro-trash with big fake titties.* He stopped outside the door of the restaurant, talking to some Middle Eastern man with a thick gray beard. *Interesting. I guess the brother does more than just screw the ladies.*

"What are you going to do?"

"Party!" he screamed. "I wanna hit some clubs, get high, drunk, sleep, and at the very least see some dick. Lots and lots of dick!" He cheered, all his Rio-ness back in full force.

Nadja

10

I shimmied into a tight-fitting chartreuse number that was much more revealing than what I usually wore. After the past few days of submitting to my mother's demands that I dress conservatively, almost covered from head to toe, I needed to assert my independence at least when it came to my wardrobe choices. Home was my own personal version of stepping into the *Twilight Zone*. Thankfully the worst was over and I had returned to my life. And the reinforcements were always right on time. Simone and Gabriella had been my roommates first at Phillips Exeter Academy boarding school in New Hampshire, then at Stanford, where we all applied to get far away from the Northeast weather. Simone was born and raised in France to real aristocracy and Gabby to ridiculous amounts of Spanish money.

As international students away from our families we three immediately bonded and formed our own version of family. Even though I was the oldest by three months, they treated me as the youngest because I refused to relinquish my virginity as if it were a prize to be given to the horniest guy. And there were plenty. Simone was a total romantic that fell madly in love with whoever she dated, while Gabby enjoyed having power over the opposite sex and changed men as often as it occurred to her. Lucky for me that after all these years they were always willing to jump on a plane to restore me to sanity at a moment's notice.

"Yay!" Gabby laughed as I entered the VIP area of the club.

"Let's drink to freedom," Simone screamed out as we clinked glasses.

"Was it really that bad?" Gabby rubbed my shoulder, always quick to comfort me.

"Worse," I said as I took another necessary gulp of my drink. "Imagine being dragged kicking and screaming back into the dark ages." This was met with screaming laughter. As thoroughly westernized women they couldn't imagine that women were still subjected to second-class citizenship.

"Wouldn't it be sooo awesome if you could have a harem?" Gabby was always looking for a way to expand her male fan base.

"I was forced to sit there covered up to my neck."

"What, no burqa?" Simone pretended to be horrified.

"Oh, don't joke. My mother would have been ecstatic to get me into one of those. And the men?"

"Were they like Ahmad?" We all locked eyes at the mention of that name.

"Worse!" I swore, which had them doubled over in pain.

"He was so dull. You would have died a slow death just listening to him talk," Gabby added.

"'Nadja, men are born to be the controller of women. You must submit your will to us.'" Simone parodied his monotone way of speaking.

"Oh, my God, he was the worst." We all laughed.

"And him?" Gabby used her soothing voice. We'd all decided to never refer to the great love of my life by name. It made it too real. Too painful.

"I just want him," I cried out.

"Where the fuck is the waitress? We need more alcohol!" Simone huffed. Gabby hugged me close to her.

"Why is this so hard for me?"

"Because good dick is much more difficult to let go of," Gabby offered. "Especially first time good dick."

"You can really say that? Out loud?" Simone challenged her.

"Yes, and I should know. I've slept with enough men to be able to judge the effects of good sex versus lame, everyday dick."

"That's not true." Simone held her ground.

"Yes, it is. You get attached if someone tells you you're beautiful," Gabby teased. "Face it, you have no perspective."

"Fine. How can we be sure it was good? He's the only man she's ever let enter the great sacred place," Simone kidded me. They teased me using the name they called my vagina in high school.

"How good was it?"

"Seven orgasms good," I whispered.

"Seven?" Gabby screamed out loud. "Hell, I would have fallen in love with him too. I was way in the double digits before I even had my first big O. I'm jealous!"

"That's hella rare for the first time. Maybe I should take this stallion out for a test drive, see if it was beginner's luck," Gabby joked.

"And I will kill you," I warned, aware of the edge creeping into my voice.

"Whoa, backup. Joke. Just a joke." Gabby stared at me until I calmed down.

"I'm sorry but I can't even kid about him."

"You got it bad!" Simone grabbed me into a hug.

"Seven orgasms, who wouldn't." Gabby sighed as the waitress brought a second round of drinks. She raised her drink in a toast.

"To Mr. Seven. May he submit to the great sacred place again and again." We all clinked glasses but I knew the chances of it happening were growing slimmer every day.

Rio

11

We were standing in front of this club suggested by the concierge after I slipped him a few Benjamins. They liked their guests to stay close to home, but for those of us willing to take chances and looking for trouble he informed me that there was a whole 'nother side to Valencia. I got dressed, threw on some smell good, and of course I had to wait for my sis to finish her fashion takeover. Girl took her style seriously and you bet to believe she made sure all of those looking at her were schooled to her fabulousness.

The line to Klub Impulso began where the cab had dropped us off. Yeah. We were in the right kind of spot. Mixed in with weed and alcohol in the night air, I could smell the money. This was bound to be my kind of ish. The long line snaking around the corner didn't faze either of us. We were OGs at getting into clubs.

"Just follow my lead," I said as we approached the chiseled, bald brother impeccably dressed in black who was in charge of keeping people from reaching the Promised Land just beyond those doors. The key was to not make eye contact and to ignore anyone trying to stop you. The brother took one look at us and opened the rope to let us pass.

Once inside the doors, my vision had to adjust to the blackness broken up every few seconds by crazy, pulsing flashes of light to the beat. Another member of the club's security staff, a bearded Spaniard with a stoic face, was waiting for us. Without saying a word, which would be hard to hear anyway over the noise, he slapped two special wristbands on us and motioned for us to follow him.

Two large railed ramps running parallel along both sides of the warehouse separated the VIP from the overwhelming crowds below. We were led up one of the ramps beyond what passed for European royalty these days: footballers, racecar drivers, whack-ass comedians, pop stars, and spoiled scions of nobility. Paris had a way of letting you know she was straight-up special and belonged with the elite even though she had way more fun among the hood rats. We ordered some drinks and sat back, studying our surroundings.

"That one or that one?" She nodded to two metrosexual dark Spaniards who looked related. They caught her eye and smiled hopeful.

"One with the gold chain on. He's spending more time at the gym." I noticed the muscles and tight abs and agreed. "What about a little girl on girl?" I asked, motioning to these three women seated to the right of us. Paris burst out laughing.

"For a gay you are so predictably male. You just looking at those big fake Euro titties. Sorry, your sister is strictly dickly but I would wear the hell out of that dress." She motioned toward the olive-complexioned one in a killer chartreuse body-hugging number.

"Sis, you'd look so much hotter."

"Right. Who wore it better? Me!" Paris chuckled. We got our drink on strong. Paris made nice with the two Spaniards who were hospitable enough to share a joint. It was obvious they were feenin' for baby sis but they were shit out of luck. The new Bruno Mars hit the table and Paris grabbed my hand and jumped up to dance. Didn't take a moment for the whack-ass DJ to cross it with some Gaga, which sounded like heavy beats and shrieking. It sent us back to our seats in a funk.

"What the hell is wrong with this club?"

"First off, the music is whack. Who the hell wants back-to-back Justin Bieber? And those techno eighties flashing lights? It's like a gay club without the gays."

"You need to go on up and school these fools." My sister got all head-rolling and hands-on-hip attitudy. We were hardcore when it came to partying so our standards were extremely high. I looked down over the railing. People were just milling around like they were waiting for somebody to take the stage or some shit. Yeah, this was not happening, and the room could have been bumping. I didn't fly halfway around the world to listen to bullshit badly mixed beats. I hit up the waitress when she brought our next round of drinks.

"Who's in charge?" I asked, 'cause the level of lameness was getting worse with every song. I left Paris sandwiched between the two brothers vying for her attention and went in search of the owner.

"You want me to fire the DJ?" Eduardo Becerra, the owner of the club, stared at me, no doubt awed by my audacity.

"If you actually want this place to work. 'Cause it ain't working."

"This is the hottest club in Valencia," he challenged me.

"Anyplace can be hot for five minutes. Look around. Do these people seem like they're enjoying themselves?" He followed my gaze around the dance floor. His customers did not look like they were particularly happy. "Clubs are all about word of mouth. People talking, tweeting, texting about this is not going to be good for business," I warned him.

"And you are?"

"The one person who can turn this shit around for you."

"You're kind of young to run a club."

"Oh, I don't usually run clubs. I party. I am a professional partier and if there is one thing I know how to do it's to have a good time. You need a great space, which you got, pretty people, you got, but the music and the mood are killing you."

"And you think you can fix this?"

"Yeah, I know I can."

"Well, we have a group coming from Amsterdam. They like to party!"

By the time I made it back to the VIP section I was grinning so hard li'l sis thought I'd had a little party of my own.

"Nope. I got a job."

"Blow job?" she had to scream over the bad sounds.

"No. A gig. Work. Real work."

"Fuck you talking about, Rio?" I could tell that I shocked the hell out of her.

"You're looking at the new assistant manager of Klub Impulso," I raved.

"What you know about running a club?" Paris didn't hide her surprise.

"I know how to party. Ask yourself: who is better at partying than me?"

Her silence was the only answer I needed. This wasn't law school but maybe it was something I could actually be good at. The one thing I knew for sure was that I wasn't going back to New York and the way it had always been. And whether my family could accept it or not, that life was over for me.

Niles

12

"Hey, man, how's it going?" Benton, the bouncer at the door, asked as he opened the rope to let me in.

"It's going," I responded as we exchanged a knuckle bump.

"Try not to take all the women; leave some for me." He laughed as I entered the club.

I pulled out my phone and sent a text: Here. I stepped up to the bar and took a quick surveillance of the spot. There were lots of pretty people in expensive finery milling around. Definitely not jumping off like the clubs I grew up partying in when I was a teenager. I looked up at the VIP section and spotted the sexy American. Unfortunately two guys I knew were vying for her attention. Something told me that she was smart enough to see through their lameness. We locked eyes for a minute until one of them diverted her attention away.

"Checking out your options?" the person I had come to meet said, following the direction I had been watching. She frowned. "I need you to keep your mind on business. You're here for a reason and it's not to wave your manhood around like a magic wand."

"Magic wand? I like that imagery," I joked until I saw that my humor was not appreciated.

"Did you schedule the meeting?"

"Of course. I'm nothing if not professional."

She slipped me a car key. "Black Mercedes SLR. Two blocks east. You'll find it in the trunk."

"Be back," I said and quickly made my way out of the club.

"You leaving?" Benton asked.

"Nah, I gotta make a call." I grabbed my phone and pretended to dial someone as I strolled up the street.

Forty minutes later I was back in the club. When I entered the VIP section I saw that the sexy American was now talking to her friend from the restaurant. Just like I thought, she had gotten away from the two idiots I'd spotted her with earlier. I started to approach until I noticed they were having a rather intense conversation. Actually, she was the one doing all the talking while the guy kept shaking his head at her. Her hand movements were getting more expressive. Whatever they were arguing about I knew I didn't ever want to be on the other end of a disagreement with that one. Clearly she wasn't the type to calmly end an argument unless she had won it.

"Everything go all right?"

"It's handled," I assured my associate as I slid her the key.

"You wanna join me and my friends? A little celebratory drink?"

"Nah, I'm good." I saw the sexy American checking us out. She turned her head as soon as she noticed me staring back.

My associate didn't miss a thing. She never did. "Way too high maintenance for you!" She laughed as she stepped back to join her party.

She was probably right, but hot was hot and this little bird was sizzling. Still I had to say something. Just as I stepped to her my associate's two friends flanked me.

"Sorry, we have plans for him," one of them hissed at the stunned American as they hustled me down to the dance floor.

"Bitch, you can have him." She snapped her fingers and turned her head.

I heard the guy calming her down. "Shhhh! Chill up in my spot."

I turned to see her raising her middle finger at me. I couldn't help smiling at her feistiness. She was the opposite of the women I'd come in contact with since landing in these parts and I wanted to get to know her better. At least once.

Paris

13

"Heeey! Sexy American! You made it! We were about to leave," Ramon screamed as he saw me hustling down the dock. They had a decent-sized crowd already aboard the yacht, which I considered on the smaller end of the scale as far as yachts go. Still, it seemed like a good party vibe. Attractive fashionistas drinking fancy drinks.

"Told you I was coming," I growled as Antonio took my hand and guided me onto the stern of the vessel.

"So your brother didn't want to join us?" Ramon looked way too thrilled that there was no threat of cock blocking. They'd hit me up at the club a couple of nights before and sweated me about this boat ride. I planned on ignoring their invitation but when Rio morphed into Mr. Responsibility with his new job I wasn't in the position to turn down a good party. It beat staying holed up in that hotel hoping I fell across a good dick.

"He had to work so I'm flying solo," I pouted. "Now let's get this party started."

"It's going to be an even better party now that you're here. We're waiting on a few more people before we cast off," Antonio said as he kissed me on both cheeks. His nice arms gave me something else to focus on besides his bad breath. Smelled like he had hummus for breakfast, lunch, and dinner.

"And there they are!" Ramon yelled as if he were greeting royalty. Did he ever speak at a normal volume? Dang.

As I cleared the stern, I turned to see exactly who was worth that much excitement.

"Yes! More beautiful people. Our party will be the talk of the festival season," Antonio cheered as I glanced at the four long-legged models strolling toward us.

And the way-too-confident motherfucker from the hotel dressed in a pair of beach shorts and muscle shirt was escorting them. I couldn't get away from his ass.

"You do have something to drink on this boat, right?" I asked them.

Aboard the yacht, I changed into my swimsuit, checking myself out in the mirror. It was a stunning designer original courtesy of the little shopping spree Orlando had generously paid for back in the city where I got my name. I couldn't believe Rio came all this way only to land a job instead of in the trouble I had planned for us. Damn, I was gonna have to find someone to keep me busy, and the best-looking piece of dick always had a rotation of groupies swirling around him.

Cocky as hell, he was leaning against a railing, looking like a young Rick Fox as I exited the dressing room. He held out a flute of champagne for me to take. From behind my Linda Farrow Luxe sunglasses, I ignored both it and his trick ass. I kept it movin' like I do. He followed me, took a few extra steps to get ahead of me, and put one of the drinks down.

"Niles Boateng." He extended his hand, playing the perfect gentleman. No matter how polite he was I knew he was one more hard dick tryin'a get it. Well, he had another think coming if he thought I was the type to join his rotation of women.

I knocked Niles's hand away, causing some of the champagne to spill onto the deck. "Nigga, please," I said with an added hiss at the end. Putting my hands up with the rest of the party people, I left Niles and sought my own glass of champagne from the yacht's crew. Now armed with a full glass in hand, I took a strawberry off of a passing fruit tray and chewed it succulently as I sashayed through the crowd, nodding my head to the beat.

The yacht party was like all the rest I'd attended. Plenty of booze, sexy bodies, and decent enough music. Other than the rough waters, the Mediterranean weather couldn't have been any better either. Would've been close to perfect if I weren't alone. I truly hated this anonymous shit. Back home, I would've had Jasinia and my girls to wreck shop with. And folks would have got in line 'cause I was Paris Duncan and not some no-name trick.

Didn't know why that guy had me so riled up anyway. Niles was obviously not a one-woman man. He'd wasted no time moving on from my dismissal. As I interacted with folk, a little game spontaneously developed between the two of us over stolen glances through the crowd.

Y'see, I'll be woman enough to admit it. Just as many women were flirting with Niles as these marks were with me. Super Euro had game. And as soon as I would make witty and delightful conversation before moving on, so would he. This nigga was taunting me with that perfect smile and pretty teeth. The game went on as we rotated around the boat from port to starboard and back again, always keeping the other visible and able to see what we were doing. Hell, what can I say? It was something to do. He easily toyed with as many bitches as I men, matching each other's skill like the deck was our own private chessboard. With each new conversational conquest and seduction, it was like I was engaging in foreplay, working myself up toward something like a thrill the more I did it. Yeah, I was going outta my mind. If I didn't get some dick soon on the trip, I didn't know what the fuck I was going to do.

My little game brought me upon a couple, both with dark, curly hair and looking to be about my age. Ramon and Antonio probably found them in the club last night as well, figuring they needed a couple of people not looking to hook up. The way the boy's and the girl's hands kept brushing against one another, they were definitely well acquainted. I'd only been fucking with singles until now, but there was no more fun a challenge to me than this. I felt it was time to get my evil on. I adjusted my bikini top, making sure my breasts were prominently displayed, before I stumbled into them. Made sure my delicious C cups brushed right up against the side of his face as I pretended to lose my footing.

"Oh! Excuse me," I said as I took a seat next to them, the blue waters below splashing just over the rail as the DJ instructed the sexy ladies to strut across the deck. I was on break, so the hoes walking about could have their chance to shine. The boy looked nice enough with his fresh little haircut and Scorpio tat on his right bicep. *Sting me, baby.* "Do you speak English? Or *parlez-vous français?*" I asked, letting my lips pucker on the last word for him to see.

"Yes. We speak English," he said with a genuine smile as his girl leaned over, briefly lifting her sunglasses to get a better look at me. She smiled, but the way her bottom lip twisted 'n' shit betrayed her true thoughts. I was used to it. But she was too weak to do something about me other than mumble in her boyfriend's ear.

"Where are you two from?" I asked, not really giving a fuck what she said.

"Santorini," he said, smiling even more broadly than before. "Do you know where that's at?"

"No," I gushed, playing young and dumb. *Like I ain't never been to Greece. Bitch, puh-lease.* "But are the rest of the boys there as cute as you?" I asked in my baby-girl voice while I batted my eyelashes. Too easy.

"Yes. There are some. You should go there and look for yourself," his girlfriend hissed forcefully for him in her choppy English. Maybe she wasn't as weak as I thought. I welcomed the challenge even more as I imitated her, placing my hand atop his other knee.

"Relax, *Maria Menounos*. We're all friends here," I taunted, waving my empty flute in her direction in a mock toast. On cue, Ramon showed up. Took my empty glass from my grasp and replaced it with a full one.

"As our most important guest, we can't have you thirsty. Drink. Enjoy," he said with a wink before he immediately rejoined Antonio, who had been intently watching me from a circular leather couch across the way. The two of them waved at me, motioning for me to drink up. Guess they just wanted to keep the only American on this bullshit floating pickup scene happy so I wouldn't go back home and badmouth their little shindig. Still, I wasn't getting pissy drunk on the high seas without a wingman to have my back. Last thing I needed was to get plastered and stumble over the side. Wind up some tragic chic in a Lifetime movie.

"VIP." I raised my glass to Miss Thing. She had the nerve to turn her back. She was damn lucky I was on this side of the ocean and not in my territory. If LC hadn't warned me to stay out of trouble shit would have gotten really interesting, but I held back. I smiled and acted like I put up with ignorant bitches like her for breakfast.

Niles

14

"And what is your name, lovely lady?" I leaned in and took her hand, kissing it for extra measure. I had begun to enjoy this game of cat and mouse with the sexy American. Antonio and Ramon had been gushing about her like they were in competition for her hand in marriage but I knew better and now I also knew her name. Paris.

"Eleni," she replied, readily ignoring her boyfriend who had been distracted but was suddenly attentive. What goes around . . .

"Niles," I said and watched her blush. This was way too easy. I shot a look at Paris and saw the slight amusement on her face.

"What's your name, handsome?" I heard Paris ask the boyfriend. I had to keep myself from bursting out laughing. His attention got diverted when I began fawning over his girlfriend. Paris placed a well-manicured hand possessively on his arm, stroking it to regain his focus.

"Are . . . are you okay?" he asked her. His concerned tone got my attention. I shifted my focus away from Eleni. Good thing I'd learned the art of having one conversation while listening to another.

"Yeah. I'm cool," she said as she took another sip of champagne. I thought I noticed a slight slur in her words. I listened closely and for a while she seemed fine. Maybe I was just paranoid because I'd heard some disturbing things about the brothers over the years. They were dirt bag rich kids who thought normal rules of behavior were strictly for those not fortunate enough to have their unlimited bank accounts.

Normally I would have avoided partying with them but I found out that one of the clients I had been priming was going to be on board. Now that I'd run into the sexy American my focus had turned from business.

"You have beautiful skin," I said to Elani, just loud enough for Paris to hear, but she didn't react. That's when I saw her jerk her head as if she had fallen asleep for a second. I'd seen that the brothers had personally refilled her glass. I thought they were trying to impress her but now I could tell it was something else. Eleni's hand on my arms distracted me for a moment. She was competing with Paris. I stood up.

"Here. Give me that." I held out my hand for the champagne glass. When she didn't give it to me I snatched it out of her hand.

"What the hell? You ain't my daddy." Paris's voice sounded wobbly.

"Maybe you should have some water or juice or something," I offered as I dumped the rest of her champagne overboard.

"Boy! What the fuck? Look . . . you don't tell me what to do," she snapped, shocking the Greek couple by the sudden change in vocal temperature. "I'm going to get me some more bubbly. Now if you'll excuse me . . ." She tried to maneuver around me but I stood firm.

"Let me help you," I offered.

"I could go to the restroom by myself," she said, sounding tipsy.

Then boyfriend, whose name I still didn't get, stepped up and offered as well. But she ignored him too and ducked down the stairs. I felt a hand on my arm. I thought it was Eleni but instead I found Nadja.

"Hey." She smiled at me. In the two years since I'd met her she'd gone from damn near wearing burqas to being comfortable in one of those tight Band-Aid dresses. I knew she was here working but she definitely looked ready to play. At least the brothers wouldn't attempt to fuck with her. Their fathers were business associates and that made her off-limits for their kinky fun and games.

Shit. I glanced around and didn't spot either of the brothers. This was not good.

"Sorry, but I have to go," I tried to excuse myself, but she didn't look happy. Nadja was a real workaholic and she could have cornered me into a workplace conversation that went on indefinitely. I raced away hoping to find Paris passed out in the ladies' room, but no such luck. There was a cocaine party in the bathroom with the scantily clad models and rock star–looking men. I had to fight my way out of there. I wasn't sure where she was but one thing was certain: I would find her.

Rio

15

"He better be worth every dime I'm paying him," Eduardo muttered gruffly.

"Actually he's worth a lot more. He gave me a discount because he owed me a favor," I told him, which stopped his bitching. Then I reminded him, "You want folks coming from all around then you have to change the vibe up in here. Get rid of the eighties disco ball techno thing. That's what they're doing at the raves and gay clubs in America and believe me it's not your crowd."

"And you're sure you can turn this around?" He was seriously stressing. I'd learned that Eduardo came from a wealthy family of bankers. When he dipped his inheritance in the seedy business of club ownership his family suggested he leave Madrid. They did not want their friends to witness the downfall of their progeny. Despite their lack of support he'd made a successful business of being a club owner. Had spots all over Europe. He'd been married and with kids but I suspected he was way more comfortable on my side of the dating fence. He'd shown me around the club, introduced me to the other employees, and listened as I read off my list of suggestions. He killed my suggestions about having naked models with hot wax being dripped onto them but I'd seen it done and it certainly kept people coming back. Who didn't like naked people with beautiful bodies? I also suggested they create some signature drinks. People liked to get their drink on and got attached to specialty cocktails. It brought them back.

"You gentlemen want another drink?" The waitress came over.

"You in a rush?" Eduardo asked me.

"Nope, my sister is out for the night."

"Then why don't I show you around Valencia?"

"How about we check out the competition?" I raised my glass to him.

"I like how you think." His thick lips spread into a smile. He was probably twenty years older than me but that better-with-age thing was certainly true in his case. Talk about fine. My brother, Vegas, made a big deal about not shitting where you eat but I'd have to find out the downside to that one all on my own 'cause Eduardo was funny and sexy as hell and, unless I was misreading the signs, interested.

A few hours later we were in it to win it hitting all the local spots. And I was right on the money. He had come out of the womb embracing his sexuality and had his family's support all the way. But he didn't have any of the obvious gayness about him. In fact, he was a football fanatic and the ultimate macho male. That probably had everything to do with him being Latin. He'd recently gone through a breakup and was ready to get back out there.

"So, Mr. Wimberly, what should we get into now?"

I almost swiveled my head to see who the hell he was speaking to until I remembered my cover name. The day after I got here Orlando delivered to the hotel a full set of ID: credit cards, phone, and driver's license. Paris and I were stunned. Neither one of us had told the family that I was here but that's them damn Duncans for you. No matter how far you run you can't hide. I was sure that LC knew I'd gotten this job, which meant it was only a matter of time before he tried to take back control of my life. I didn't care what he pulled; I wasn't going back to that life he'd planned for me. Even Paris, who had more mouth than all of us kids combined, always did exactly what LC told her, including attending that badass school in Switzerland. But I was suddenly on some other shit and unless I was kidding myself things were starting to really look up.

"Whatever you want!" I responded to Eduardo and pierced him with a look that confirmed I meant every word. He did a double take, staring back at me. I returned the look, letting him see that I meant it. Damn straight.

Paris

16

Below deck, I felt suddenly consumed with nausea. After it kept getting worse, I tried to make myself hurl, but I only succeeded in making my eyes water. Placing a cold, damp washcloth across my face didn't help. I almost wanted to cry. I suddenly felt so alone and vulnerable. Paris Duncan getting all fucked up in some foreign country like some amateur. It didn't make no sense 'cause I ain't even mixed my alcohol.

When I exited the restroom, both Ramon and Antonio were waiting for me. Maybe these two brothers really were gentlemen.

"We heard you were ill, pretty lady," Antonio chimed.

"Yeah. No biggie though. I . . . just need some air," I lied as my world began spinning.

"No. You need to rest," Ramon offered as he went to steady me. "Come. We have a place for you to lie down. You can rejoin the party once you feel better."

"Nah. Nah. I'm all right. Just need some air," I said, trying to get my bearings and head past them in the narrow walkway.

Neither one of them listened to me. Instead, they lifted me off my feet, each taking an arm, and carried me down the hall, speaking rapidly to one another in Spanish. I tried shaking my head to fight off the sluggishness but I couldn't resist them.

In a darkened room they tossed me onto a bed and slammed the door shut behind us. One of them must have turned on the lights because it was suddenly really bright. When I tried to sit up, I was forced back down onto the bed by Antonio. That's when I really got worried.

"I'm not playing. I will fuck you up," I said as I clumsily tried to catch him with a heel strike and missed. Even though I acted stupidly sometimes, I wasn't stupid. These mother-fuckers had drugged me, caught me like a sloppy amateur.

"Since you haven't given any indication which one of us you'd prefer, we're going to share you," Ramon said as he pulled down his shorts, pencil dick on hard. Antonio stayed on the bed, trying to keep me from getting away while he tried to undress too, exposing his black bikini briefs.

That's when I saw the camera on the tripod aimed squarely at the bed.

Oh God. Daddy's gonna kill me for killin' 'em. Because I swear that's the first thing I'ma do if I get outta here, I thought. But despite my confidence in my skills, I wasn't so sure what would happen once Ramon and Antonio finished their little film with me. The drugs had me at a disadvantage.

Antonio managed to snag my ankle. But I spun away, slipping free and finally kicking him upside his nose with my other foot. Some of my reflexes were coming back. *Maybe I had a chance,* I thought as I tried to push through the fog.

"Puta!" Antonio cursed as he held his face in pain yet still tried to keep me corralled on the bed.

Ramon laughed at him then said to me, "I will give you this cock good, *la negra.*"

But just as Ramon pushed play on the camcorder, someone knocked on the cabin door. When I tried to scream for help, Antonio leapt across the bed. His sweaty naked body landed with a thud, stunning me as he fought to get his hand over my mouth.

"Shhh. We have to be quiet," he shushed in my ear just before licking my face. Now the loud music playing topside felt more ominous. This might have been my only chance for someone to hear me. I cried out, but he muffled it.

From the hallway, someone called out in Spanish in a nasally voice. Ramon said something back to them, to which they quickly replied. He looked at Antonio, who was trying to feel me up while kissing on my neck, whispering something to him.

"*Una momento,*" Ramon called out as Antonio tightened his grip over my mouth. Something topside must've needed his immediate attention. Pulling his shorts back up, he went over to the door, obviously pissed. I was still squirming and trying to bite Antonio's fingers when Ramon unlocked the cabin door. As he peered out into the hallway, the door smacked him in the face. Antonio was rolling me onto my stomach in the bed, dry humping my ass, so I couldn't see what happened next.

I heard the sound I knew to be a body hitting the floor. But whose? Before I could give it much thought, Antonio was suddenly yanked off me. He blurted out two words in Spanish before his voice suddenly fled. As the drugs began to take even more of an effect I struggled to roll over and sit up. I saw Niles hovering menacingly over Antonio, holding him up by his arm with a fist drawn back ready to strike him again.

Seeing me looking at him, Niles let Antonio fall to the floor with a thud. In the blink of an eye, he leapt through the air and was standing over me in the bed. Before I could even thank him or put together a coherent sentence, he yanked me to my feet then dragged me along to the cabin door.

"Wait . . . what—" I fumbled around, weakened by the drugs.

"Don't move! Wait here," he calmly instructed as he left me slumped over in the hallway and slammed the cabin door shut once again. He was alone in there with Ramon and Antonio while I could do nothing but collapse on to my ass.

Niles

17

I left Paris in the hallway and went back inside to put an end to the brothers' reign of terror on innocent females. There was nothing I hated more than limp-dick niggas taking advantage of a helpless female. Something told me that if they hadn't drugged this one she would have given them a real fight. American prisons were lined with assholes like this but here in their world they were untouchable and they knew that. As a man that loved women, respected them, there was no way I could stand by and let them continue their reign of terror.

When I stepped out of the cabin and saw her, I smiled. "Can't believe you actually listened," I said, closing the door behind me; but she wasn't ready to lay out the gratitude.

"*Were you in on this?*" she asked, which stopped me from moving forward.

"Don't piss me about," I snarled, dragging her along again. "I just saved your ass back there."

"Fuck you. I'm a grown-ass woman," she pouted through slurred speech. She didn't do "damsel in distress" very well.

"Bollocks. You're a hardheaded little girl," I scoffed. "And out of your league. Somebody needs to watch your back."

"Watch my back? Is O paying you?" she asked. I had no idea what she was talking about and wondered if the drugs were having some residual effect.

"Who?"

"Never mind," she mumbled as we reached topside, music blaring once again, but in Spanish this time. Our little Greek couple was in the middle of a heated argument now and didn't see us. I guided her through the crowd of partygoers, grabbing a bottled water from an ice-filled tub as I moved us to a quieter location.

"When we get back to shore, they gonna pay. Best believe," she swore in a fit of rage.

"If," I corrected her. A lot could go wrong between now and getting off this boat. "I need you to leave this alone. We don't need complications in a foreign country. Especially involving people with their kind of influence. Their father owns the largest construction company in Spain. Who you think the *policia* are going to believe, you or them?"

"Shit!" she cursed under her breath. "So you just beat their asses? I know you did. That's the only reason they didn't come after us."

"Because I told them not to," I replied as I flashed the camcorder's memory card between my two fingers before hurling it into the Mediterranean. "Now drink that water."

Nadja approached me, watching us closely. I could see that she was trying to figure out what was going down. I nodded my head, motioning her to keep it moving, but that just made her more determined to stand her ground.

"One second," I told Paris as I stepped aside to talk to Nadja.

"What's this one's problem?" she asked, annoyed at the distraction. "I thought we were going to talk."

"I'll meet you for breakfast. We can go over everything then."

"Get rid of her and we'll talk now," she pressed me.

"I can't."

"Why? It's not like you won't replace her in five seconds."

"Nadja, tomorrow. I got to handle this." I walked off, leaving her pissed no doubt. Women!

"What is this with you and these skirts? Are you some kind of gigolo?" Paris asked, half serious.

"My work and my capabilities between the sheets are two entirely different talents," I assured her.

"You knew they were going to spike my champagne? How?"

"They were stalking you as if you were their prey after handing you the champagne. Was planning to talk you out of drinking it, but you were too fast. And probably too thick-skulled to listen to me. When they were through with you, you could've found yourself sold to human traffickers and never seen again."

"*Stalking. Prey. Human traffickers,*" she repeated. "How you know this shit?"

"All this and I don't even get a thanks. Why you gotta bust my chops like that, ma?" I asked her.

Her mouth dropped open wide like she didn't have no quick comeback. "What did you just say?" she asked, looking me in my eyes for the first time since boarding the yacht.

"You heard me. Got sumthin' against a brother?" I prodded.

"You some kinda comedian? Listen to Jay-Z on a loop or some shit? You're good. Almost had me fooled for a minute." She chuckled.

"Yeah, I got jokes. But my accent, it's called growing up there."

She stared, giving me the once-over. "Boy, getthefawkout-tahere," she challenged.

"I'm serious as a heart attack. Marcy Projects."

"Whoa whoa whoa! Don't you think you're taking the ode to Jay-Z shit a little far?" She still wasn't getting it.

"We came up in the same hood but different times. As bad as things were back then, you makes me miss home. Furreal." I could tell by the way her mouth softened that she finally got it.

"Then why in the fuck are you out here pretending to be British 'n' shit?" she whispered.

"People are comfortable letting one of their own handle their dollars. If a change in accent gets me into these rich fuckers' pockets, then . . ." I said with a shrug.

"Or panties," she tried to diss me.

"Hey. I'm not gonna apologize for being single. Got no kids. And I do what I want, ma."

"And you like it that way?" She stared at me for confirmation.

"I did," I said and let the rest drop there. We both went silent after that. But before things had a chance to get awkward our Greek couple took center stage. They were in a full-blown brawl. Eleni busted her man in the head with a champagne bottle so the party was really over for them. The poor boy's blood sprayed those unfortunate to be wearing all-white ensembles, screams and groans escaping their mouths in response. The captain of the boat ordered a crewman to have them brought ashore immediately in the smaller craft docked onside.

"Ready to get outta here?" I grabbed her hand, ready to flee.

Nadja

18

I'd spent an extra hour hitting the bag at the hotel gym. My girls had plied me with drinks and an assortment of eye candy to keep me from spiraling. There wasn't enough type B in my personality to balance me out. I was type A squared and it took more than a few cocktails to get me back in party mode. To say I was peeved was putting a very mild slant on it. The fact that Niles dismissed me in front of that American didn't exactly endear him to me and it was my job to have his back. I wasn't sure what exactly was happening with that one but it wasn't his normal modus operandi. Something had gone down with her that he didn't want to share with me. Instead of letting me in on things, he acted really overprotective of her, which threw me. Niles and I were not only friends and coworkers, but as his employer it was my job to make sure things went smoothly. That meant no extra added drama with the revolving door of women he slept with. I couldn't afford for him to become unreliable or distracted.

The work we did was too important to too many people, mainly my father. I was trying to prove to him that one day I could take over his business and I wouldn't allow anyone to compromise that goal. The hardest part was getting my father to see that my sexual persuasion was not reason enough to exclude me from being in charge. One thing had become glaringly clear and that was that I had to keep an eye on Niles. One false move could topple everything I had worked to build and I wasn't about to let that happen. My father trusted him, which in and of itself said a lot because he usually viewed his employees as easily replaceable. So for entirely different reasons we had both come to value Niles as an important asset. I needed to trust him and to know that no woman was capable of shifting his focus and loyalty away from my family.

"We have a problem," my father's voice rang out on the line.

"Yes, Papa."

"That job you just handled? Well, it came with more complications than we originally thought. The contract cannot be finalized until these two other issues are addressed. One should be easy but the other is going to require a more delicate negotiator."

"How soon does this need to be finalized?"

"Twenty-four hours would be an acceptable timeline. Like I said, the second part of the contract requires a lot more work."

"Consider it handled," I assured my father.

"I will send you all of the particulars via courier. Good thing you stayed in Valencia an extra night. You saved yourself the travel."

After my father hung up I called my assistant, Navid. "Got it," he said after getting all the particulars. "You okay?" he asked.

My assistant was always concerned about me. *Why can't I be attracted to men like him? It would make my life so much easier.* Coming from the same culture, Navid and I shared the struggle of parental expectations that neither of us could live up to. Neither of us could ever tell our parents what we wanted in a mate. We each wanted what we wanted: someone who would be taboo in our culture. Because of that bond, talking to him always made me feel so much better. That's why I had to stop myself from lamenting to my assistant about the man I wanted; so instead of going on about my broken heart and the man I loved, my only response to him asking about me was, "I'm fine." Then I hurried off the telephone, thinking about all the work in front of me. Part of that work had to do with debriefing Niles as soon as possible. I picked up my phone to call him, but he didn't bother to answer—another bad sign.

"Phone me as soon as you get this. We need to talk." Call it instinct or just knowing him too well, but something told me he wasn't sleeping in alone.

Paris

19

I groaned as I rolled over when the sunlight hit me. The angle of the sun had it directly shining in my eyes. The night had been brutal getting the drug out of my system; yet, Niles stayed by my side through it. The series of vomiting and sweats made me even angrier for being the fool. But once I fell asleep, I slept like a baby. Roofies are a real motherfucker.

"How long have you been sitting there?" I asked Niles, who was sitting at the foot of the bed, sporting a charcoal-gray business suit. I glanced around. Although the rooms were exactly the same, everything in here was positioned the opposite of mine.

"Not long. Slept on the couch, just took a shower. I wanted to check on you," he answered as he patted me on my thigh.

"Thanks," I replied. "You know . . . you could come join me. I'm feeling better. Really."

"About fuckin' time. And I'd like nothing better than to *get with the joinin'*," he said with a wide grin. "But I have to go downstairs. Work calls. Last day of the conference and I've skipped out on way too much as it is."

"Yeah. From chasin' too many bitches around town," I teased as I sat up. The sheet slipped away, exposing my bare breasts, which I did nothing to cover. I was buck naked and surprised by him not trying anything. Kinda pissed me off. "Well, suit yourself, homie. I ain't gonna ruin your money game. Or tell 'em you're frontin' with the British shit."

"Thanks. Appreciate that," he said, effortlessly shifting to his phony accent for my amusement. "But I have another request of you."

"Shoot."

"Leave that stuff on the yacht behind you, Paris. Those two are dangerous. And I don't need any complications in my business dealings. Or being dragged into something that's way over both our heads."

"Selfish prick," I said, smacking my lips. "Why it's gotta be all about you?"

"Because I'm all about my paper. So let it go, Paris. A'ight?" he growled, Brooklyn proudly bellowing through his lungs again. Niggas from BK was always trying to be the boss.

"Yeah. A'ight," I agreed. Just to shut him up.

Niles leaned over and kissed me on my lips. "Good," he said just as my phone rang. I was going to ignore it but it was a specific ring, which meant it could only be one person. I dived over to the side of the bed and grabbed it.

"This better be damn important 'cause I'm looking at the hottest piece of light chocolate in Europe."

"The world," Niles teased.

"I'm sorry I didn't come back last night. I got into a little something." Rio responded.

"So did I," I said, still staring at Niles. "What happened to your ass, or should I say who?"

"It ain't like that . . . yet." Rio laughed. "I'm hella crazed. Gonna head back over to the club in a minute. Got lots to do."

"It don't make sense having my brother here if I ain't gonna get to see him," I pouted as Niles gathered his things.

"Yeah, but I'm throwing the hottest party this little town ever seen tomorrow night. You better be there."

"You know it," I responded

"I'll catch you later." Rio hung up.

"My brother," I answered Niles's questioning gaze before he could ask.

"That's who I saw you with in the restaurant?"

"Yeah, 'cept he took a gig at Klub Impulso or some shit! They're having a party tomorrow." I smiled up at him.

"I suppose I'll have to go with you to make sure you stay out of trouble." Niles kissed me on the forehead.

I frowned. Did this brother want to get it or not? I got up and grabbed a robe as he hit the door. "I need to go." I threw on my heels, letting the robe open as I stood up. *Yeah, check out what the hell you're missing,* I thought.

"You making it hard for a nigga to concentrate on his work." Niles smiled at me as he stepped into the hallway.

After I made my way back into my room and grabbed a shower I retrieved my Ruger .380 from out the air vent where I'd hidden it. Ramon and Antonio were going to get got by my hand and this, the precious bit of steel in my hand, was a start. I was loading one into the chamber when my phone rang.

"Yo, you put me in the middle of some bullshit, O," I answered, recognizing the number.

"Paris?"

"D . . . Daddy." I gasped, clumsily dropping my handgun onto the floor.

"How are you holding up?" LC asked. "I hear your brother made his way there too?"

"Yeah, I guess he didn't like the idea of me being alone," I slyly responded as I snatched my handgun back up.

"Then what 'bullshit' were you referring to?" he pressed, his already-deep voice deepening even more.

"Huh? Oh that," I scoffed. "There's a business conference going on at the same time. Bunch of old people and their money, s'all."

"Well, maybe Orlando did you a favor. You might learn something about the value of money from those 'old people' as you call them. Just make sure that you and Rio stay out of trouble. Maybe with the two of you there you won't get bored and cause trouble."

"Daddy, I understand why you wanted me here. After what happened with Vegas and all."

"Enough," LC reprimanded me. I knew why he wanted me to stop there. This phone was secure, but you never know. Now wasn't the time to be slippin'.

"Sorry, Daddy," I humbly offered.

"Paris, we'll talk another time. Soon. But for now, just listen to your brother. And don't create any more problems than we already have."

He ended so quick that I didn't even have a chance to tell him I love him. I carried my gun over to the desk in the living room and logged on to the hotel's Internet. Wanted to find out more about Antonio, Ramon, and the construction company their father owned. I had been taught not to give in to emotion and just wild out, but to do my research first and strike when the time is right. The Web site clicked on the local news.

The main story froze my finger atop the mouse, daring me to click away. But I couldn't. There had been two deaths overnight in Valencia.

The sons of a major construction magnate, both dead from what looked to be apparent drug overdoses. On their yacht.

Their names were Ramon and Antonio Villaragosa. Known on the party scene. The article said that brought the total deaths in two nights of the festival season to three, the first being the accidental death of a Pakistani businessman Mr. Hamid Khan the night before.

"No fuckin' way," I cursed as I leaned in closer to the monitor, refusing to believe what I saw. I recognized his face as the man who I saw talking with Niles.

The connection among all three of them was . . . Niles.

Maybe Khan really did die by accident. But the other two? They were mine. And I knew he had something to do with it even if they were calling it an overdose. Did Niles pay someone to off them after we got off the boat? Of course, I never saw them leave the cabin. Maybe Niles did it himself then lied to me. Now I was really buggin'. Who was this guy?

Well, whatever. That sneaky motherfucker was gonna pay for lying to me.

I quickly finished dressing, putting my hair in a ponytail, and forgoing a nice pair of heels for some Nikes, then headed downstairs.

I took both my knife and my gun with me.

Hadn't decided which one I was going to use on Niles, but I was sure I'd figure it out when I saw him.

Bitch-ass Brooklyn nigga. I was gonna show him how Queens gets down.

Rio

20

I rolled over to see Eduardo staring down at me. Nigga had been watching me sleeping. Hell, I knew I was fine but he was looking at me like he wanted to take a bite and couldn't get enough. It would have completely creeped me out except it felt really good to be with someone I didn't have to pretend with.

"What?" I leaned up on my elbows so we'd be face to face.

"Are you sure that was your first time?"

"Going all the way? Yep. Trust that I would know if I'd done that before."

"How can that be? You were amazing!"

"Maybe I'm a natural."

"But why now? Why me?"

"Luck and timing. I was ready, you were here."

"I may never let you leave."

"Valencia or your bed?" I laughed.

"Both. You have honored me by giving me such a gift."

"Hey, I spent a long time following somebody else's rules and now I've decided to make my own."

"So is that why you landed in Valencia?"

"You can say that."

"Let's say that I'm just glad I was able to have the pleasure. I am certain I am not the first to want to get to know you better."

"Not exactly." I smiled, thinking of all the opportunities I put off for fear of anyone finding out the truth.

"You going to tell me more about why you decided to settle in Valencia or leave it up to my imagination? You running from an angry lover or two?" he asked, and as much as I wanted to not think about my family I decided this was the right moment to perfect my cover story.

"Well, I was bored and looking for the next thing. My sister came here for vacation so I joined her. And when I saw that your club had some whack-ass things stopping it from being the business I got my answer."

"And your family? They're just okay with you being here?"

"Aside from my sister I'm not really that close to my family. They're a lot more traditional."

"So you've up and left?"

"I've been on my own for a long time fending for myself." I thought of the pocket full of credit cards in my wallet with bills I'd never see or have to pay. I liked this story better. It fit with my new plan to eventually own a club.

"Well, you don't have to be on your own anymore." He gave me one of those "sprung to the max" stares. Shit, I guess I did know how to put it down. "I can take care of you so you never have to worry about anything."

"What I want is to build your club up. Make it the reason people jump on planes and come to this city. I want them lined up desperate to get in: rich, famous, young, pretty, and every wanna-be across the globe begging. That's what the fuck I'm interested in."

"That's it?"

"Yeah. I been out the closet for less than a week. You've had your time out there. I know you remember those days. Ain't like you stayed with your first?"

"High school."

"Let me guess. The high school football star?" I kidded him.

"Impossible. I was the high school football star. My first was the chemistry teacher."

"You dirty bastard."

"What? Girls do it all the time."

"True." I wasn't into hearing about his past. It made me think of him with other people and that wasn't making me feel special. I quickly changed the subject. "Don't you think we need to get up and get moving? There's a lot to do today. Gotta get a car to pick up the DJ, meet with the lighting crew and a couple of mixologists."

"You really are all work." He smirked and raised his eyebrows at me.

"Oh, I'm about my business but I don't mind playing. Plus I have to find an apartment."

"Why? I have plenty of room. You can stay with me."

"Excuse me?"

"I enjoy having you around and until you get acclimated it might be nice for both of us."

I looked at him, not sure what the hell to say. Homeboy's crib was definitely palatial with views of the water, a pool, tennis court, full staff, and wings and things that went everywhere. I would have to give this some serious thought 'cause I certainly would be one comfortable and fly Negro up in this palace.

"What you tryin'a do to a brother?" I laughed.

"I'm trying to make sure you never want to leave." He laughed. Dude had game and he had some fly shit but he didn't know that I was a Duncan. I was born with a platinum card in my mouth and the knowledge about how to use it.

Nadja

21

By the time Niles graced me with his presence I was in a rage. This was the way I'd been treated back at home by my father's underlings, but here in the free world I expected to get the respect that I deserved. Had I been a man, there was no way he would have ignored my phone calls, texts, and e-mails. He'd even had the hotel block his messages so that his phone didn't ring in his room. I didn't know what he was up to, although I did have an idea. But this was work and the one rule in my business was to handle your duties first, even if that meant getting the booty later. Men! I had to check in with my boss.

"Papa." I spoke quietly into the receiver, glancing around the restaurant to see if anyone was listening. It was past the normal breakfast rush so most of the crowd had thinned, but you could never be too cautious.

"Are we on track to handle that last bit of business?" he asked.

"Yes," I assured him.

"This is a slippery situation so have our guy use extra precautions."

"He went in yesterday to make sure there would be nothing holding up the finalization."

"Good. And you, daughter?"

I could never hide my feelings from my father. He caught the slightest shift in my speech. I didn't know how he did it but it was eerie. "I'm fine. There are just a lot of moving pieces."

"This is why you need a husband. You need a partner to comfort you when you're working this hard."

"Papa, please!" I begged him. He said the one thing that hurt the most. Didn't he know that I would give anything to have a husband, but I wouldn't settle for just any man? I wanted him. The one I would never have.

"Your mother said you refused to give any of the suitors she chose serious consideration. Nadja, you must think about your future."

"For now my future is work." I looked up to see Niles strutting into the dining room, dressed in all black.

"My client is here. I will phone you when the deal is done." I hung up and glared at Niles.

"What? I'm ready!" He threw up his hands.

"I ordered you breakfast but it got so cold they took it back to the kitchen. I don't appreciate being kept waiting and not being able to reach you," I fumed.

"Have I ever let you down?" Niles answered all smooth and confident.

I wanted to punch him in the nose. Instead I opened my briefcase and handed him a file. He opened it and studied for a minute. "This for real?"

"Yes, and it's quite generous."

He turned back to the folder, going over the papers in more depth. He reached over and grabbed a piece of cold toast out of the basket.

"Fine. I'll order you breakfast." It took awhile but eventually Niles managed to get on my good side. He had me laughing about the craziness on the yacht.

"I can't believe you ditched us. I wouldn't have even gone if I knew I'd have to spend the night getting hit on by complete idiots."

"Nobody told you to wear bandages and call it a dress. What were those boys supposed to do, offer to buy you tickets to the ballet?" he joked.

"You should have protected me. Technically you are my family's head of security."

"Technically." Niles winked at me. "So what trouble you getting into today?"

"Work, work, and more work." I sighed.

"You gotta lighten up, Nadj." He smushed my hair.

"Hey, that took work. Not all of us can just roll out of bed. Speaking of bed, what happened to that little damsel in distress last night?"

"Oh, she is hardly that. She's around."

"Stay away from her. She's got high maintenance written all over her. And she's already distracted you."

He nodded his head noncommittally.

"What's that mean?" I asked.

"I don't know. Hey, let's focus!" He had the gall to reprimand me.

By the time he left I knew he'd be ready for the job. As soon as he walked out the restaurant that chick he was with on the boat stepped in, searching for someone. I followed her out in time to see her watching Niles getting into a cab.

"You missed him, whore," I wanted to scream but she jumped onto a scooter in hot pursuit. Shit, this was not good. Whatever the fuck was going on with them it had to end. And quick.

Paris

22

I rushed outside just in time to see Niles taking a cab. I could've let it go, but I still wanted to confront him about what happened on the yacht with the Villaragosa brothers. There seemed to be more to this guy and I wanted to find out what it was.

As the taxi cab pulled out onto Calle de Eugenia Viñes and took off, I raced to the edge of the street behind it. A scooter rental service for beach cruising was open at the curb, and since I was rocking my Nike active wear, I decided why the hell not.

"Pronto! Pronto!" I hissed to the elderly gentleman in the straw hat as I put on my sunglasses and waved a handful of Euros at him, cutting in front of about three people. He mumbled some instructions to me in Spanish, telling me when to return the Vespa and some other shit, but I'd paid him too much to bother listening. I gunned the throttle and scooted into traffic.

Remembering my training from finishing school, I stayed back several car lengths. Wasn't hard to do as I couldn't get much speed out of the scooter anyway. Lucky for me, the cab I was tailing took it leisurely. At first, I thought they might be going to the airport, but that wasn't the case. Niles's cab instead left Valencia, travelling northwest into the countryside. After about forty minutes I was beginning to get bored with the slow-speed chase. I almost turned around and went back to the hotel, but I sucked it up and stuck it out, telling myself I would be a fuckin' tourist and at least enjoy the nice scenery. If Niles was leading me out here just to hook up with some local, I might kill both of them just on principle.

It looked like Niles's destination was a town called Lliria. At least that's what the last road sign said before the cab slowed and pulled off beside a tiny cantina. Afraid of being noticed, I continued down the highway. I pulled over beside a bunch of other Vespas parked outside a sports bar just down the road.

From my Vespa, I watched the cab pull out and continue past me. I started up my Vespa and resumed my chase. Around one of those sudden, winding curves, I was startled when I came upon the cab stopped in the road for no apparent reason. With no other traffic to distract him, Niles would probably recognize me, so I swiftly ran the scooter off the road and into the minor brush alongside. Turning off the motor, I laid it down and crouched low next to it.

Peering from the tall grass, I watched Niles exit the cab with his briefcase then hustle out of sight up the hill and into the thick growth.

"What the fuck?" I whispered to myself as the sputtering cab turned around and drove past my hidden position. Picking the scooter up, I got back on the road and began cautiously walking it toward where I last saw Niles.

"Niiiiiiiles," I sang, trying to be somewhat sexy. I knew my hair had to be kinda messed up from the humidity and sweat. "I know you saw me. And I don't scare that easy, so you can come out now. Unless you're naked, that is. Then I can come find you."

Niles didn't reply. I came to the spot where I saw Niles enter the woods. There was a fresh, barely visible trail that went up the hill.

"You better not jump out and scare me, boy," I sang as I prepared to follow the trail, glad I wasn't wearing anything expensive.

Not a peep came from him.

I removed my .380 from my purse and slowly moved up the trail. My senses were heightened. I was looking and listening for anything that might tip me off to Niles's position. I wasn't liking the feeling I was getting. Something just wasn't right.

Without warning a loud, echoing shot not of my doing rang out. From its sound, it had to be a high-powered rifle. Either this area had hunters or that shot had something to do with Niles. Going on pure instinct, I raised my gun, ready to fire back. I spun around 180 degrees, making sure nobody was running up on me. The sounds of an engine revving and racing further confused me. I was trying to pinpoint exactly where all of these sounds were coming from. Snapping branches and creaking metal brought my focus back to the hill in front of me. There was an old Jeep rumbling down the hill, coming dead at me. It was going to run me over and there was nothing my little cap gun could do about it. With no time to spare, I dove to the side and rolled clear just in time. Worse than almost killing me, Niles was behind the wheel.

The barely controlled Jeep shot past me on its descent, taking a final bounce before landing on the highway, sparks flying from underneath it. It just missed crushing my scooter as Niles corrected and sped away back down the road.

"Niles! Wait!" I yelled but he didn't stop. Now I was intrigued. I had to find out what he was doing here and why he was in such a hurry.

I was mashing on the throttle, picking up speed on my descent, almost to the main road when a trio of black Audi sedans streaked across my path.

"Shiiiiiit!" I screamed out.

Reacting as fast as I could, I hit the brakes and laid the scooter down, going into a slide. The black Audis had moved on, all heading in the same direction as Niles's Jeep. There was no way I was going to catch up to Niles now. I hopped back on the scooter and made it to the main road. It was a T-shaped intersection, left or right my only options.

I could've taken a left and returned to Valencia and given grandpa back his rental, but I don't live life safe. I'm a Duncan. Besides, it would serve Orlando right to send me somewhere I could die. Daddy would kick his ass.

I twisted the throttle and made that right. A mile down the road, when I figured I'd definitely lost them, I saw the Audis. Where the road split to the right, smoke poured from under the wrecked hood of one, the back of it smashed in also. Just beyond it rested another one flipped on its side. The skid marks in the street were Niles's doing, no doubt. Seeing the shape of the skid marks I assessed that he must've faked taking the road to the right then slammed on his brakes, causing those two to wreck before jumping the curb and continuing on the road to the left. So Niles was not only a playboy hustler, but a stuntman.

In the air, I could still smell the fresh rubber and antifreeze as I passed them: two bloodied men in black suits, staggered about, cursing and screaming; two more huddled around a cell phone, while another appeared dead.

It wasn't them that made me nervous, but the fact that there were three cars in pursuit and only two Audis accounted for. Somewhere ahead, the chase was still on.

My gas was getting low as I headed deeper into the countryside, dodging the occasional broken taillight piece or shell casings. They must've been bustin' serious caps, getting closer to him. But I hadn't seen any blood or Niles's body yet.

Paris, don't be stupid. Daddy didn't raise you to be stupid. Just turn around before you get stranded out here . . . or worse, I thought. Guess I could be hardheaded to a fault because I pressed on.

Off the tiny road, I spotted a trail in the gravel with two separate sets of fresh tire tracks. Would've smooth driven past if this thing had any speed. I turned off onto the trail, which led to a bunch of buildings that looked like an old settlement or something. It had long ago been deserted and now only held graffiti, memories, and maybe homeless people if this country had some. I figured somewhere in the middle of the buildings were Niles and whoever was in the Audi. The dust I began to kick up could be seen, so I decided to go in on foot. I removed my gun and knife from my purse and camouflaged the Vespa near the road as best I could.

The closest building afforded me shelter once I got to it with no one trying to take off my head. I eased my way around its perimeter, trying to figure how best to conduct my search without somebody getting the drop on me. I had no idea of the numbers involved or even why they were after Niles. But I wasn't stupid. Whatever he was involved in was bad. Most of those thoughts disappeared when a barrage of gunfire broke out a few buildings away. *Fuck it*. There was no time for being a stealth bitch today and, besides, guns blazing was probably more fun anyway. With a smile I rounded the corner and took off running, ready to unload on whomever I chose.

I found the Audi with its engine running just beyond the third barely standing building. Its driver was still behind the wheel, but his ass wouldn't be driving anyone anywhere. What was left of his head and skull looked to have been shot through the windshield of the A8 with . . . a high-powered rifle.

I found all the remaining parties making nice inside the last building, a mixture of wood and clay. Stepping over another dead body in fine Italian loafers just outside its entrance, I snuck up behind a group of three that had Niles cornered, heckling him in Spanish as they eased from different spots and slowly approached the large tractor tire at the far end of the building he was using as a shield. Niles probably chose to make a stand here because anything beyond would be open space for at least a quarter mile. Sheer suicide with the odds and ammo against you no matter how fast you think you could run. Niles didn't know it, but I was gonna do what I could to even those odds a little bit.

Either go hard or go home, bitch, I thought as I unzipped my Nike jacket a bit and messed up my hair. And I was a loooong way from Jamaica Queens. Crazy. The one thing I remember most was having to pee when I stood up and went with something that didn't make a bit of sense.

Niles

23

"Help me! Help me! He . . . kidnapped me."

I looked up, shocked to see Paris enter screaming. She staggered wearily inside, announcing herself to the three men in loud English. Shit! I didn't understand why she was here or who could have kidnapped her. *What have I done?* I poked my head out and locked eyes with her for a minute. I motioned to the door, prodding her to run. None of the men had bothered to fire their weapons yet. I couldn't risk her getting hurt. Then one of the guys approached her. She fainted straight to the ground. I knew if I took one step toward her to help they'd spray me with ammo. The guy bent over to help her and she jumped up, and shanked him with a single thrust beneath his rib cage. Her move shocked me so much I almost fell out and let myself be exposed.

I could have sworn I saw her smile at him as she pulled out her blade. Another guy sprang to action. He shifted his gun away from me and aimed it straight at her. She picked up the corpse, using it as a shield; then she drove both of them as fast as possible toward the one wielding the shotgun. I kept the last guy distracted once I realized that she could handle herself. Fearing more for his safety than that of his friend, the gunman finally let off a shot. The force smashed into them, but the human shield took the brunt. Poor guy couldn't get another round chambered before Paris and the dead guy fell atop him.

He started screaming and yelling in Spanish. She scurried like a little rabbit over the dead body sandwiched between them and pointed a nice little Ruger. Placed the barrel against his right eye and let off a fatal trigger squeeze, bringing her total body count to two in under a minute. Boo-yah.

I saw the third guy take aim. Just as he prepared to shoot I came flying through the air off the large tractor tire, wielding these two curved blades that look like fangs, one in each clenched fist. I couldn't let anything happen to her. For a second, I just hovered there high above. I came down upon him with a thud and drove those things into the poor man's chest from behind. As soon as they dug in, I yanked them upward and back, ripping and tearing all they'd dug into. The man screamed as if his soul were being removed—arms just a-flailing as all control to them was severed—and dropped to his knees. With simultaneous flicks of my wrists, I removed the blades from the sobbing, wounded man's body, then brought them across his back in an X pattern before slashing each across the man's exposed throat. The instant silence was more disturbing than the man's screams. Amid the outward spray of blood, I removed the 9 mil from the newly departed's hand just as the body fell over dead.

"Paris? What the fuck are you doing out here, yo?" I asked, ditching my fake English accent again as she stepped over the man I'd just killed.

She was a completely different animal than I thought. As I guess I was to her now too.

"Apparently saving your fucking ass," she replied, as hard rock as she'd been toward me until today. She jumped up to her feet with the Ruger still in hand.

"You sure about that?" I said, spinning the newly acquired Sig Sauer around on my hand like somebody from out the Wild West.

I aimed the 9 mil at her.

Looked like the final score was gonna be tied.

Paris

24

"Oh! Is this your way of thanking me?" I asked angrily as I turned my Ruger on him as well, aiming straight center mass on his chiseled frame. Beaten down, his dress shirt stained with dirt and familiar streaks of pink and red, and he still looked hot. But I was prepared to gladly add his body count to the mess. "Now . . . whatcha wanna do?" I asked, adrenaline flowing.

Niles didn't flinch though. Seeing what I was packing, he cautiously took a few steps back while keeping his handgun trained on me. Not out of fear, but from being cagey as fuck. He didn't have to say it, but I got it; could see the look in his eyes. He knew the range of the Ruger being pointing at him. And that its accuracy dropped off dramatically the greater the distance from its target. His? Not so much. Niles sidestepped the heap made by my two victims. Not missing a beat he reached down with a gloved hand, making sure they were both dead.

"Who sent you?" he asked coolly.

"What the fuck! No one sent me. And what the fuck did you do to make these fools come at you? Stole their money?" I asked, having a hard time controlling my frustration.

"Nice. Good one. Had me fooled for the longest. Good looks and attitude. My weakness, no doubt." He chuckled, not making a bit of sense. "Now . . . I'ma give you one more chance. Who sent you? You freelancing?"

I shot at his feet, making him jump. "There's your 'freelancing' right there," I replied. Yeah. I could still hit him. Got a gold fuckin' star in marksmanship back at school.

Without wasting a word, Niles shot back. The bullet grazed my jacket without hurting me. But almost made me pee on myself. "You stupid ass! You coulda killed me!" I yelled as I thrust my gun toward him in anger.

"But I didn't. Look . . . we only got about fifteen minutes tops before their friends find us. And you do not want to be around here when the numbers are on their side," Niles said, his eyes glancing down at the bodies around us. "So you gotta tell me. Who are you working for?"

"Myself, bitch. And you need to stop pointing that gun at me. Seriously. Unless you plan on killing me like Ramon and Antonio. Yeah. I saw the news and came downstairs to have a 'talk' with ya. I only followed you when you skated out of your meeting back at the hotel."

"If we're done with the standoff and your anger over that yacht mess, we need to go. Now. We can talk about this later. Somewhere else."

"Like how you talked to Ramon and Antonio on the yacht? Drug overdoses, my ass," I argued. "I also read about that Pakistani businessman. The one I saw you talking to at the hotel."

"Stop right there before I suddenly have a situation on my hands. A situation you really don't want, ma," Niles said as he motioned at his near miss. "Now I'm about to walk out of here. You're welcome to come with me or stay. But if you stay, you better scrounge up something more than that LCP .380."

"Like you did much better," I said, lowering my gun as I begrudgingly followed him. "Yeah. They had you hemmed up behind that tire over there, boss. And I'm still waitin' on a 'thank you, Paris' or sumthin'."

"Yeah. Thanks. But the plan wasn't for me to get caught," he groused as he casually fired a shot into the body that lay in the entrance then kept walking.

"I got a scooter. A Vespa in the grass near the road. Over there," I said as I pointed toward the road where, according to Niles, more trouble would be coming. "But it needs gas."

"Really? A Vespa?" he said with a sneer. "Yo, we gotta roll. And roll hard."

"That raggedy Jeep you got there ain't fast either," I shot back . . . verbally. "Maybe they wouldn't have caught you if it was."

"I'm not talking about the Jeep," he said as he walked over to the still-running Audi with the dead body in the driver's seat.

"Who shot him? You had some backup, right?" I asked as I looked a little more closely at the shots placed through the windshield into what used to be the driver.

"Nah," he said as he grabbed the body by its jacket collar and pulled it out onto the ground. "Did it myself with that," he indicated with a bit of pride.

I spied the discarded black rifle lying on the ground by the Jeep. And a Halliburton briefcase left open and on its side. It didn't hold paperwork after all, but had foam cutaways inside.

"Was someone shooting at you atop that hill?" I asked, figuring the answer even as I asked.

"No. I was the one doing the shooting," he said as he wiped some of the dead guy's brains off the steering wheel and changed the radio station.

"Eeew," I squealed as my face scrunched up. "That is just nasty. Hope you plan on throwing away those gloves. And using some hand sanitizer, too."

"Quit playing and get in because you're gonna be driving."

"What?" I blurted out.

Niles

25

We were on a road, working our way back toward Valencia, and both of us were stressed the fuck out.

"You got me sitting in the mess you made. Know how gross this is?" she asked, trying to get comfortable with the blood and stench of death on her clothes. "And why in the fuck do you have me driving anyway?"

"Because with you at the wheel we stand the best chance of us making it back. The ones still alive didn't see you," I said from my reclined position in the passenger seat, my gun aimed at her side since we got on the road. Every few minutes or so, I would raise my head to peer out the window.

"Why are you in Spain? For real," she asked.

"Just doing a job," I calmly replied as if we were just going for a leisurely drive, never mind the fact that we had racked up a body count and the day wasn't over. "I took out a very big some-one in one of his villas. Straight sniped him from the hilltop above while he was tending his garden. Lliria's his hometown. This was supposed to be a place where he felt safe enough to be without his usual security entourage. At least that's what my contact, that man you saw me with, told me. Shame on me for believing him. And shame on him for trying to be greedy and change the terms of our agreement."

"So you're not a money manager at all." Paris actually sounded shocked and hostile.

"Ding-ding," I replied. "Just my cover for my being here. Mixed in a little fun, too, took in the local sights . . . to keep up pretenses."

"Uh-huh. That's what being a ho is called? And why are you being so forthcoming now?" she asked.

I watched the cars passing us while wondering if I should instead be concerned about the woman driving the car. "I dunno. Maybe because I don't think we'll make it outta this alive. Or maybe I've decided to kill you when this is over," I said. I rested my finger on the trigger with the safety off just in case. "Where'd you learn the craft anyway?" I asked, referring to that which we both seemed to do oh so well. "One of those schools?"

"Yeah," she answered.

I'd heard about a certain kind of school that trained you to become a cold-blooded killer. I knew better than to dig too deep. Apparently they swore you to secrecy once you enrolled. "Did you attend one?" she asked me.

"Nah," I replied. "No 'Hogwarts for Hit Men' for me. I didn't have some rich sponsor to put me through one of them. Picked up my talents on the streets then worked my way up. On-the-job training for this boy."

"And that British accent? What about that? I ain't no expert, but I've been in Europe for a minute. You got 'em straight fooled."

"My moms met my dad in New York, but she was from the UK. A pale white lady from Dover speaking all proper and hooking up in Brooklyn with a hard mofo from Ghana. Life is funny as fuck. God really got a sense of humor, yo," I admitted. Even gave her a mischievous smile. "And what about you, princess? You came here to merc someone too?"

"Hell nah. I came here to chill. Furreal," she said with a laugh. "My plan was to stay out of trouble."

"Yet here you are," I muttered. "Deep in the shit."

She'd taken a route bypassing Lliria and sticking to the smaller roads. But as we got closer to Valencia, both the traffic and tension picked up.

"We'll need to ditch the car soon. Probably burn it or dump it in a lake or something. Don't want anybody connecting us to all this mess or tracking us back," I said, bringing up my seatback. "Maybe we'll walk the rest of the way in. Or catch a cab. Pull over up there," I instructed, pointing to a spot half a mile up where a little side road branched off toward a farming community.

Our luck ran out though on that final approach to Valencia. We were so busy talking that we got caught slippin' to the point of not noticing the Audi A8—one identical to ours except minus the guts, gore, and bullet holes—until it passed me. Oh. And as its brake lights flashed in the rearview mirror we remembered the other distinct difference.

The men inside that fucker wanted to kill us.

"It's them!" I yelled at Paris, hoping she could handle the wheel. "They just lost their boss. Believe me when I say they ain't gonna stop and ask which nigga did what no matter how pretty you look."

She floored the Audi, needing no direction about what to do. I was impressed. But where to go was another matter.

"Where am I going? Tell me where to go," she shouted at me.

"If we head back into the city, the cops will probably get involved. I don't kill cops, so take the road where I told you to pull over. Do it now!" Just as she swerved onto the asphalt road heading toward the farm, our back glass exploded. Shards of glass flew throughout the inside, pelting us as the sound of rounds striking the trunk and taillights drove home how fast things were going south.

"They've got a fuckin' assault rifle!" I screamed to Paris, wanting her to take extra precaution.

"No shit!" she yelled back over the racing of the engine while snaking the A8 back and forth across the lanes to avoid another direct hit like that. Paris briefly went off the road, cursing over the near miss we had with a truck carrying goats. In my side-view mirror, I could see them somehow gaining on us.

Another shot landed, this time sparks erupting as they took out the door mirror the moment we switched lanes again.

"They're trying to take out the tires," I cursed as I glanced back. I undid my seat belt and rolled backward into the rear seat. Risking death, I carefully took aim and fired a single shot at our pursuers. I saw them respond to the bullet striking their windshield by backing off.

But not for long as another hail of gunfire erupted in our direction. I dove for cover just as the first bullet missed me and struck the dashboard radio, causing all the electronics in the car to blink out for a second. "If we're not going to outrun them, we gotta get them closer," I called as I checked the number of rounds left in my clip. "You down for that, Paris?"

"Closer. Yeah," she replied through clenched teeth.

Yeah. We were dead.

Nadja

26

I tried to stop that crazy American from following Niles but she was moving too fast. He didn't have a phone—not a great idea in case things went badly—so I couldn't warn him, and the last thing I could do was follow him. Shit! I was going out of my mind waiting to find out if he had successfully completed the assignment or if she had destroyed the entire operation. I did not want to be the one to tell my father that I'd allowed some horny American bitch to interfere in our work. And I hadn't even considered the possibility that she was some plant and out to hurt or even kill Niles. This was much worse than I thought. I needed to find out exactly who this woman was and stop her in her tracks.

I approached the concierge at the front desk.

"Hello, may I help you?" She smiled, ready to fix all my problems.

"Yes, there is a *mujer Americana negra* staying at the hotel?"

"Madame Hosseini, I am not sure to whom you are referring!" she said, even though we both knew there was only one black woman in the entire hotel.

"She looks like that singer Beyoncé?" I reached in my wallet and pulled out a bill large enough to loosen her lips. "We were supposed to meet for drinks and I've forgotten her name."

"Oh, you must mean Madame Wimberly."

"Ah, yes, Wimberly. And her first name?"

"Paris, like the city."

Humph, typical. "And where is she from?"

"America!" the hostess pronounced excitedly as if it was her dream to go there.

"Yes, but I mean do you know where in America?"

"No." She nodded. "America!"

"Thank you." I stepped away from the desk, already working my Internet. I didn't know where she was from but she was now in my world and I had a few things to teach Miss Wimberly.

After an hour of intense Internet searching I did not come across anyone who matched the description of our nosy American. She didn't strike me as the type of woman who filed easily into the background. It was obvious from my inspection of her couture wardrobe and Cartier diamond watch that she was only comfortable among the finer things in life. The Wimberlys I discovered online were all in the South and of a lower to middle social and economic class. No, this bitch had been exposed to some things 'cause she walked around like she owned shit. Maybe she was the mistress of some rap star or athlete. But that would mean that she was cheating with Niles. I could say one thing and end her cushy existence. Yeah, I was about to make this whore sorry she'd ever stepped one foot into Valencia. I did a quick search of all the black gossip sites. An hour later I'd gotten absolutely nowhere.

I picked up the phone and dialed Navid. He wasn't just an assistant; his tech skills were part of the reason he made five times what my second assistant received. The other part was his loyalty. There wasn't anything I couldn't share with him.

"Get me everything you can find on a black American, Paris Wimberly. She's probably early twenties. I don't care if you're busy; this takes precedence." I fumed as I hung up, frustrated and ready to throw something. I wasn't about to let this floozy ruin everything I had been building. She was a nothing and a nobody and the sooner I got her away from Niles the better.

Paris

27

A sandy dirt road between the rows of fruit trees caught my attention. I gambled, ignoring Niles's squawking, and made a hard right turn onto it, thankful the car was able to handle it. I held the pedal down, having no time for worry as Niles finally righted himself in his seat. In my rearview mirror, I could see nothing but gravel and dust flying up behind us. This would've been fun if not for Niles's sobering bullet holes in the windshield directly in front, reminding me what being on the losing end meant.

While plowing through rows of fig trees, Niles told me of the desperate idea he'd come up with. After hearing his bat-shit-ass plan and agreeing to it, I slammed on the brakes, partially running the Audi off the modest road and into a cluster of trees.

"Are you ready?" Niles asked, checking his weaponry: the Sig Sauer and those crazy curved knives of his. I still had Daddy's gifts, but was down to only a few rounds in my clip and my blade for who knew how many were coming for us.

"I got no choice, so yeah," I replied with a genuine smile. From our first meeting on the hotel elevator to the yacht to now, I was willing to admit I enjoyed his company no matter how crazy the drama.

With our time fleeting, Niles kissed me tenderly. Perhaps to say good-bye, but it felt like we were just being introduced for the first time: a girl from Queens and a guy from Brooklyn. Made me want to tell him who I really was and how I ran things, but we didn't have time for my scorecard. I could hear our pursuers almost upon us, hard charging in their car with dark intentions on their minds.

"Now," Niles said, putting our plan into action.

When they caught up to our car, I said a silent prayer to get us out of this mess. From the limited view my vantage point gave me, I watched five men slowly exit their Audi and methodically surround the car we'd abandoned. We'd left all its doors open to confuse them as to how many people they were up against. I also hoped the blood all over the driver's seat and my ruined Nike jacket left on the ground would make them think they'd shot me and I'd fled.

As best I could tell, the men were carefully fanning out, as they spoke Spanish at a rapid clip. One man, the one apparently in charge, sat on the hood of their car screaming orders, and even slapped the head of the one carrying the automatic rifle: a black H&K from what I could tell. As they moved about and out of my limited line of sight, I didn't dare move a muscle for fear of giving away our position. Niles was crouched over beside me on his knees in an impossible position, but his muscles hadn't failed him yet as he stayed immobile. In the dim light we had, his eyes were on overload, blinking rapidly. We struggled to hear what was being said. It was a critical time, because we only had, as that old Mr. Scarface's song went, "A Minute to Pray and a Second to Die."

My heart beat like a nightclub soundtrack while the veins throbbed in my head. I was almost afraid to breathe, worried that even the sweat about to drip off my face would be heard by one of the men milling around us. *When? When?* I frantically thought as minutes felt like hours. When Niles brushed his hand against mine, I had my answer.

Now.

In the darkness, I smiled as all my fear and nervousness dissolved. I gave a hearty yank on the emergency release inside the stuffy trunk where'd we been hiding. We had been using the bullet holes provided by these very same men with whom we were about to get up close and personal to peer out. Niles thrust upward against the trunk with his back, having been pressed against it since we scurried inside. As we popped up like a couple of badass jacks-in-the-box, ready to engage, I was so happy to be free of the tiny, hot space while fortunate that they hadn't unloaded on our hiding place as a precaution. In unison, Niles and I quickly found targets before they could react. I used my Ruger on the closest one, a Versace-wearing thug who had his foot resting on the bumper while he lit a cigarette. I gave him a light of my own right in the middle of his forehead, his smoke hovering in the air for a moment as his limp body fell away. Niles chose his target well, dropping the boss with a shot into his open, startled mouth less than a second behind me. Simultaneously, we jumped down, fully exposed as we rolled clear of our only shelter. Niles went to the left while I went to the right to cover ground more quickly as there were three remaining.

Both of us had the idea to go after the biggest threat and we found him: the man with the assault rifle. From both our spots, we had him in our sights, standing three feet in front of the car. Unfortunately, he saw us too and shot first. Niles and I both reacted in time, diving for cover behind the car as rounds flew everywhere. Ducking low, we regrouped as the remaining windows to our car were shot out, pieces of glass raining down around us as he moved in closer for the kill. All this noise was going to bring the other two running as well, so we knew this had to end quick. But either one of us would be nothing but a target if we revealed ourselves.

So we did something unexpected and improvised. When the shots stopped coming, on the count of three, we came out simultaneously, making him decide with Niles to his left and me to his right. Sexist pig thought more of Niles and his Sig Sauer, aiming at him first. Conserving my ammo, I had my open blade in my hand by then and hurled it overhand as hard as I could. The stiletto was true as it tumbled end over end through the air, finding its mark in his neck just as he fired at Niles, his H&K making a distinct "Brrrraaap!" sound that carried through the quiet grove. My attack only wounded him, yet threw his aim off just enough for Niles to scamper for cover behind the car once again. When the enraged man turned to shoot me instead, Niles returned the favor, running across the top of the car and leaping off its roof while leveling two rounds dead in his chest before landing atop him with a body tackle. *What was up with*

Niles's "flying through the air" shit? Must've thought he was a daredevil or something.

"Thank you," I mouthed as Niles gracefully rolled onto his feet near his fresh kill as if a cat.

"I just wanted to get my hands on his Heckler & Koch before you did," he softly joked (I think) as he removed my blade from the man's neck, closed it, and tossed it back to me. "Now . . . stay here," he tersely instructed.

"Wait! Where are you going?" I whispered.

"Hunting," he answered as he held up two fingers for the stragglers out there amid the trees.

"But . . ."

"Paris, listen for once. Stay here and wait for me. Won't be long," Niles stressed, now brandishing enough firepower in the form of the automatic rifle he got to before me.

"Argh! Fucking asshole!" I cursed, clenching my fists. Would serve him right to take one of these cars and leave, but I waited like he knew I would. Random gunfire caught my attention though, leading me to take cover against the undamaged Audi and get my guard back up. Another few shots told me the action wasn't in our immediate vicinity, but Niles could've been flushing the last two back my way.

When I heard footsteps running toward my position, I trained my gun sight and waited for the little birdie to fly across my path. But a fucking farmer, coveralls and sweaty bandanna around his neck, came scampering from out of the grove instead. Poor thing was so terrified by the suited bodies strewn all around him that he didn't see me until it was too late. When I saw he wasn't a threat, I stowed my Ruger.

"Help me! They are shooting," he pled in Spanish, pointing back in the direction of where Niles had gone to tend to loose ends. He untied his bandanna and used it to wipe his brow while his eyes darted from body to body.

"Calm down. *Tranquilo*," I said to the wide-eyed, gritty-faced man as I cautiously approached him, still worried we weren't out of the woods yet until Niles came back alive and in one piece. "These were bad men . . . *hombres muy malos*. You will be okay."

As I reassured the farmer in my terrible Spanglish, Niles emerged from among the trees, moving the leaves aside with the extended H&K, smoke still visible from its barrel. His eyes were cold and his shirt stained with fresh blood as he made a zero with his thumb and index finger, signaling all five were accounted for. *Game over, bitches.*

"No . . . no," the farmer begged as he saw Niles, and began looking for somewhere to run.

"It's okay. It's okay," Niles said as he dropped the assault rifle to his side, sliding back into his disarming British accent. "See?"

I breathed a sigh of relief as Niles's posture softened. "We have money. *Mucho* Euros. No speak to anyone, okay?" I said as I motioned with my hands to further calm the farmer.

"*Sí, mi amigo. No problema,*" Niles agreed as he placed a hand on the wary man's shoulder. But it was only to steady the poor soul as he shot him in the head, point blank with the Sig Sauer he'd retrieved from his waistband with his other hand.

"What the fuck!" I shrieked at Niles, drawing my Ruger on him again as I took a step back in disgust and shock. "He's a civilian!"

"Who saw both our faces," Niles matter-of-factly commented, turning and ignoring my gun, which was aimed at him. To get his attention, I shot once at an olive tree to his right. He didn't even flinch. "I hated doing it, but had no choice. You think he would really keep quiet?" he asked me, looking back.

"No," I replied, relenting. Just because he was right didn't mean I liked it.

"Good. 'Cause I ain't spending the rest of my life in prison. Too pretty for that. Paris, there are hard choices you have to make if you're serious about doing this kind of work. Now help me."

Under Niles's instruction, I got a crash course in crime scene subterfuge, moving the bodies around and repositioning guns. Did enough to confuse even the best CSI while implicating a poor simple farmer in the mini massacre.

The final touch was to stuff rags made from his bloody shirt and my ruined jacket in the gas tanks of both cars then set them afire. The fire was bound to spread to some of the fruit trees and maybe the poor man's home as well. A shame that he'd never again enjoy the literal fruits of his labor.

As the two of us beat a hasty path across the farmland, amid lemons and grapefruit, one of the cars' gas tanks exploded, making us look back to acknowledge the cloud of black smoke. Our plan was to cut across the property and intersect back with the main road to town. Niles, sweating in his undershirt, slacks, and dress shoes beneath the hovering sun, recited our story as we briskly jogged over a hill a mile from where we started. "When we get back, just act normal. I'll say I was with you after the conference seminar. We were in your room having sex, okay?" he stated, rather than asking.

I stopped running. Niles, so focused on getting his story straight, continued a few steps before noticing I'd even stopped. "What's wrong?" he asked as he turned around with that "what the fuck" look etched on his face.

"If we're going to claim we had sex, might as well keep it real," I said with a smile and much more than that blossoming between my legs.

Hot.

Sticky.

Wet.

Niles went to argue against it . . . before his smile came to match mine.

"Paris, this place is gonna be crawling with *policia*. Soon," he weakly offered.

"Then you better work your magic quickly," I responded, lazily cocking my head.

I tossed my gun and knife aside, after which Niles followed suit.

As much trouble as he's gotten me in, the dick better be good.

Niles

28

I put my hand up to block the sun and checked my watch again, calculating how much this unforeseen shit had jacked up my timetable. The job was supposed to be simple. Just a clean hit and get out. Should've been long back at the hotel playing my role again, but Kahn must've tipped De Banderas's people off. Turned this into a warzone, which made me not regret offing Kahn's greedy ass one bit.

And now this.

Paris Wimberly.

Or at least that's the name she was using. She seemed proud enough of it that it probably was indeed her real name. Amateur move even if she was just on vacation.

As much trouble as she's causing me, pussy better be good, I thought as I smiled and disarmed myself, tossing my gun and my karambit blades aside. But not too far away in case I needed to get to them in time. People had different ways of softening up their victims and she might be that fuckin' crafty.

But in addition to being beautiful and too sexy for words, Paris had saved my life at least once today. Something I couldn't just forget . . . or that she would let me forget.

Girl was still raw, but had skills. Showed promise and had a ton of arrogance to go along with it, which was why I'd never admit how grateful I was for her help. Looked like we had the makings of a good team, and maybe something more if we didn't kill one another first.

But here in the Spanish countryside? With too many bodies to count and two burning cars only a mile away?

Shit. We weren't even outta the woods yet and she wanted to stop for a quickie?

"Yo, are we gonna do this?" she asked as she stopped in the middle of slipping off her pants, probably sensing my hesitation. Mmm. Those legs and that exposed ass as she bent over like so could've made the spread of many a magazine. But it was those eyes of hers, the desire in them that overwhelmed me. That desire in them I'd dreamt of seeing since first laying my eyes on her. Yeah, she was a New York girl to the fullest; from Queens, not Brooklyn.

But it would do.

"Yeah. Why the fuck not?" I replied, already hard as fuck as I unfastened my belt.

Paris pranced over seductively in her tennis shoes, absent her pants as if unfazed by our surroundings. I'd gotten my slacks and briefs down to my knees when she jumped into my arms, daring me to drop her. I caught her, holding her firmly in one arm while I slid her shirt up for a taste. I dragged my tongue lazily up her taut stomach, her sweet sweat assaulting my senses as she dug her nails into my back as if they were mini versions of that knife she liked to throw. As I took one of her perky breasts in my mouth, Paris kissed around the edges of my ear before purring all raspy, "Brooklyn, go hard."

If I wasn't hornier than a mofo before, there was no question now. I had no snappy comebacks for this sexy bitch because I had a mouthful of titties just then, my teeth masterfully nipping at her lovely, attentive nipples. Paris's gasps and the forceful thrusts of her pelvis told me I had her gushing as I pulled her close to me, kissing her neck before wantonly giving her my tongue. The two of us stumbled around on the uneven ground, maddening lust overruling caution, until we bumped up against a tree.

Rather than complain about her back striking the trunk, Paris instead reached up with those toned arms of hers and grasped the branches overhead, wrapping her legs around me as she coaxed me inside her.

"Hurry," she panted, her eyes cast in the direction of the billowing clouds of dark smoke for which we were responsible.

"You're crazy," I commented at the sight of her suspended before me as I slid inside, warmth enveloping my dick as I attempted to navigate the strong currents of her lovin'. I moaned with pleasure, ignoring my survival instincts, my training, as I gave in to something more primal deep within me; something longing to escape.

"Yeah. Crazy for this dick," Paris grunted as she began bouncing on me, the branches she held relenting then returning in rhythm with the slap, slap, slapping of our bodies.

I took a hold of Paris's ass, going more forceful with my strokes as she panted, "Beat. This. Pussy. Up." Began a tug of war for dominance as she came then came some more all over me, her essence delivered on the winds to my nostrils by my heavy breathing.

"D . . . damn," I stuttered, overcome by how good she felt as I tried to push through the moment. Tried to tell myself it was *just another shag* as I'd gotten used to saying in my adopted English tongue around here. But she had me feeling more punk kid than porn star, more student than stud.

"Go hard, Brooklyn. Go hard." Paris giggled with a tease, followed by a grunt of agreement. She relented as I took over our dance, her fingers slipping from their sure grip above as I now controlled her bounding body, matching then surpassing her intensity as she worked her ass cheeks, making them clap to each stroke.

All talk ceased as Paris wrapped her arms around my neck and held on for dear life, latching those deceptively powerful legs as if to prevent my escape. With that door shut, I forged ahead with my strokes that had her eyes rolling back in her head as she spouted gibberish. I stood strong, holding Paris right there in the moment as I briefly took in her beauty. Admired the curve of her lips, the tip of her nose, the sound of her breath, before letting that which I'd been keeping at bay claim me.

For the queen from Queens, her Brooklyn came hard, my very being spewing forth as my leg muscles tensed and tightened. As I erupted, Paris held firm, taking control back as she came with me, her dam giving way.

I was weary and drenched in sweat as I slowly let Paris down, our heat more than that of the afternoon Spanish sun. I watched her, unsure of what to say in this instance.

Paris replied by quickly picking up her Ruger before even retrieving her pants from off the ground. She had me cut off from my weapons with my slacks around my ankles—literally caught with my pants down. I tensed, ready to accept the double cross that happens in the world in which I live . . . the betrayal that's just the cost of doing business.

But Paris didn't shoot. Keeping her eye on me, she reached down for her pants and her blade.

"Get your shit. We gotta go. Remember?" she reminded me, that sass and brass having returned despite the smile of satisfaction she couldn't hide.

Rio

29

Eduardo lent me his Bentley and driver to pick up my boy from the airport. He was working hard to seduce me into staying up in his crib. Shit was fly as fuck! It wasn't like I wasn't used to high-end shit but the Euros didn't play with their flossing. I got out the car when I spotted my favorite DJ coming out the door.

"What's up?" DJ PLUS 1NE grabbed me in a bear hug. We went way back. "Fuck, you the mayor of this bitch already?" He motioned to the car and driver who had already collected his bags and put them in the trunk.

"Working on it." I laughed. Damn it felt good to get a taste of the States.

"I'm just doing this thing. Thanks for taking the cut."

"Shit, I owe you big time."

"Congrats on your nomination. A Grammy, right?" I said.

"Yeah. Actually two nominations. Who'da thunk it," PLUS 1NE joked.

"I always believed in you."

"Shit you put me on the map. I'd be back in Nebraska shucking corn if it weren't for your hooking me up with your connections."

Teddy, as I first knew him when he landed in the city post high school, was now one of the hottest DJs out. I helped put this lanky, introverted white boy from Lincoln in the game by featuring him at some venues and private parties around New York and Jersey. One of the bonuses of having older siblings is that folks let you do shit way before you're legally permitted. Paris and I got into clubs from the time we were fourteen. They knew not to serve us drinks or let us get high so it was mainly about the beats. We love to get fly and dance. When we turned seventeen we were able to have a drink, maybe some weed. Not legal but that's what kids our age were doing. Using hardcore anything was off-limits, which I learned the first time I tried cocaine and my brothers busted me. I thought I was acting normal but they saw right through that shit. They explained that weed was no problem but anything that had a high addiction factor was straight-up *no*. They didn't have to tell me twice. Helping people throw great parties by introducing them to the next best thing was like my addiction. Folks knew that if I suggested someone that meant they should give them a chance.

Five years ago when we met, DJ PLUS 1NE had been my running buddy. DJ, for those that don't know, is really shorthand for dick jockey. Once he started spinning at clubs he had lines of females ready to throw him as much sex as he could handle. When you're hanging out with celebrities and getting hired for their private events you become a celebrity and by extension so does the chick on your arm. In fact he'd dated more than a few household names but nobody ever locked him down for long. I had a crazy crush on him but his pussy parade ran so deep there was no way I'd step to him and ruin a good friendship.

But now that he was here in Spain and looking fly as hell a guy could dream. Eduardo was fun and I had plans to go back for more but nobody could get this for long. I wasn't close to being gettable but I couldn't help wondering what it would be like to go for a ride with my passenger. He'd earned the nickname PLUS 1NE because when he blew up, people would say one man wasn't capable of doing what he did. Some hotshot had him change the spelling to PLUS 1NE just to be unique.

He pulled out a pouch he'd snuck into the country. Waved it under my nose. "They call it 'Dragon,'" he offered.

"Paris is gonna lose her mind. She's been feinding for some good stuff."

"Shit, the fabulous Paris around too? Sounds like a hell of a start to a good party."

"Don't forget the name thing," I whispered so that the driver couldn't hear.

"Fuck yeah; I'm all about the Wimberlys." He winked at me as we pulled up to the hotel. "Speaking of Paris. Isn't that her not looking her normal fly self?" He pointed at my sister and Mr. Big Feet dashing in front of the car and into the hotel. I didn't know what the fuck my sister was up to but it didn't look good.

Nadja

30

After pacing frantically around my room, waiting for some kind of information about the job I'd sent Niles to handle, I decided to head down into the lobby. That way I'd be present when he returned. And even though I didn't want to think about it one word kept haunting me: if. There was always a chance in his line of work that things wouldn't go so well. That he'd get hurt, or wounded, or, worse, captured. And if that American bitch had anything to do with him not returning in one piece there would be no place in the world for her to hide.

I hit redial on my phone. "Did you find out anything?"

"No, it's like she came out of thin air." Navid appeared to be stumped.

"That's impossible. She exists and you must find out who the hell she is and where she comes from and if she's connected. Just do it!" I slammed down the phone.

The lobby was literally overrun with people, those at the business conference and others checking in and out. I took a seat so that I would be facing the entrance. *Come on, Niles; get your ass back here.* It had been four hours, more than enough time for him to handle things and return if they had gone well. It made me think back to the first time we'd gone on an assignment together. When things switched from me hating him and thinking of him as one more arrogant prick I had to put up with.

We'd returned from a particularly hairy endeavor with the Russians. I'd arranged passage for us out of the country, which we made with bare minutes to spare. After crossing the border we were helicoptered to Nice and a five-star hotel suite. It was the only room available, which meant we'd have to share. We were both functioning on pure adrenaline, having come dangerously close to being discovered. I'd made some calls, handling the cleanup, so he'd showered first.

As I entered the room finally clean and relaxed I stopped when I saw him staring at me. The look he gave was pure, deep, penetrating lust. Forget about undressing me with his eyes, his intense gaze went much further, ravaging me wholly and completely. I stumbled, caught under the power of his seduction. In that split second everything changed.

"I'd like to do things to you," Niles's husky baritone threatened.

My body reacted as if there were some invisible thread drawing me toward him. Next thing I knew my clothes were off and he was down between my legs, devouring me. His hands were manipulating my nipples, twisting them in sweet pleasure. My body tensed up because I felt like I was going to pee on myself. I tried desperately to hold it back but then it switched and I suddenly felt this sensation unlike anything I'd ever experienced. My breath was coming in aggressive spurts and I felt as if I were losing control of my body. Everything started convulsing into earth-shattering pieces. Each nerve ending in my vagina burst and spilled over, taking me with it. The room started spinning as I tried to gather myself and gain control to no avail. Finally after what felt like forever I was able to lift myself up on my elbows, my face flushed and confused. He stared down at me, a huge satisfied grin etched on his face.

"Oh, my God. That's what sex is about?" I murmured in between short gasps of breath.

"No, darling, that was the warm-up," he replied all smooth and confident.

Sex. I rolled the word around in my head. Feeling shy I grabbed his shirt off the bed and threw it on, covering myself. I'd never been naked in front of a man in my life. He moved to me, pulling his shirt open.

"Beautiful." He leaned in and began licking my nipples, first gently then more forcefully. He grabbed a handful of my hair in between his knuckles, jerking me to him. His mouth crushed mine as he licked and sucked my lips. I felt myself go completely limp.

A couple of hours later, wet and satisfied, I lay beside Niles feeling deliriously happy and completely unfamiliar. Everything hurt but felt good at the same time. My inner thighs burned as if I'd been riding my prized stallion for too many hours, and my vagina was throbbing and pulsing. Pain and pleasure. Pleasure and pain. This man had done things to me I'd never imagined before that day. And the version I did know about from books and movies was strictly forbidden in my family, and frowned upon in my culture without the bonds of holy matrimony. It made me remember Amir, my fiancé. I winced when the vision of him entered my mind.

"I have to call off my wedding," I shouted, panic rising in my voice.

"For what?" Niles reacted.

"For us! Isn't that obvious?"

"No! I don't mind teaching you what you need to learn in the bedroom. I've never been with a woman who was as good as you were your first time but I don't expect you to leave your man."

"Of course I will. I can't marry him now. Not after this." I couldn't believe I'd have to spell it out for him.

Niles sat up, staring down at me. "Whoa, Nadja, I've never been a one-woman man. I'm simply not capable of it."

"But? What about today?"

"Today was two grown adults playing their version of 'Let's Get It On' like a seventies song." Niles grinned at me, pleased with his rhyming.

"But I'm not a whore. I don't sleep around; for that matter, I've never slept with anyone. I have been saving myself for the man I am going to marry. And now that we have slept together—"

Niles cut me off. "I've never been able to commit to any one woman. It's never been about the women. Like you. You're amazing and any man would be lucky to have you but I just have this block. Maybe it's one of the hazards of my job. I can't afford to allow myself to be that vulnerable in my line of work."

I was shocked by his coldness. It was always my vision that I would marry the first man I slept with and now he was telling me that wasn't the case. I was hurt. I felt used and didn't know how to react. "I want to be your one and only woman," I assured him.

Two policemen rushing into the lobby along with a civilian tore me away from my memories. It was obvious that they were looking for someone. I hoped to God it wasn't Niles. Minutes later he entered and Paris was with him. The civilian turned toward them.

"There." He pointed at Niles and Paris. This was bad. Very very bad.

Paris

31

After the long hike with Niles, we hitched a ride the last five miles back into Valencia where we had someone buy us a quick change of clothes. The Hotel Balneario Las Arenas Balneario Resort never looked so good when I limped into its impressive lobby, legs feeling like licorice.

Two municipal police were strutting around the lobby. Place must've served damn good coffee otherwise the hotel guests were gonna begin to think maybe this wasn't the nicest place to be spending their money. I went to complain about the po-pos to Niles, but in just that tiny moment of distraction, he'd gone ghost on me without a trace. *Well, fuck that nigga.* I'd finally gotten some dick, so I was just looking forward to a long, luxurious bath followed by a deluxe down pillow beneath my head anyway. Many of the business conference attendees were checking out, so I kept it movin' and charted a path to the elevator through the guests and luggage-filled carts.

But as I moved, one of those fuckin' po-pos spotted me for real this time, no mistake. Damn me for looking so good; I always stood out even when I was tore down. It was hard being a splash of mocha goodness out here. And no denying it or attributing it to weed-based paranoia this time. His eye was trained on me as he stepped lively in my direction, saying something I couldn't yet hear or understand.

"Aww, mother fuck me," I muttered under my breath, too worn to put up a fight anymore. I could already feel myself being fitted into a prison jumpsuit and the cuffs tightening around my wrists. And that's not the kind of jewelry I like. *If they're going to pin all those bodies on me, I'm gonna be a legend on the inside . . . unless I get the death penalty,* I thought, trying to find a silver lining in what was to come. Did they even have a death penalty in Spain? *Damn you and your bitch ass, Niles.*

But life threw me an underhand toss for once.

"*Es el!* That's the one!" the voice from an old man alongside the po-po squeaked. "She took my scooter and didn't return it!"

The Vespa? They were here because of the Vespa?

I would've laughed with relief if it wouldn't have caused more trouble for me than it was worth.

"Excuse me, señora," the other officer who'd cut off my path to the elevators chimed in. I kept his eye contact with one of my smiles, hoping he wouldn't focus on my myriad scrapes and bruises I'd done my best to conceal. "May I see some identification?" he asked.

"It's up in my room," I replied, glad he'd find no weapons on me if I was suddenly patted down. "Is something wrong?" I asked all innocent-like.

"Humph. *Americano,*" the officer standing beside the old scooter rental guy snarled in near perfect English for my benefit. Somewhere I was sure I could scrounge up a bullet for his *Mario Kart*–lookin' ass.

"Is there a problem here?" a familiar British accent said. Niles had reappeared to my defense, acting all gentlemanly and suave again. Had even switched into one of his power suits. So he hadn't abandoned me? Points scored.

"Señor, it is none of your problem," the smart aleck one said to Niles as he stepped forward, waving him off.

"It is if you're mucking about with my girlfriend. The Yank's with me," he retorted, asserting authority as he stood his ground. Heh. He called me his girlfriend . . . even if he did call me a "Yank," too. "Now . . . what is the matter?" Niles stressed.

"The señor here. He claims this woman took his scooter and didn't return it."

"Well, she couldn't have done that because she was with me. She rented the Vespa. And I, being foolish, took it for a spin and got it stolen. I was embarrassed and assumed she'd paid this gentleman for his inconvenience while I was attending these dreadful mandatory seminars. Honey, did you pay him yet?"

"I . . . I was just about to, *muffin,*" I replied, going along with it while batting my eyelashes. "I'm sorry."

"I'm sure we cost you some valuable income due to its absence. How much will it take to solve this?" Niles asked as he produced a wallet and promptly removed a wad of cash. Looking at him now, you would never know he was a hit man. Something I could take to heart in the future when I needed to dial it back and hide in plain sight.

"*Mucho gusto,* but we still need to file a report." And as he said the words, the bitch who tried to grab Niles attention on the boat appeared at his side.

"Officer, I am Madame Hosseini," she snapped. "These people are my business acquaintances. I can vouch for them. Surely this isn't going to become a problem?"

"Oh, Madame Hosseini, of course not. No problem at all." The policeman bowed and scraped to her as if she were some damn nobility.

"So you will accept the money and understand that it was a mistake. Americans do not function with the same rules and class as Europeans." She gave some fake-ass smile, which made them all laugh as they stared at me. I was about to go off on her but Niles squeezed my arm, warning me to calm me down. "I'm sure we can work something out?"

"Of course, Madame Hosseini."

"What about the Vespa? It's—" I was whispering to Niles but he cut me off.

"The cleanup crew will handle it." Damn he was sexy as hell when he took control. Bitch liked that but that Persian heifer was about to get schooled. Paris style.

"Paris!"

I turned to see Rio and DJ PLUS 1NE stepping to me. I fled in their direction, squeals and hugs all around. This had been our running buddy for years before Rio and I went off to school. In the meantime he had blown way the fuck up. Leave it to my brother to get the very best. I turned to see that bitch studying us. She was already too damn far up my ass for my comfort. I would have to find out her story.

"You're not your normal fabulosity." DJ PLUS 1NE twirled me around.

"Decided to take a ride on a Vespa. Fell and shit." I groaned dramatically.

"From the look of the grass stains you didn't fall alone." Rio nodded toward Niles, who had his head pressed together with that chick.

"You coming to see me work?" DJ PLUS 1NE grabbed my attention.

"Got my fly dancing shoes ready to move." I made a little move to signal my readiness to hit the dance floor.

"You heading up to the room?" Rio asked.

"A room!" I responded, winking at my twin. "I got some trouble to get into first." I laughed. "I'm sure I'm not the only one." I pointed to the two of them, who were looking awfully cozy. Yeah, shit was going down all over this hotel.

I stepped over to Niles. It was time to interrupt his little discussion. We weren't done with our one-on-one just yet. They were obviously in the middle of an intense discussion but I couldn't care less. I grabbed him by the arm. "Let's go!"

"Excuse me but when someone saves your ass you should thank them," she snapped.

"Nobody asked for your help. I could handle it myself."

"Just go away. You rude American." She dismissed me, turning back to Niles.

I maneuvered so that I was standing next to him again. Gave her a glare that said "don't push a bitch." "Unless you want to watch some nasty catfight you better get me out of here. I'm ready to go!" I gave him a look that said everything. Smart boy took the bait.

"Nadja, if you can handle that loose end. We'll talk later. I've got to get cleaned up," he finished, almost apologetically.

"Yes, I need a shower." I slid my hand into Niles's, shot Miss Thang a satisfied smirk, and stepped toward the elevator. Yeah, even busted I knew how to get my man.

Rio

32

DJ PLUS 1NE and I high-fived watching the Paris show. My little sister certainly had her game on ten when it came to getting Niles all to herself.

"Get your man." I snapped a gay finger in the air.

"She is the business!" He laughed.

"Don't fuck with Paris. She always gets her man." I smiled, watching her saunter to the elevator with her prize in tow. "So do all of us Du . . . Wimberlys," I stumbled before spitting out my cover name. "They just got to decide if they want it."

DJ gave me a stare, letting me know that he was still way up on my jock. Who'd have thought that after all these years and him blowing up so big he had his pick of DL brothers and straight up out the box guys that he'd still give me the vibe that I was his preference?

"So nobody locked you down yet?" I wondered out loud.

"Eh! When you spend your life in the clubs for a living the DJ groupies become nameless, faceless chicks who don't even care that you're gonna use them and throw them away. It's like they just want to say they had some. I get so much action I'm getting bored with it. It was crazy when I started but after I blew up I couldn't tell who wanted me and who wanted the perks of dating me. You know how that shit can go, all the way to the new reality show, *DJ Exes*," he joked.

"Don't kid. How many no-talent, no nothing cling-ons landed clothing lines and can now charge fees just to show up at the clubs? This is all just because they were fucking the right people. It makes a guy wanna back all the way the fuck up."

"I hear you." He nodded.

The bellman led us up to DJ's room. I insisted on the best hotel but Eduardo let me know that he wasn't swinging for a suite. Still, the room was nicer than most folks' houses. He handed him a tip and closed the door.

"Shit, Rio, you knew me when I was sleeping in the storage rooms of clubs 'cause I had nothing. Hell, you were the one who hooked me up with my first place."

"I couldn't have you homeless."

"So, you're still confused about why I been holding out hope?" he added, which knocked me the fuck out.

"What?"

"Oh, you didn't know I work the whole pendulum. Close your mouth." He laughed at me.

"You're gay?"

"No. I like sex."

"So you're on the down low?"

"Beats being low down but, no, I prefer women; but I ain't gonna turn down no good dick."

"Serious?" I was floored by his admission. Was this really happening?

"What about this?" He leaned over and shoved his tongue in my mouth. "Let's just say Paris wasn't the only one inspiring brothers to play Marvin Gaye songs." After finishing his seductive kiss and stunning the fuck out of me, DJ pulled out his weed and rolled a spliff.

"Want to get high?"

"Nah, man, I got work to do," I reminded him.

"I work better high." He took a hit, getting blazed. Tried to give me a contact but I leaned away from him.

"Long as you bring it. I gots a lot riding on tonight."

"And I got a reputation to uphold," he said, and we both knew he wasn't talking about DJing anymore.

Niles

33

"Mmmm," she moaned, which was getting me excited.

I fought back the urge and commanded myself to stay calm. I knew exactly what she was feeling. While she showered, I'd surprised her by arranging a romantic couple's massage. After the day we had, dodging bullets and risking life and limb, the least I could do for the woman that saved my life was extra relaxation. Not one, but two sets of hands touching all over my achy body: one doing my upper body, while the other concentrated on everything from my tapered waist down. The aromatic oils being coaxed into my sore muscles by the two masseuses flooded my nose, relaxing me even further.

I turned to Paris. "You like?" I mumbled, watching her getting a rub on the table beside me.

"Yeah," she purred softly, briefly opening her eyes to smile at me.

After the first hot stone went atop my back, I felt ready to forget all about the day we'd had. It was the expert touch of those thumbs pressing against the soles of my feet that put me all the way under. It was one of those intense sleeps where you wake up wondering if you've been drooling. I was certainly snoring when I woke, realizing my massage was still going on. The hot stones were gone and only one masseuse was working on me, hands skilled yet more forceful in their glide over my body. At the base of my skull, strong fingers pinched both sides of my neck, making me mumble something that made no sense. My body responded, going limp, as those hands navigated from my neck down my back, thumbs working like powerful little rollers along my spine. I motioned for the masseuse to leave as I rose and approached Paris.

Her body responded as I slid the sheet off of her and began to rub oil on the small of her back, then smoothly traversed the slippery slopes leading to her buttocks. My strong hands began working her ass cheeks.

"Ooooh, boy," she cooed, enjoying every single touch.

"*Aimes-tu?*" I spoke in French even though we were in still Spain.

She strained to move her head, opening a lazy eye long enough to spy me working her. "Well, all right now." Her lips parted in a happy smile.

"Yeah, baby. You like?"

"*Bonne,*" she hissed in French as I spread oil over her ass cheeks. I lowered my face firmly between them. My tongue slithered about at first, teasing and titillating before I put my lips on hers for a little mouth-to-kitty resuscitation. Between each kiss, I paused to lick her from pussy to asshole and back again. Her body responded with shivers. She came just from my breath hovering about her pussy. I forced my face deeper between her legs and sucked on her clit. She cried out in ecstasy. She came again, this time hard and fast.

"Take the pussy, daddy. Take it," she begged me. I dropped my towel and climbed onto the table. I entered her, my dick more swollen and desperate to have her.

"Ooooh," she muttered as I got into a groove.

She arched her back, welcoming me as I worked every stroke, riding her like she was the wave and I was the surfer. My pelvis slapped against her ass again and again, my big dick determined to tickle her cervix. I wasn't going to stop until I wore the pussy out.

"Paris," I whispered in her ear, consumed by my need to be close to her.

"I want it, boy," she gasped back in response. "Give me that."

She kept bucking her hips as I fought to get even deeper inside of her. As we battled, I bit at her shoulder, showering her with foul words of praise. My pumping became shorter, more intense, as I shifted my rhythm and stroke. I reached out and intertwined my fingers with hers.

"Paris, I . . . um . . . oh shit, oh shit. I'm . . ." I babbled, sweat now forming between the barest of spaces that separated us.

"Yes!" she yelled, closing her eyes as I did a deep final thrust. We both erupted in pleasure. I felt our bodies shudder in a sticky sweat swirl of ecstasy.

For the longest I remained motionless atop her, with the only sound being the rapid rising and falling of my chest.

"Damn," I eventually said almost as a gasp of escaping air.

"Yeah," she replied, barely able to speak.

"I dreamed of this, Paris," I admitted, sliding to the side on the table to make her more comfortable. "Back when I first laid my eyes on you. It never left my head. For real."

"Even when you were bodying folk? And fuckin' them other bitches?" she asked jokingly. Well . . . half jokingly.

"Yeah," I said with a laugh. "You were such a distraction. Probably why I was off my game."

"Boy, I don't see nothin' off about your game," she teased as I pulled her tight, spooning with me.

"I like this." As I said the words I realize just how unfamiliar and true they were. This . . . whatever this was right now wasn't going to last. We both knew that. She'd have to get back to school and I'd be off to my next assignment. Shit. So I might as well enjoy it because for once I wasn't ready to be by myself. I liked this.

Paris

34

"Where you goin'?" I groggily asked Niles, hating to see the light of day coming through the curtains.

"Just going take a shower. Go back to sleep, Paris. We'll have breakfast on the patio later on . . . when you're ready," he declared, dick still impressive in its non-aroused state as he stood naked over me. If my pussy wasn't taking a rest, I would've reached up to coax it back to full attention.

Instead, I rolled over in the canopy bed and obeyed him this time. I slid one of the extra pillows over my head, content with my memories of last night. It was impressive that he actually kept getting better. Hell, I didn't even think that was possible. I smiled, thinking how I came all over that dick in this very bed.

I heard Niles rustling, probably looking for a change of clothes, but why was the shower still running?

That question was enough to leave me unsettled when I should've been afloat in dreamland. When I sensed Niles reaching for my purse, that's when I slid the pillow from off my head to see what the fuck was up.

As I sat up, I discovered why the shower was still running.

Because Niles was still in it.

"Paris Wimberly," the woman in all-black Adidas gear with pretty amber skin said, reciting my name off the ID Orlando had given me. The ID that had been in my motherfuckin' purse until now. "Hello, Paris," she said as she finally greeted me with a snarky smile. She was the bitch who I'd seen Niles with on the boat and the one who kinda saved my ass yesterday.

I could tell she meant business by the compact Ruger she pointed at me with her other hand. It was similar to mine that I'd ditched back in Valencia.

No time for second-guessing. Without taking my eyes off her, I reacted. I snatched the alarm clock on the side of the bed and hurled it in her direction, its freed chord flailing behind it as it sailed toward her face. As she shielded her nose, the Bose struck the back of her hand. Yelping in pain, she dropped her gun as I hoped she would. I wanted to dive for it, but I'd only slowed her with my throw because, like some sort of mixed martial artist, she came around with an axe kick to make me think twice.

She just missed me as I rolled away. Her foot dropped onto the soft mattress with more force than I expected. On the opposite side of the bed, I came to my feet. Standing there naked, I spied Niles's karambit blades resting on the dresser, right where he'd placed them last night. Before he proceeded to some deep dicking.

Damn, Niles and his dick getting in my head at the wrong moment. But at least he left something out that I could use.

And, being the excellent pupil, I'd seen how he worked 'em.

I hurled myself toward her just as she began to bend over, those blades of Niles's flailing through the air in my hands. She had to pull back just to avoid her face being sliced open. Judging by her looks and the extensive upkeep, bitch had to be as vain as me. As she fell onto her butt, I landed atop her, trying to pin her arms with my knees as she squirmed around.

That cocky look of hers faded as I raised the curved blades overhead, preparing to paint the room red and end her before she had another chance to end me. The bitch didn't go out like that though. Getting a single hand free, she stunned me by reaching up, digging her nails in, and squeezing the fuck out of my exposed left tit. When I reacted, she used my surprise to toss me off her.

"You crazy bitch!" I yelled as we simultaneously came to our feet.

She replied with something in Farsi that didn't sound too nice either, but somehow she'd got her hands back on her

Ruger. Just as she was about to take aim and I cocked back to throw Niles's blades, a voice roared, "Stop!"

Both of us froze, turning to see Niles, who'd emerged from the bathroom in a towel that barely hung around his waist as he dripped water all over the carpet. He was breathing hard, mean-mugging first at the bitch in black then me.

After running his fingers through his hair and quickly surveying the room, he snatched his blades back from me while leaving the girl with her gun.

"Hey!" I yelled over him rudely disarming me like that and leaving me literally naked.

"Paris," he said, pausing to think. "This is Nadja . . . my travel agent," he said, motioning toward our visitor, who was glaring at me.

There was no way this bitch was a travel agent. *He must think I'm a real stupid bitch.*

Niles

35

"What the fuck is she still doing here?" Nadja snapped as Paris hastily wrapped herself up in a sheet.

"Unlike you, stalker, I was invited," Paris snapped back. "Sorry I can't say the same for you."

"She's my company," I replied, coming between the two of them as Nadja still wielded her gun.

"Yeah. I can see that," she said as she flipped Paris's driver's license—which I'd already checked—in Paris's direction. If it was a forgery, it was a good one. "But what the fuck is she doing here in Valencia? How do we know she's not a plant?" Nadja demanded. Damn her and that temper.

"I'll show you what I'm doing here, bitch! No sneaking up on me this time!" Paris snarled as she tried to get by me to Nadja. Even unarmed and wearing a sheet, she was still crazy as fuck.

I thought physically blocking Paris would do, but I wasn't dealing with an ordinary bird and she outsmarted me. She suddenly draped her sheet over my head, twisting it around my neck and pulling me aside so she could get to Nadja. As I yanked the sheet from off my face, I saw the naked Paris deliver a kick to disarm her. Then, in a split second, she was atop her.

"Say sumthin', bitch!" Paris yelled as she rained down strike after strike on Nadja. Lucky for Nadja, Paris was obviously holding back and hadn't gone for a kill strike. Nadja knew how to defend herself, blocking or deflecting most of the blows.

But I knew Nadja, and her gun was still close enough to grasp, so I had to be decisive and charge into the fire.

"Don't. Move," I instructed both of them, holding a single karambit blade to each of their necks. Nadja knew me, so she immediately relented. Paris thought she knew me, so I dug the blade into her neck ever so slightly to get my point across.

"Okay. I've stopped. Now what?" Paris said as she unclenched her fists and relaxed. She was still breathing heavily. Being so close to her after our night of fun, my bare skin on hers, was powerful. Yet, I didn't fully remove the blade from her neck until she stood up and backed away from Nadja.

"This is just a misunderstanding," I explained to both of them. "Nadja, how come you didn't call or text me first?" I asked, not bothering to hide my irritation.

"Didn't know I had to and since you had your phone off it wasn't possible," she countered as she came to her feet, leaving her gun on the floor until I nodded that it was okay for her to pick it up. Nadja had killed before, but she wasn't a killer. Paris, on the other hand, I had seen her in action and she was definitely a killer. The direction this could take was nothing short of dangerous. I needed to defuse this bomb before it went off.

"Paris, Nadja and I are pretty lax so it's usually fine for her to show up unannounced. You just surprised each other, s'all."

"She snuck in here and had a gun pulled on me. So, if you expect me to apologize, it ain't happenin'," Paris pouted.

"What I do expect is for you to put something on," I barked, finding it hard to concentrate while she looked so good.

"Nigga, you need to put something on too. You're almost naked," Paris shouted at me, reminding me I was barely in a towel after running out the shower. I saw a look of shock pass on Nadja's face when I didn't put Paris in her place but instead just tightened the towel around my waist. She knew I'd never put up with shit from women. I usually kept it moving on to the next one, always staying free from drama.

"Humph. Definitely American," Nadja chimed in over Paris's outburst.

"Bitch, I will—"

"Stop it! Both of you!" I interjected. "Nadja, could you wait in the lobby? Please. I'll be down in a moment."

Nadja cut her eyes at Paris, but reluctantly agreed. "Don't keep me waiting!" she snapped as she headed out the door.

I stood around, surveying the room while thinking about how bad this could've gotten. "Paris . . ." I started, but the icy-cold look she gave stalled my speech.

"You fuckin' her too?" Paris asked with a laugh, not expecting an answer as she bumped past me, heading toward the shower. "Guess you better get dressed. Don't want to keep your little Persian waiting."

Now I remembered why relationships weren't my cup of tea.

Nadja

36

"What the fuck was that?" I hissed like a snake uncoiling to strike.

"You shouldn't have let yourself into my room without my permission," he snapped back at me, which really set me off.

"Since when is that a problem?" I asked. "It's not like this is some kind of relationship," I pressed, knowing he was the same person that swore to me he wasn't capable of being a one-woman man. And I swore to myself that if he did become ready for a real commitment it was damn well going to be me and not that bitch.

"How's your face?" he asked, genuinely concerned. "What went down with you and Paris should never have happened."

"Don't ever put your damn silly knife to my neck again," I warned him. "And why do you need armament here?" I grilled him.

"Just a little practice," he replied.

"A rifle? Uh-huh. Sounds like more than practice, Niles," I said with a raised eyebrow.

"I'm serious. Just some practice. If I don't keep my edge, then I'm out of a job."

I didn't push any further. Instead I moved on to what was really on my mind. "That girl back up in your room, she's not one of your typical bedroom conquests. She knew what she was doing. Quite deadly."

"Yeah, I know."

"That mess with Kahn?" I asked.

"Yeah. Greedy bastard betrayed me before I arranged for his accident," he admitted. "After I did the hit on De Banderas in his villa, his men were all over the countryside after my ass. I was outgunned and outnumbered. Paris saved my life."

"And you don't find this Paris girl too good a coincidence to be true?"

"I see what you're saying, but . . ."

"Is that what you think? The trail of dead bodies and fuck-ups, not to mention me having to send someone to return the scooter before it was found near the bodies?"

"Our source set me up. Nadj, seriously." He tried to cajole me with his charm and grin but it wasn't working today, not when that woman was lying in his bed.

"And do you think that's some kind of accident? How dare you invite that person into our business?" I shrieked at him.

"That person saved my life. If it hadn't been for Paris I would have been dead."

"Did you ever think that maybe she's the reason things went so poorly today?"

"Of course I did and I checked it out. It's fine."

"No, it's not. You can't just rule her out as a hit man just because you like fucking her. She could be working with one of the other families to take you out."

"I've always trusted my instincts and they say she's not involved with this," he insisted.

"And you don't think it's odd that she just found you in the middle of nowhere?"

"If she were a man, sure, but she's a woman and none of you can know how to mind your own business. You're like super sleuths when it comes to finding out what you want to know," he said, clearly protecting that bitch.

"I don't trust her. Do you even know anything about her?" I screamed, trying to get him to wake up.

"She's from New York and I trust her."

"Enough to stake your life on it? Because that's exactly what you're doing."

"She's not a threat," he swore, trying to convince me.

"Did you see my face? Niles, I want her gone."

"Nadj, come on, lighten up."

"Let's go to dinner and you can try and convince me to do that." I tried to get the conversation to a more friendly tone.

"Can't. Paris's brother is working at Klub Impulso and I promised to go."

That was not the answer I wanted to hear. I couldn't stand the fact that Niles was going to blow me off for some idiotic club. "This isn't serious is it?"

"No, of course not," he tried to assure me, but I wasn't buying it. He was acting different with this girl. I had never seen him react to a woman the way he was with Miss Paris. It was making me boil inside.

"Good, because we don't need anything getting in the way of your work. Now go play at your little Klub Impulso."

Before he walked out the door he turned to me. "Nadja, I got this." Then he left me standing there alone. No matter how cocksure he sounded something told me that this one wasn't like all the rest. That she may actually matter to him. And for me, that was going to be a problem.

I picked up the phone. "This is worse than I thought. You need to get on a plane and get here. We have a little problem that you need to help me solve." I hung up the phone.

Having Niles in my space made me sooo horny. I couldn't get my mind back on work. I knew exactly what I needed to do. Slipping off my dress, I stood in the mirror in my La Perla lace under things and the black thigh-high boots the salesman had convinced me were every man's fantasy.

I lay back on the bed, legs spread apart, threw my head back onto the pillow, and imagined my hands didn't belong to me but to Niles. I licked my fingers, wanting them to belong to him, and ran them down my thighs until they touched my Brazilian-waxed great sacred spot. Memories of him down between my legs, bringing me to life, sent my body erupting in waves of pleasure. Just thinking of him brought me to the threshold of orgasm and within seconds I had slipped over into the real thing.

For a while I lay there, basking in the glow of the memories of him making love to me. As I came back to my cold, lonely reality I swore that if I couldn't have him then neither would she. That meant that I was willing to do whatever it took to get rid of Miss Wimberly.

Rio

37

By the time we got to Klub Impulso the line was snaking around the block. DJ PLUS 1NE had developed a worldwide following. Thanks to all the social networking, folks were excited to hear him do his thing. There were signs out front announcing him. Eduardo greeted us at the door. I introduced them and could tell that Eduardo was tryin'a figure out what team DJ batted for. I definitely liked the same kinds of guys Paris did. If you could tell they were gay then they weren't for me. I preferred a man's man: sports fanatic, car guy, sometimes thug. After I introduced them, I led DJ to the booth where he would spin. Of course, he had his laptop, which was all you needed these days to do your thing. I looked up to see Eduardo staring at me.

"You good?" I asked DJ before heading off to see if the boss needed anything.

"Did you date him?" Eduardo asked me out of the blue.

"What?" I looked at him like he must be smoking the pipe. My personal life was exactly that. Personal.

"That DJ? He your boyfriend? That why you had my fly him all the way over here?"

"You high? Why don't you step outside and clock that line around the block? That's why he's here. Two Grammy nominations."

"But you're more than friends?"

"I got work to do to make your club more than a temporary placeholder for bored rich kids," I said as I went back to handling my business. *What the fuck was that about?* I thought as I went to check on the mixologists.

A few minutes later Eduardo found me. "I'm sorry."

"It's cool. I already let it go."

"Yeah, I'm just nervous about tonight."

"It's handled. Just trust. I know what I'm doing."

"Got it. I'm just not used to handing over the reins."

"And that's all it is?" 'Cause homie was acting a little sprung, which I already knew wasn't going to work out for him.

"Yeah, nerves. I really want this club to succeed."

"Me too. Then we're talking the same thing." I couldn't help myself so I decided to throw him a bone even if it wasn't really true. "FYI, he's straight. Watch the line of women fighting for his attention tonight."

"Oh, I'm sorry.

"It's cool. We both want the same thing. For Klub Impulso to be on the map. So, I better get on with it."

Paris

38

When Niles walked back into his suite I was standing there dressed, ready to put an end to whatever the hell this was. No way I planned on putting up with no thirsty whore thinking I was dumb enough to believe this shit was all business.

"When you look at me, what do you see?" I asked him, stopping him in his tracks as he entered the room.

"Huh? What kind of question is that?" he responded, having no idea where this was going, and I refused to be seduced out of my pissed-off state by his charm or big dick.

"Just answer the question and please don't play stupid. You're way too smart for that," I urged, keeping an eye on him.

He came closer, studying me. "I see someone who's deadly."

"Ooo, you're smart. Go on," I said, not taking my eyes off of him.

He added, "But who's also a bit of a princess."

"Excuse me?"

"Traveling around Europe first class, with an expensive wardrobe and an attitude that says 'I'm used to the best of everything.' You've obviously been spoiled by someone. Maybe an ex-boyfriend?"

"Yeah. Close, but not a boyfriend. I haven't gotten around to getting myself one of those yet," I responded. Actually it was my daddy LC who was the only man I'd ever let spoil me. And even he was a hard ass, but that was private information.

"Really? So was it this man that set you on this career path?"

"Nah. Always had a knack for beatin' a bitch ass and a badass temper. It was suggested by someone that I put both those to use. I have a low tolerance for putting up with bullshit." I punctuated my words with a cold, hard stare to make my point.

"And you're angry with me?"

"I want to know why you put me in a position to have to fight with one of your women. I'll kick a bitch's ass but not over no man. Ever."

"Whoa! Nadja is technically my boss."

"I thought you said she was your travel agent," I said with an attitude.

"I'm used to having to lie about who she is."

"So, technically, she another one in a long line of thirsty hoes wanting more of your dick?"

"It's not like that!" he swore and then fixed me with one of those looks like I was all drama.

"You tryin'a tell me you two ain't fucking? And before you answer, remember I'm a woman and I can tell when a bitch has peed on a nigga to make sure other bitches know to stay the fuck off. That was the vibe girl was giving."

"Yes, I slept with her. Once. Over a year ago and that's it." And as he said the words I almost felt sorry for him. Why is it that no matter how many women a man sleeps with he can still be dumb as hell when it comes to the opposite sex? Men fuck and move on, women fuck and move in. At least in their fantasy of what they want to see happen.

"You may have thought of it as a one-off but I promise you she wants something more." I watched the confusion on his face.

"No. No. You're wrong," he swore, tryin'a convince one of us, and I wasn't the one that needed convincing.

"And you're blind." I laughed, despite my plan to stay pissed. He was just seeming so pathetic not understanding that Nadja was still in love with him.

"And what about you? What does Paris want?" He grabbed me around the waist.

"I haven't decided yet. But tonight I want to get dressed up and dance my ass off." He covered my mouth with his. I pulled away. "And if you're really good and incredibly lucky you may get some more pussy."

"It's like that?" Niles said, kissing me on the neck.

"Yeah, it's like that," I said, but the words rang hollow in my ears because I wanted more right now.

Niles

39

After smoothing things out with Paris, she went back to her suite to change for the evening at the club. We planned on meeting in the lobby, and when she walked out of the elevator it took all my self-control to not drag her back upstairs and tear it up. She looked so damn tasty in a body-hugging couture dress and straight-up fuck-me-now shoes; but tonight was a big deal for her brother and so here we were at the club. Klub Impulso was packed and for once, thanks to the new DJ, the beats were on point. Even in a house packed with every kind of beautiful woman, Paris stood out and she knew it.

One of Chris Brown's numbers was on when we entered so I grabbed Paris to see if she could move on the dance floor as good as she did in bed. Three songs later and I started wondering if this woman was just good at everything. I couldn't help smiling at the reaction she was getting from the men. Made me feel possessive, which stunned me, because I couldn't ever remember feeling that way.

"What?" Paris saw the look on my face.

"Nothing. Like your moves. Let's go get a drink." I played it off that I was shocked by my possessive feelings.

We stood at the bar where I ordered drinks. A buxom brunette tried to get my attention at the other end of the bar. Paris didn't miss a thing and shot her a dirty look, which didn't faze the woman at all. She took a seat at the end of the bar, her big rack visible from anywhere in the club as she sucked seductively on a straw to get my attention.

"Learning to curb those violent urges in public. I'm proud of you," I laughed.

"No. Just ain't gonna check a bitch who's beneath me," she responded.

"You use the word 'bitch' a lot." All my humor leaving.

"Yeah, so? Problem with it?"

"I know most of the time it don't mean anything, but I heard that word way too much growing up. From my dad."

"Oh. One of those situations," she commented, her tone softening.

"Yep. Wasn't no term of endearment or slang when he used it with my moms."

"An abusive pops. That's what got you on this career path?" she asked, staring at me.

"You can say that. You think you know everything?" I felt myself loosening up again with her.

"What I do know is I got ya. And you know what you got? Me on loan for a few more days," she teased.

"Damn. Like that?"

"Yup. There's an expiration date on this *date*."

"And if I refuse to let you go?"

"You wouldn't want me to compromise my education," she flirted just as her phone blew up. She glanced down at it. I saw her wobble for a minute before ignoring it.

"So much for having you on loan. Trying to make me jealous? Because you know you don't have to do that. I like games . . . just not right now," I said as I pulled her close to me. This woman had saved my life and then she proceeded to fuck the shit out of me. Paris swung on the continuum from life to death and everything in between. Letting her go was starting to feel like less of an option.

"Hello, Niles." Two stunning women in short, tight dresses leaving nothing to the imagination stepped up to us. A Eurasian beauty and a Nordic one who obviously knew my name although I was certain we'd never met.

"Hello," I said, my arms still holding Paris, letting them know I was with her. My second reason was to make sure she didn't beat their asses.

"We wanted to invite you to an orgy." The blonde gave a seductive smile.

"Yes, your reputation is that one woman is never enough for you," her friend added.

I tightened my hold on Paris, who had a smile on her face.

"I don't do groups. Never been good at sharing," Paris said, trying to end this conversation.

"Ever?" I joked, wanting to see how far I could go.

"I'm exclusive." She stared at me without any hint of humor. She was dead serious.

I addressed the two women. "Can't. I'm exclusive." I kissed Paris on the lips.

"But that's not possible," the dark-haired beauty pouted.

"You heard her. She's not good at sharing and, well, neither am I."

"Bye-bye." Paris waved them away. "There are plenty of men in here willing to buy what you are selling, so step off." The edge came back to her voice, prompting the women to take off in the direction of the VIP area.

"What is it with you and all these thirsty bi . . . hoes?" We both broke out into laughter.

"What's up?" Rio came over to us.

"Damn, bro, you sure this the same club? 'Cause I had to get on that floor tonight."

"Right! Yeah, it's coming together. "

"Great job! Definitely a step up." I gave Rio a high five just as a waiter approached him.

"Duty calls. Hang out. I'll see you guys later," he said as he hurried off to handle his duties.

"You probably want to pop expensive champagne, princess? Maybe make it rain? Or '*just dance?*'" I asked, jokingly quoting the song by Lady Gaga. As we stood watching the excited partiers I could have sworn that I saw Nadja up on the balcony, but when I did a double take she was gone. Definitely for the best that I didn't see her. Last thing I'd want tonight was to get Queens all fired up.

After DJ PLUS 1NE's set ended I turned to Paris. "So with that outta the way, I'm down for whatever you wanna do."

"For real?" She used a really sweet girl voice on me.

"After vacation . . . when you return to your school," I said, pausing before I continued. "What do you plan on doing when you're finished? I mean . . . are you going to work for a family? Or freelance like me?"

"Haven't decided yet," she replied. "I'm not one to brag, but I think I'll be a pretty valuable commodity. Why you ask?"

"Just wondering," I replied. "Let's break out of here and go find some trouble."

Paris

40

Just as Niles took my hand to lead me out of the crowded club my phone started blowing up again. I almost didn't answer I was so hungry to get naked and horizontal. I checked the number and had no choice but to take the call, especially if I wanted to avoid World War III.

"My sponsor checking up on me. Gotta take it," I lied as I motioned I'd be back.

"If you say so. Don't make me come looking for you," Niles taunted as he pointed his finger at me, making an imaginary gun. Yeah. Real subtle.

"Uh-huh," I said as I quickly turned and walked off for some privacy amid the throng of people coming and going. As I left I spotted Rio at the bar talking to some hot Persian dude. At least he wasn't wasting any time thinking about things back at home.

"Paris, what the fuck is going on?" Orlando's voice boomed in my ear when I answered.

"Huh? Whazzat?" I said, putting my finger in one ear to hear better over the thumping bass and screaming crowds on the other side of the club.

"Is that music? Where are you?" Orlando pressed.

"Yeah, it's music. And? I'm out partying like a girl my age is supposed to do."

"Are you okay?" my brother yelled clearly.

"Of course. Why wouldn't I be?"

"Bodies," Orlando called out in that tone of his that irritated me, but got my attention. "Lots of 'em piling up out there.

Heard about it over here. Valencia, Spain turns into Bagdad and you act like you haven't heard about it? Don't play with me."

"You ain't Daddy, so don't speak to me like that. I'ma say it once. I ain't got shit to do with any bodies out here," I yelled, restraining myself from adding a "bitch" at the end. Damn Niles and his stupid lecture.

"You're right, I'm not Daddy, but if he finds out you been wildin' out there he'll go ham on your ass. You better be staying under the radar."

"Don't lecture me. I'ma do me. You tuck me away in this sleepy-ass town like I'm some leper the family is ashamed of."

"Just stay out of trouble, Paris. I'm warning you."

"Whatever."

"Grow up, Paris. I gotta go. Check back in on the regular. And stay away from idiots."

"If I'm to avoid idiots then how am I supposed to check in?"

"Cute."

"I most certainly am."

"Bye, sis," Orlando muttered.

I returned upstairs in time to witness those two hoes flirting with Niles at the bar. One tried pulling him to the dance floor to complete her seduction. I could've fucked both them up but my family was in the middle of a fight for their survival back in the States, making this seem even more trivial. My education was paying off. I was learning.

Rather than arguing, I walked into Niles's line of vision.

"Paris!" Niles shouted over the music.

I turned as if unfazed. "I want to fuck. Coming?" I asked, ignoring his present company.

Niles followed me out of the club, the two of us riding back to the hotel with a wall of silence between us. Kinda liked making him think I was pissed at him for that thirsty one back at the club. The sexual tension rising as he squirmed only made me hotter while I pretended he might not get this.

On the elevator ride up to our suite, I suddenly hit the emergency stop after the last guest exited two floors below us.

"What the fuck, Paris! Why'd you do that?" Niles barked at the elevator screeching to a halt.

"Because I needed to get you alone. Now seemed like a good time," I matter-of-factly replied. Niles kept his distance, even maximizing it in the tiny confines. Then he drew those damn karambit blades from out of nowhere, his eyes showing he was prepared for a fight once again. Made me wonder how much betrayal he'd experienced in his life to assume I meant to harm him.

"Damn, boy. Relax," I said as I took a cautious step toward him. "I just want to thank you for tonight."

I came closer. Got down on my knees before him and carefully unzipped his jeans.

"What are you doing?" he asked, those blades still looming perilously over my head.

"Well, I certainly ain't tryin' to kill you," I cracked as I pulled his dick out.

Nadja

41

"He didn't want what we were selling," China, the Eurasian hooker I'd hired, pouted as she stepped in front of me. From the way she deflated it had become obvious that she'd never actually been rejected.

"He said he was only with that woman," Kareena, the Nordic blonde who was right up his alley, added. "What made her so special? I command a much higher fee."

"What did he say?"

"We offered him a three-way. An orgy like you said," China said. "What man in his right mind turns down an orgy with this?" She motioned to her best assets.

"And she told him that she was exclusive," Kareena cried.

"Yes, and?" Thank God these women used their bodies for a living because their brains were on a permanent state of pause. "What did he say?"

"He said that he too was exclusive," Kareena finished.

"With her? He said he was exclusive with her?" I felt my temperature rising.

"Yes, with her."

"Maybe you misunderstood him. Maybe he said 'for to-night.'" I offered them options but they just shook their heads in unison.

"No. And they kissed. He did not see us. He only wanted her."

"What do you want us to do now?" China pouted.

I turned to my assistant, who had been quietly listening to the exchange. "Pay them." I looked over the balcony down at Niles, who had his hands around Paris, hugging her as if she were some precious thing instead of one more ho to add to his scorecard. What was it he saw in her? She seemed like American trash to me. I picked up my phone and called the one person that could help me.

"I need a job for our security guy. He's getting distracted and that can become a problem. It needs to be as far away from here as possible. Yes. Immediately. Tehran, Jordan, Mozambique, Antarctica for all I care. I don't give a shit as long as it isn't in Spain." I hung up the phone. If I couldn't get rid of her then I'd do the next best thing and separate the two. By the time he got back home memories of the rude American would be long gone.

I stole another look at Paris Wimberly. Less than a week ago Niles had never even heard of her. Neither had any of the people I'd put on her case. Who exactly was this woman and what did she want with Niles? She had no idea who she was dealing with or the lengths I would go to eviscerate her. Whatever game she was playing, Miss Wimberly was about to find out that she was way out of her league. From the balcony I trailed my assistant to the bar, a little surprised that things had suddenly gotten a whole lot more interesting.

Rio

42

"I ordered breakfast," my host informed me as I emerged from the shower. I had to admit that other than this gig he had proven to be my best surprise.

"I'm starving," I responded.

"Yeah, you should be." He laughed, stepping over to the living room area of his suite where he had them set up the food. "I took the liberty of ordering you an American breakfast." I opened the various serving dishes to find all my favorites. Course, none of them could touch Mom's cooking but it might be awhile until I had a real home-cooked meal, Chippy style. Oh, well. I pulled the plate of pancakes close, grabbed some bacon, thrilled I was one brother who stayed on the swine. I dove in, forgetting all my home training.

"Sorry, I haven't eaten anything since lunch yesterday."

"Well, if that's what it took for last night to be such a hit."

"It's not just me?"

"I'd get on a plane anytime if the club is throwing down like that. You must be so proud of yourself," he said, and I nodded 'cause a brother had overproduced. The receipts were so flush, which made DJ PLUS 1NE pay for himself. He had a real international audience. One tweet and all of Europe landed in private jets, ordered Dom and Cristal by the case. Eduardo all but apologized and tried to lock me down to a contract at the end of the night. All I wanted was to bask in the glow of my first real success. Hooking up with my host made it sweeter.

"So you didn't tell me much about yourself last night. Except that you came to visit your sister? Does she live here?"

"My twin," I said. Usually people got all touched when I revealed I was a twin. Wanted to know if we had psychic abilities and twin intuition, which we damn sure did. "No. She's in school in Europe so it made sense."

"Are you two alike?" he asked just like I expected.

"Yes and no. We both like to have a good time, love to shop and laugh, but she's a hell of a lot tougher. I'd rather negotiate." I laughed, thinking that was the reason LC wanted me to become a lawyer. From an early age, I used my brains to get out of things while sis would kick ass and ask questions later. "And what brings you to Valencia?" I asked him.

"Vacation. Getting far away from people."

"So you can do you? The gay you?" I couldn't help ask. I'd always met so many foreigners who came to America on a gay holiday because back at home they had a girlfriend, fiancée, or wife.

"Is it that obvious?" he asked, looking guilty.

"Hey, a week ago that would have been me."

"Serious?"

"Yeah, and let's just say that when I came out the non-reception made me jump on a plane."

"So your parents are traditional too."

"Oh, the D . . . Wimberlys have their moments. They're traditional when it comes to certain things."

"Like their son's sexuality."

"Exactly! But that hiding it ride is over."

"How did you bring yourself to do it? To tell your family that you were gay? Did they insist you get married?"

"No. There is no pressure to head down the aisle in my family. But my dad is ol' school, which means no son of his is going to be gay."

"Are you the only son?"

"Naah, I got three older brothers, which you'd think would let him lean up off me; but, no, we all got to be straight. My dad is from the hood in Queens and he can't tell his important political connections that he's got a fag in the family. Not LC."

"Lacey?"

"No, LC, my dad's initials. Everybody calls him LC."

"Does the L stand for a city?"

"Nah, although all my siblings except my brother, Junior, are named after cities. Shit, we're so busy talking about me I barely know anything about you."

"I'm from Armenia, the middle of four kids, two older sisters and a younger brother. My parents basically arranged my marriage in the womb."

"I didn't think people still did that."

"Oh, yes, they do."

"What are you going to do when you actually have to sleep with your wife?"

"I'm going to think about you." And that's when I felt myself stop hating my father. For better or worse I'd never be expected to marry some woman against my will, and even though that didn't change anything, it was a start.

After breakfast, I gathered my things and was about to run, even though it was only three flights up when Navid stopped me.

"Rio, I wish I were brave like you."

"You can be. There are a whole lot of other countries that you can move to," I joked, which helped lighten the mood. Brother started feeling really good about life. New job, new freedom, and lots of available dick. *How could it get any better?* I thought as I stepped on the elevator.

Nadja

43

"Tell me everything. And leave nothing out!" I barked at Navid as he entered my suite after pulling a very necessary all-nighter.

"Everything?" he raised his eyebrows in jest.

"Pertaining to information about that tramp!" I said as he walked past me and sat down at my computer.

"He and Paris are twins."

"That should be easy."

"Get this. All of his siblings except one are named after cities."

"Oh, how horribly ghetto." I sighed.

"Except I don't think that they are. He mentioned that his father has lots of political connections in Queens." Navid's hands were already working the keyboard of my laptop.

"Anything else?"

"That Paris attends school in Europe."

"Yeah, one of those Swiss killer training places."

"Those really exist? I thought that was urban legend."

"Our last security consultant was a graduate."

He raised his hand in a quiet motion. Normally I'd have his ass for that sign of disrespect, but accessing this information was way more important than catering to my ego.

"Oh, they are wealthy and very well connected." He turned the computer to face me. LC Duncan was the CEO of Duncan Motors Imports and an extremely powerful man. Named one of the top campaign contributors of the year. Father of six: Junior, Vegas, Orlando, London, Rio, and Paris. I did a quick

Google search for Paris Duncan images and there she was at the Met Ball, Mayor's Ball, the white party in the Hamptons, her cotillion at the Waldorf Astoria, and along with various celebrity socialites. There were a few I recognized and even some I knew personally. They were the children of people that worked with my father. Very important associates as he liked to refer to them. Damn! This was not good.

"Why is she using an alias?" I said out loud.

"Maybe they're running from something? Hiding out?" Navid, ever the conspiracy theorist, asked.

I grabbed my phone and dialed a number. "Papa, hello."

"Daughter, it is a father's greatest wish to see his daughters married." He started in immediately on his favorite subject.

"But I am considering the men Mother so generously introduced to me," I lied.

"Good. Every day you grow more like rotten fruit when it comes to getting a suitable husband. You are giving me no choice but to become less choosy."

"Yes, Papa. Can we talk about that another time?"

"It is always another time for you. What is it?" My father sounded annoyed.

"You have dealings in America, and I wondered if you had ever heard of a gentleman: LC Duncan?"

"LC, why yes. As a matter of fact we are in the process of completing a very lucrative deal with Mr. Duncan. One that I hope will continue for years to come."

"But what if something goes wrong?"

"What are you talking about, Nadja? The Duncans are a very powerful family and whoever they do business with comes under their protection. It is in our best interest to make sure this deal goes through."

"But, Papa, are you sure? What do you really know about them?"

"Enough! Nothing will stand in the way of this transaction being completed. Understand?"

"Yes, Papa."

"Good. You just worry about choosing your husband."

I hung up the phone, my father's wrath now ringing in my ear.

"What?" Navid caught the look on my face. "You're scaring me."

"Then imagine what fate I have in store for Paris Duncan."

Niles

44

After hastily toweling off, then donning a white tee, khaki shorts, and some sandals, I told Paris I'd be back. When she refused to answer from behind the locked bathroom door, I left her. I knew that meeting Nadja would not go over well with her but this was work. She would just have to get over it.

When she saw me, Nadja stood up from her wingback chair in the lobby where she'd been wrapped up in her iPhone. Her slender shape looked even tinier in the black Adidas gear she favored. We kissed on both cheeks, as was our custom these days.

"You look well . . . as always," she remarked. "Can't believe you got any rest."

"C'mon. Let's walk. Outside." I was never comfortable talking real business indoors.

We went poolside, leaning over the wall as if admiring the Mediterranean below. A palm tree shaded us from the prying eyes of others.

"Your ID and passports are done."

"Thanks, but what about Paris? I need you to get hers too."

"After the damage she did to that last job? I don't want you going near her!" she barked at me; her concern sounded like it had a real basis but I didn't care. I could handle things.

"You don't have to worry about Paris. We're just having a good time. She's not going to get in the way of my work again," I assured her.

"But you fancy her," Nadja answered for me as she jabbed her slender finger against my temple. Her fingernail dug into my skin, making me blink. "Damn, Niles. What is it with you?

Because she's a fellow American? You've been away from the States for a very long time, chum. No, wait. I got it. You feel some connection with her because of some shared 'black experience.' Is that what's going on here? Something *soulful?* You found yourself a *soul mate,* mate?"

"Ease up on the mouth, Nadja. You're about to cross a line we won't come back from. Are you jealous?"

"As much as you'd love it, jealousy is not what this is. Our past is just that. I'm just saying how can you trust her? I don't believe in coincidences. And for someone with her kind of skills to suddenly show up . . ."

"Relax. She ain't here to off me, Nadja. I'm sure of it. She's a student at one of those kill mills for the rich. She was at my hotel on vacation. Almost got herself raped at a yacht party until I stepped in. If she's professional, sure could've fooled me."

"A yacht? Humph! I know you like the long-distance kills . . . or with those bloody karambit knives of yours, but you can stage a mean suicide. Tell me you had nothing to do with the Villaragosa overdoses. Just tell me that. Their father can be an evil bastard."

"Had to. When I broke up their little video session with Paris, we were out to sea on their boat. Couldn't have them creating a scene after I fucked 'em up. Especially when I had the De Banderas hit to do. Put them away nice. And got off the boat with Paris."

"Does she know what you did to the Villaragosa brothers?"

"Uh . . . she didn't at the time."

"Damn, Niles," she cursed. "Very sloppy. How many unnecessary bodies this time? Ten? Twenty? And to top it off, your friend up in the room knows all about it? I don't need that kind of attention."

"It won't happen again."

"You need to ditch her permanently," Nadja said in parting as she began walking away.

"I trust her."

"Then you better make damn sure you can trust her, because if you're wrong it might not just be your life she takes, but mine too." She turned back toward the exit.

"Wait," I called out.

"What, Niles? You want a quickie or something? For old time's sake?" she said, batting those eyelashes teasingly. Good taunt as she vowed to never let me get so much as a whiff of her pussy again.

"No," I replied, not letting her rile me. "But I might need something else though."

"Such as?"

"An ID . . . for Paris. Just in case we need it."

"We? You are not talking about taking that girl with you any further. I forbid it. Totally unacceptable, Niles. Her tagalong ends here!"

"Just see what you can do," I said. I wasn't sure where this thing with Paris was going but it was not going to end today. Shit, just thinking about that girl made me want to hurt somebody. Her.

Paris

45

"Lovers' spat over?" I asked as Niles entered the room.

"Get your stuff. We need to go somewhere," he said, gathering some things.

I was in store for a quick cab ride to the other end of the town. No romantic vibes this time; and the driver definitely was not a gentleman, hurriedly driving through stops signs without an ounce of conversation. Maybe he just didn't know much English.

"Where are we going?" I asked Niles, deciding on small talk as we wound through the twisting streets.

"Shhh," he said, daring to rest his hand on my knee. *No, this nigga didn't just shush me.* Almost smarted off, but then I recognized this face from before.

Niles was on a job.

Our journey ended on the west end of Playa de Palma, a less-opulent accommodation than our hotel. It was some high-rise hotel for vacationers on limited budgets, no doubt.

When he got out, I got out. The cabbie didn't even ask for payment before speeding off.

"He'll be back later," Niles commented from behind his black Ray-Bans, anticipating my question. "C'mon," he muttered, looking around the area before crossing to the beachside of the street.

"*Hola,* Señor Tomas!" the man at the front desk gushed when he saw us. I almost looked over my shoulder to see who he was referring to before realizing he was smiling at us. Unless Niles had been here before—and I doubted it—something Niles was wearing must've tipped him off.

"I need to see my locker," Niles calmly stated as he high-fived the man with greasy hair who smelled of cheap cologne and cigarettes. His eyes said he found me attractive and wanted to say something lurid, but knew better with Niles around.

Responding, the man stepped aside and motioned for us to step behind the counter and down a short hallway directly behind him. At the end to the right lay a doorway with only a burgundy curtain blocking it. Niles entered first with me wanting to stand guard for fear of being trapped or caught in a double cross. As Niles kept walking toward a row of expensive, fortified lockers that didn't match their surroundings, I hesitated.

"It's the only way out. Good girl," Niles commented with an approving smile. At the front counter, the man had stepped back in place going about his regular duties. I stayed put, splitting my attention between him and Niles, who was matching a key he produced to the correct locker. With a swift click, Niles retrieved a briefcase and an envelope from the locker and left the key in place. But not before wiping his fingerprints from it.

"All okay, Señor Tomas?"

"*Sí*," Niles said, slipping him a few Euros. I kept pace, following behind Niles as we entered the hotel's lobby. But rather than leaving this shitty-ass place, Niles turned and headed toward the elevators.

"What the fuck?" I let escape my lips before blindly following.

On the ninth floor, we entered a unit using an old-fashioned key in the lock. Place reeked of cigars and disinfectant and I was afraid to even touch the bedspread. Felt like somebody packed up a slice of Jersey and moved it to Spain. Niles set the briefcase on the desk and opened his envelope instead. Inside was another passport along with an Italian driver license and other papers. "Close those blinds, would you?" he asked of me.

When I complied, he opened the briefcase. A disassembled rifle lay inside, each piece safely cradled in protective foam casing.

"Here?" I asked.

"Yep," he answered.

"No Pakistani dude gonna double-cross you this time, huh? 'Cause I don't want to have to rescue your ass again."

"Nah. This one's pretty straightforward."

"That Nadja bitch trying to overwork you?"

"Actually I found this job myself," he said as he finished assembling what looked to be a modified Austrian Steyr-Mannlicher.

"Uh . . . you forgot a piece," I called out before he shut the briefcase.

"Good eyes," he said, snatching up the firing pin and removing part of the rifle to accommodate it. Fucker was testing me. "Now I need you to be my spotter," he said as he handed me the scope. "Look down at the beach below through those blinds. The target should be there."

"Okay. Gonna tell me what you're looking for?"

"European, white male, balding, black hair, black swim trunks, white shirt," he rattled off.

"Could you help me out some more?" I stressed.

I waited for him to answer me, scanning from left to right across the beach for something fitting Niles's description. "Gold chain," he finally added. "He's supposed to have a gold chain."

"And he's supposed to be somewhere directly below?"

Niles read from one of the papers in the folder. "Yes. He should be directly below this unit. Time is ticking."

"Wait," I said before Niles began working my nerves. "I see him."

"For real?"

"Yeah. He's at ten o'clock. Missed the shirt because he took it off. He's sitting on a blanket. Putting on suntan lotion. But there's the gold chain."

"Good. Knew you could do it."

"Okay. So once you do the hit, what's our escape plan?"

"Don't worry about it. I've got that part covered. Once you do your part."

"Niles, what are you . . ."

"Here," he said as he took my scope, affixed it back atop the rifle . . . then handed it to me. "Need to see if you got what it takes in this business."

"Thought I already proved that to you. Remember?" I stressed, picturing the tally of bodies left on the mainland.

"Those were easy decisions, Paris. Need to know if you can make the hard decisions."

"Sounds like you're talking about the future, Brooklyn," I said, grinning.

"Just focus on the job in front of you," he commented, no grin.

"Uh . . . this is sweet and all, but if I do this, I want a cut of the money. I ain't stupid," I said. No need letting Niles know I was loaded and didn't need whatever this job was paying. But I could most def go on a sweet little shopping spree with it.

"Show me you can make the shot . . . and you get the whole pot," Niles offered as he cracked a smile.

"Okay," I agreed as I swiveled around and cracked open the sliding glass door. I adjusted the weight of the rifle in my hands then chambered a round. "I got lard ass in my sights," I said as I extended the barrel into the open air.

"Good. Anyone with him?" Niles probed.

"Nope. No . . . wait," I said as the man's situation had changed just that quick. "He has company now. His wife, a son . . . and a little girl."

"Okay."

"You sure this is the man?" I asked as I lowered the rifle and glanced over at Niles, still seated at the desk. "Looks like just some poor schmuck chillin' with his family. Maybe you should take a look."

"Are you saying I shouldn't trust you?"

"No. I'm saying that maybe there's another balding dude wearing a gold chain on this beach. Just come over here and double-check. I don't want you cheating me out of my money," I cracked, trying to hide my case of nerves.

Niles looked over whatever instructions were on his sheet of paper. "That's him, Paris. Don't be nervous."

"I ain't nervous!" I yelled. "I'm just wondering why it has to be now in front of his family."

"Because it's not him, Paris."

"Huh?"

"The man's the identifier. The target is his wife."

"What the fuck are you saying?"

"I need you to kill his wife. Now," he said as he stood up from his chair and walked over beside me.

"Why? I need to know why."

"We don't always get the whys in this business, Paris. We're weapons . . . with someone else's finger on the trigger. Just point and shoot."

"But you know the whys this time, don't you?" I pushed.

Niles looked over that damn sheet of paper once more before balling it up and hurling it across the room. "Because that man down there pissed off the wrong folk. And to punish him, he was given the option of whether to kill his wife or his kids. Paris," he said with a pause, "he's sitting there because he knows she's about to die. And if we don't do it, his entire family will be taken out by somebody else . . . horrifically. Now . . . I'll say it again. Pull the motherfuckin' trigger!"

I raised the rifle and put the scope to my eye once more. "Niles, you are a bastard," I cursed, almost wanting to cry.

"Have to be sometimes. So will you, if you're serious about this life. Now, I'll ask you . . . are you 'bout this life?"

"Yeah. Fuck yeah," I replied, regaining my composure as I lined up the man's poor wife in the crosshairs, cinched the rifle butt against my shoulder . . .

And squeezed the trigger.

Nadja

46

"Get me Gavin on the phone," I said to Navid.

"Gavin Gavin?" he asked, his words questioning more than the name I requested.

"Yes, you heard me."

"But I thought you stopped working with him when your father chose to employ Niles."

"This job isn't right for him."

"Nadja?"

"I need to make Miss Paris Duncan disappear," I said in no uncertain terms.

"But you're doing that. You're sending Niles to London."

"Yes, but he would like me to secure identification for her. Do you know what that means? He's falling for her and I can't let that happen," Just the thought made my blood boil.

"You can control a lot of things but not a person's feelings for another person," he said but I didn't care.

"No, but I can try," I said adamantly, "and with her out the picture, we will see where his feelings go."

"But that may still not get you what you want. Just because you extinguish the competition is no guarantee that he will fall in love with you."

"Leave that up to me. I've been waiting an entire year for him to be ready for a relationship. You think I'm going to just let this whore come in here and take what is mine?" I stared at him, feeling myself grow more determined to carry out my plan.

"But what about your father? He's not going to be very happy with you," Navid, ever the sensible one, warned me. "Take a step back. Think about this."

"You are my assistant. Not my fucking conscience. Your job is to assist me, which you have done very well. Now get Gavin on the phone and assist me in making sure that come tomorrow Paris Duncan is one dead bitch."

Navid picked up the phone and dialed the number. It didn't matter to me what he thought or my father or even Niles. I knew that if I were to ever have any chance with the man I loved I had to get rid of the competition.

"Gavin, nice to hear your voice. Oh, don't be that way. It was a business decision." After I got off the phone I felt a million times better. Like I could finally relax. I turned to Navid.

"One more thing. I need you to find a gentleman to help relieve my stress. And if he's also a masseur then that's a bonus."

"Yes, ma'am," he responded, letting me know that he didn't agree with me.

"And for all your hard work and loyalty, especially in helping me solve this dilemma, you can take the rest of the day off to enjoy the sights," I said as I reached into my purse and handed him a wad of spending money. One thing I always did right was take care of my employees. They weren't like family. You had to pay them for their loyalty but in the end it would be worth every penny.

After he left I thought about Niles and how good it would feel to be back in his arms. An hour later I lay spread-eagle on the bed as Tomas, my masseur slash adult escort, happily munched my vagina, licking and sucking me into orgasm. He turned me over, his tongue following the crease between my ass cheeks as he thrust his finger deep inside of me, causing my body to writhe with pleasure.

"I want to fuck you," he grunted as his dick strained against the fabric of his pants.

I sat up, throwing on my robe. "I have work to do." My voice took on an authoritative edge. It was one thing to let him go down on me and give me pleasure but that's where I drew the line. I wasn't in the mood to explain to him that I had only ever had one man inside of me and he was the only one who would ever penetrate me. I walked over to my purse and pulled out a couple of hundred dollar bills.

"But I really want to satisfy you," he whined, not getting the hint that his work was done. I handed him the money and walked over to the door. Throwing it open I waited until he had gathered all of his things and locked it. I couldn't believe I'd done anything like that and for some reason I felt unclean, like I had cheated on Niles.

Niles

47

Click.

She squeezed the trigger and it went "click."

Not a bang, pop, brrrrack, or boom.

Click. Paris lowered the rifle and came flying toward me.

"You . . . motherfucker," she cursed.

"Never put the firing pin in. Sleight of hand. See?" I said, producing it for her. "A whole other lesson that could save you in this job."

"So those people out there . . . that family," she said, angry as hell. "Who . . . who are they?"

"I haven't a clue. Made it all up," I admitted. "Figured you'd find somebody matching the description I gave you."

"But the paper you were reading from . . ."

"Oh. That," I said, letting a sliver of a smile form.

She hastily picked the paper I'd balled up and thrown, unfolding it and attempting to read from it.

Not easy to do, since it was a blank sheet.

"Pleased with my acting?" I asked. "I had to be sure you could handle a pressure situation."

"Did that b . . . cunt you work with put you up to this?" Her voice dropped to almost a whisper.

"Nadja wanted to make sure you could be trusted but—"

"Did I pass your bullshit-ass test?" she interrupted me, coming closer.

"With flying colors," I responded, feeling really proud of her. I motioned her to come into my arms. She had done so much better than I expected. Her first throw almost hit me when I caught her fist in midair. She flailed, connecting with various parts of my body.

"Paris, stop!" I grabbed her, binding her arms in front of me, hugging her against her will.

"Let me go! Motherfucker, let me go!" she screamed out but I tightened my arms around her.

"You gonna be calm? I'll let you go when you calm down," I warned her. Almost immediately she stopped fighting me. I opened my arms and let her go.

"Finally," she said then clocked me in the head with the butt of the sniper rifle. Down I went, a mix of pain and surprise escaping my lips. I placed both hands over my forehead, trying to stem the blood trickling from the wound. "Because when I squeezed the trigger, I wasn't aiming at anyone," she completed.

"Damn, Paris. I'm bleeding all over the place. You could've put an eye out. Think you could've hit me somewhere else?" I groaned as I wobbled back onto my feet.

"That's what you get for playing games. Besides, you were too pretty anyway," she cracked as she dropped the sniper rifle onto the desk. "Oh. And don't you ever put a blade to my throat again," she called out.

I stumbled to the bathroom and looked in the bathroom mirror. My blood was readily flowing into the sink as I acknowledged the image staring back at me. Not sure if I were angrier at Paris for striking me . . . or myself for not anticipating what she would do. I'd gotten spoiled on way more pliable women. Last person to really push me was Nadja.

And thanks to my arrogance and ego, I knew how that turned out.

Paris was American though. More than that, she was a New York girl.

And I'd disrespected her.

Served me right if she was already on her way back to our room, prepared to pack her shit and get on with the remainder of her vacation. I'd ruined it for her, I supposed. But she'd made my time in Spain so much more memorable.

Once I'd washed up enough, I gathered the bloodied towels and bagged them up in the trash can liner. Even though this whole scenario wasn't a real hit, any trace of me was not to be left behind.

"Paris," I muttered, trying to hide my surprise over seeing her still in the room. She sat at the desk, holding the rifle and aiming it at me.

"Like how it feels?" she asked.

"You really weren't angry at me?" I responded, genuinely surprised. My forehead was convincing enough to me.

"Didn't say that," she said, keeping the Steyr-Mannlicher trained on me. "But y'see, there's something my real teacher taught me. About using emotion as a weapon, too. Kinda like that whole sleight of hand shit you played earlier."

"And my firing pin?"

"Oh. It's right where it's supposed to be this time," she replied, tapping her hand against the side of the rifle.

"What lesson are you supposed to be teaching me?"

"I dunno yet," she said with a shrug. "Maybe that I am here to kill you. That I have been the entire time. And was just waiting for a moment like this. Once I figured out what you were all about. Which ain't much."

"Damn," I said with a chuckle. "You really are here to kill me?" I asked, scanning the room to determine my next move.

"Uh-uh. Hands up," she instructed. "Don't even think about those fucking blades of yours. And move away from the lamp. I've learned your tendencies."

"What do we do now?"

"Nothing for you to do except die, babe," she said as she squeezed the trigger.

I lunged at her knowing I was too far away to stop the shot and she was too good to miss. Saw images of my moms telling me it was gonna be all right and to just let it all go. I guessed this was the way it was gonna end.

Except nothing happened.

Just a click.

Just like before.

Except now I looked like a fool.

"I didn't lie. Firing pin was in this time," Paris admitted, smiling. "But I emptied the clip and cleared the chamber. Lucky for you. *Now* the lesson's over, Brooklyn."

"So where do we go from here?" I asked, not sure where we stood and glad I hadn't peed in my pants.

Rio

48

I scribbled a note on hotel stationary, letting Paris know that her brother was off to work at his j-o-b where he was killing it. Wasn't sure when she'd get it since she hadn't slept in her bed very much lately. No question where she had slept and I use that word loosely because if I knew my sister she put that stallion to good use. Apparently she and Niles were knocking boots and getting along just fine. Maybe this was some holiday fling for Paris but I wasn't used to my sister lighting up the way she did when she looked at Niles. Hell, I welcomed the distraction since it kept me from having to explain what the hell I had been doing last night. Hated to admit that I was quickly learning that I had as much ho in me as my twin. I had a lot of catching up to do, which clearly wasn't going to be a problem.

The one thing I hadn't considered about club life was the nightly hookups. Yeah, it felt real good to be away from the 'rents and the expectation of what I was supposed to be doing. Here in Valencia I had the real pleasure of doing what the hell I wanted to do twenty-four seven and that felt real good. So great that I was starting to see this place with a real sense of permanence, which made me want to take a look around my new city, check out some real estate. I wasn't sure what standard of living I could afford, especially if I suddenly found myself cut off from the Duncan dough, but you know I needed the finest things. Turning my back on Harvard Law in favor of running a club—co-running, but it was only a matter of time—was the kind of thing that might make my dad angry enough to issue an ultimatum. Shit made me want to get stoned just thinking about really being on my own, but if it meant being my own man I was down with Valencia all day long.

"Hello." Navid appeared surprised to see me get on the elevator. Shit, we were both staying up in this bitch; if I had known that I may have thought twice about hittin' it and quittin' it. *I definitely don't need no drama while I'm establishing myself as the club king of Valencia.* After a silent and awkward elevator ride down we stepped off and his eyes suddenly darted around the lobby like the po-po wanted him for some shit. Probably thought his family had spies checking to see what he was up to. Shit seemed way too serious for me, but then I remembered that I had been in his position less than a week ago.

"Hey." I decided to play nice. "What's going on?"

"Nothing. I figured I'd go sightseeing."

"Yeah, I'm gonna learn my way around, check out some real estate, grab lunch."

"Can I come along?' Navid looked so damn hopeful I didn't want to hurt ol' boy's feelings, plus I decided it might be nice to have someone to run around with. After consulting with the concierge we hopped in a cab and headed to the Valencia Street Circuit where they hold the European Grand Prix. Some kind of race had peeps flying into Valencia from all over. Got to the track, folks were dressed like they were at the Kentucky Derby or some shit. We hung for a quick minute then broke out. Looked at two, three places but they wanted long-term leases and I needed something on a month-to-month. Navid proved to be a great negotiator, helped me land a one-bedroom with a view of the sea for practically nothing.

"I'm treating you to lunch. Man, you got it done." I thanked him for stepping in and using his negotiation skills. He had that MBA degree from Wharton and put it to use for my benefit. Didn't have to be at the club 'til eight, which meant seven hours to chill. For a minute during our lunch I thought he wanted to tell me something. He started to nervously say something then stopped himself and changed the subject. I wasn't about to push it though; the last thing I needed was some guy professing his undying love after a one-night stand.

Navid had done his research so we hopped in a cab and went to Old Town Valencia, which was basically boys' town.

Restaurant, bars, and businesses flew rainbow flags in the windows letting the whole world know that they were gay friendly. We ducked into a place, ordered up some beers and food. I was starting to feel real comfortable around Navid and figured I would try and connect on a personal level.

"What was that back at the hotel?"

"Huh?"

"You were acting like somebody was after you. Figured your parents may be tracking you?"

"Yeah. You can never be too careful."

"But you're all right hanging out in the gayest part of town?"

"It makes no sense. I know."

"Dude, family don't ever make sense."

"No, it doesn't."

"But at the end of the day, they're all we have. Mine makes me crazy but they love the fuck out of me. You gotta meet my twin. Paris would fall on the sword for me."

"You two are very close?"

"Closer. That shit people say about twins is so true. Sixth sense and shit. We're tight in a way most people will never have. From the beginning we were two halves. She happy, I'm happy. I hurt, she wants to hurt somebody and same here."

"Even though you live apart? Aren't you used to being away from her?"

"Yeah, long as they got phones and Skype and airplanes. My dad went all crazy on me for, well, being me. I jumped on a plane, didn't even tell her I was coming. Just needed to see my other half. Hell, we're always gonna have that."

"And if she moved too far away or you couldn't talk to her anymore . . ."

"What? No, I wouldn't even want to live in a world without her and that's real." I spit it because, well, it's the truth. "And if anybody ever did anything to hurt her, there isn't a corner of the world they'd be able to hide."

Paris

49

"So where do we go from here?" Niles asked as I put his rifle aside and stood up.

"Well, I didn't kill you."

"And I didn't kill you either despite not knowing what to do with you. Now what?"

"I . . . I want to come with you. Learn more. But . . ." I admitted, stopping before I said anything else foolish. Yeah, I wanted what my sister London had: someone to love. And maybe, just maybe, I'd fucked up and found that in Niles. But I was a soldier. And I had my orders. Running off with Niles wasn't in the orders under any circumstances because family came first.

"Is that all you want? To learn from me?" Niles pushed, flashing his cockiness.

"I dunno," I lied, hearing my daddy LC in my head and seeing his disapproving scowl.

"You're prepared to leave your school early without any thought as to what that might do to your career and reputation?" Niles asked. "'Cause you know whoever is sponsoring you ain't gonna wanna hear that noise."

"Yeah. I mean . . . no," I said, flustered. "What I know is, you have to leave and . . . I don't want you to," I admitted, resisting the urge to take his hand. Spain had been scary, crazy, sinful . . . and magical.

"I don't want to do you like that, Paris. Tell you what. Meet me on my next job. It's a real one. Then you can decide whether or not to leave your school."

"Both reasonable and sexy. I like," I teased while considering whether I was up for hearing Orlando's mouth this time.

And boy would I. So much for laying low and out of trouble. Of course I'd also have to tell Rio that I was going somewhere with Niles, but he probably wouldn't question it and he didn't. Once I explained that Niles and I were off on a romantic excursion Rio stopped listened and wished me a quick bon voyage and told me to enjoy the dick.

So the next morning, per Niles's instructions, I dressed way down for my flight. Hated that I had to fly solo but I respected him for taking precautions. He wanted to protect me in case something went wrong. But I knew that together we could handle any shit came our way.

I walked briskly, keeping it movin' from beneath my fitted cap and sunglasses, looking like a broke college student. Had just turned my iPhone back on when it rang, M.O.P.'s "Ante Up" blaring as my ringtone. No telling how many calls I'd missed, but if anything, my brother was persistent.

"What the fuck are you doing in London, Paris?" Orlando screamed in my ear, sounding like he was about to stroke out. No use asking how he knew where I was as he probably had my credit cards and expenses monitored. "You were told to stay put."

Shit. I had just cleared customs at Heathrow International Airport and was in no mood for his bullshit. "Just a quick trip then back to Spain. I'll hit a few stores, check out a club or two, *non-VIP style*, then jet back. Besides, no one knows I'm here." I worked overtime desperate to sell my lies to him. But he wasn't about to let me off the hook that easily.

"I do, Paris. I know you're there! And if I do, others might too. As far as another shopping trip, I know you. And you don't go to London to shop. You go straight to Milan or your namesake."

"Hey. You treated me to beach gear in Europe. It's not so warm here. And I needed something more subtle than what I was rocking out there, right? Low-key is what you said. Well, that's me," I stated, hating my baggy and downright boyish attire as I strolled through the airport, heading to the exit.

"Paris, why you always gotta make me worry about you?" he groaned, his voice dropping in volume. "You can't even follow simple instructions. You had the setup in Spain and yet you still couldn't handle it and just leave shit alone."

"Maybe because I'm restless and want to do something to help y'all. But y'all being some bitches and won't let me," I griped as I perused the overhead signs, seeking my exit.

"What's his name, Paris?" Orlando asked way too calmly, seeing through my bullshit somewhat. Perhaps that's why I couldn't stand his ass sometimes.

"Huh?" I mumbled in the middle of picturing Niles's face.

"What's his name?" Orlando repeated. "Whatever part-time relationship you've got yourself into that has you in fuckin' London all of a sudden."

"Puhleeze. If I was with some nigga he woulda paid for my ticket and your spying ass wouldn'a called me."

"Paris, get your ass back to Valencia as soon as possible. Or I will find you and personally fuck up whoever this dude is."

"Yeah, you wish," I scoffed, laughing inside at the one hundred different ways Niles could shut Orlando down if that run-in were ever to happen. But it wouldn't just be Orlando Niles would be facing. I shuddered at the thought of Junior and my father showing up.

"*Excuse me?*" Orlando responded.

"Nothing. Stop hovering over me. I'll be back in a day or two."

"Paris—"

"Look. My luggage is coming up on the hamster wheel. Gotta go," I blurted out as I cut him off and ended our convo. But my only luggage was in the basic backpack already strung over my shoulder. Niles had said to travel light.

"Queens!" a voice bellowed from the crowd of people greeting the new arrivals.

"Brooklyn!" I shouted back with a smile as I ran toward it.

The sea of people parted ever so briefly, revealing Niles waiting for me with his trademark smile and New York swagger. No need for the English ruse here; he wore a thick denim jacket, white tee, jeans, and a pair of Tims.

I ran into his arms, kissing him like a long-lost love. My fitted brim bumped him in the forehead, making both of us giggle.

"Didn't know if you would show up," he admitted as our lips parted.

"Didn't know if you'd be waiting," I shot back. "But I kicked it around and decided what the fuck. You coulda paid for my plane ticket though. I ain't made of cash."

"Nah. Had to be sure it was your decision to come," he said as he took me by the hand to leave the airport. "Also, it's better this way. No way to connect us. Besides, Nadja wouldn't have planned your itinerary anyway."

"Does she know I'm here?" I asked.

"Been to London before?" he replied, sidestepping my question with a smile. I found this extremely interesting but decided to let it go . . . for now.

"Yep, school vacation," I remarked, knowing he was going to think I meant recently; but it made me think back to our family vacation the year I turned twelve. In the airport parking garage, we took a Vauxhall Corsa Niles had rented before my arrival, and quickly departed.

"You ever work in the States?"

"Nah, but suddenly I'm thinking of making that happen." He shot me a goofy look. "Ever see or hear from your people in Queens?"

"Nah. Ain't seen my parents since I was a wee little thang. They're probably dead and gone," I said, having arrived at this story on the flight over. My school had a class on establishing covers, which I aced. Lying did come a little too naturally to me. I continued, "Bounced around in foster homes all around the county until someone figured out there was a use for my temper. And shipped me off with passport in hand."

"And here we are," he said, smiling so true that I couldn't say if he believed my bullshit. For all I knew, his story was a lie too. That was us: two little liars up in a tree, k-i-l-l-i-n-g.

"Where are we heading?" I asked, playing with the radio to find a decent station.

"A little romantic spot on Le Lac d'Ailette, outside of Paris," he seductively cooed.

"Wow. Like that?"

"Hey. What can I say? I missed you, ma," he said as he ditched the white wave cap he'd been wearing.

"But we've only been apart twenty-four hours."

"Hey, that's a lot of masturbation!" he joked. I think.

Our journey south ended. "C'mon," he said, grinning again.

"It's kinda cold, yo," I commented as I watched the joggers in their insulated technology.

"I'll keep you warm, love," he assured me, slipping into his English charm again as if that would have a better result.

"I like that, but I'd like me and you and a hotel room and some room service a little better," I said as I reached over the gearshift and placed my hand on his inner thigh. I knew he was hot for me no matter how long he was gonna try to play otherwise.

"Live a little, spoiled princess," he cracked as he hurriedly exited the car.

I rolled my eyes but I joined him on the walking trail.

"What are some of the methods you've used?" I asked, thinking Niles was supposed to train me too, not just blow sweet nothings in my ear.

"Um . . . rifle. Pistol, switchblades, wine bottle," he said, fighting the shiver from the breeze coming off the lake. "My babies," he continued, referring to those karambit blades of his. "Poison, garrote, uh . . . car accidents, falls, drowning, a rock . . . once, explosives, asphyxiation, and a paperclip."

"Paperclip?"

"Yep."

"Why you gotta fuck with me, yo?"

"Hey. You'd be surprised what comes in handy at the oddest of moments, ma. You know how many times I had to poke the damn clip to kill him? An all-day job, yo," he said with a hearty laugh like he'd reserve for his boys or something. Well, the sooner I could get outta this awful gear, the sooner I could remind him I wasn't one of his boys.

"Damn. How many have you bodied?" I pushed.

"Uh-uh. Something you don't ask in this profession," he said. "Because we're all liars. Either wanting people to under-estimate us or to build up our cred."

A man was selling balloons on The Thames, waiting for the few kids that might come out I supposed. Niles beat a path toward him, his arm wrapped in mine as he guided me along. I hoped the poor slob wasn't Niles's target and was just trying to be a sappy romantic.

"Ahhh, good afternoon to the lovely couple!" the man who was Eastern European in appearance and demeanor chimed.

"Hello, sir," Niles responded, matching his politeness. "How much?"

"For a woman as lovely as she? Free," the man with dark, messy hair and visible razor stubble replied. "Besides, no chil-dren will be coming out for these today." He sighed. Probably depended on this gig to keep the heating oil flowing. I kinda wanted to break him off some of this funny money I had in my pockets. Instead, Niles rewarded the frail man handsomely despite him at first refusing it.

"What color?" he asked us.

As I was about to ask for a red one, Niles cut me off. "Yellow," he said assuredly.

"Hmm. I only have a single yellow one, so you are in luck. If it escapes your hand, may it lead you to your destination," the balloon guy remarked as if rehearsed to impress the locals.

"Thank you," I said as I took it in my hand.

We left the balloon guy and headed back toward the Sentra. Weird that Niles hadn't even kissed me on the walk.

"Well, the balloon was a sweet gesture . . . even though I wanted red. I'm about passion and heat. This yellow . . . is about friendship."

"What's wrong with friendship, Paris? We weren't friends before lovers?"

"Uh . . . I don't know if we were exactly friends. But I like you mentioning love."

Niles produced a paperclip in his fingers, as if by magic, and proceeded to uncurl it.

"Gonna try to prove something with that? 'Cause I will shove that so far up your ass," I chimed.

"Nah," he said a split second before he popped my balloon with it.

"Asshole!" I yelled, startled by the pop.

"Sorry," Niles offered as he reached for the rubber shards in my lap.

And removed the tiny, rolled piece of paper from among them.

"You sonnuva . . ."

"Business," he said with a shrug as he unrolled the paper and read it.

"Is that telling you what your job is out here?"

"Nah. I already know what my job is," he admitted. "This? This is telling me where to find him."

Nadja

50

Relaxation wasn't an option at the moment as I waited for that phone call. The one that would inform me that my biggest obstacle to getting what I wanted had been dealt with. I needed to handle some business to take my mind off of Paris Duncan but Navid was nowhere to be found. Apparently when I offered him a working vacation he chose to put the emphasis on vacation. I couldn't help but fantasize about having Niles back to myself. I didn't mind him sleeping with other women as long as they were all a one-shot deal, eventually reminding him that I was the only one he really trusted, and trust invariably always leads to love.

I'd given Gavin all the necessary information once I knew she'd be following Niles to London. Made more sense to have him handle her in another place. That would make it harder to tie to me. Besides, the crime rate in Valencia didn't compare with the numbers in London, even with Niles's horrible fuckup. People got killed in London. He knew to make it look like a local crime and not a hit. Actually I hadn't heard from Gavin since I called him back with the details yesterday. Was I the only person that actually gave a fuck about professionalism? Finally my phone rang. There were only three people I wanted to speak with—Niles, Gavin, or Navid—but when I saw the number, ignoring it was not an option.

"Papa," I murmured sweetly. Today was the Sabbath, a day my father usually abstained from business, which meant it had to be personal. Lord, I hoped he wasn't phoning on my mother's behalf.

"Nadja, I have sent the jet for you. Be in my office in two hours." And my cell went dead. Shit.

Two hours later I found myself walking into my father's office. Seeing both Navid and Gavin already seated caused my stomach to sink. This seemed incredibly bad, which meant it was probably worse. My father's fixed expression hadn't loosened or lightened either.

"Whatever you are doing? Stop!" my father ordered.

"But . . ."

"I've talked to Gavin and he just informed me that you ordered a hit on Paris Duncan. The daughter of the man I am in negotiations to do business with."

"She deserves it." I didn't care if he was mad. The fact that both Gavin and Navid had betrayed me to my father and treated me as if I were a child pissed me off.

"You used company resources to handle some personal vendetta."

"But you do it all the time," I reminded my father. "How could you call it off?"

"This is my company. Who is this Paris Duncan to you?"

"She is someone that should have respected me when she got the chance."

"Respect has to be earned and right now you have lost mine."

"If I were a son and not a daughter we wouldn't be having this conversation." I pleaded with my father. "You would just trust me."

"If you were a son then you would not risk my business and my reputation by making an emotional call that could bring wrath onto this family. LC Duncan is a very powerful man and from what I hear he is not the person to have as an enemy."

"But he would never be able to trace it back to us. Gavin is a professional." I motioned to Gavin to talk to my father.

"I am often retained by Mr. Duncan." Gavin gave me the real reason he had sold me out to my father. "And he is not the man to cross."

My father nodded to both Gavin and Navid to leave. "Daughter, I have made a grave error bestowing so much power on you. For the longest time I have remained blind to the realities of allowing you to remain so fully westernized in our world. It is a mistake for you to believe that you are the same as men. Had your uncles gotten wind of your plans I could not have saved you from their wrath. I may be the boss but there are still people that I must answer to. Your mother is right. The time has come for you to marry and bear children."

"Papa, no. I will not marry just to satisfy some outdated belief that without a husband I am nothing."

"Without a husband you are too dangerous. You must have a man to ground you. I give you one week to find a suitable mate and then your mother and I will choose one for you. Now go. I cannot bear to look at you."

"But . . ." There was so much I wanted to say, but I knew that my words were useless against my father's anger and disappointment. I stood up and walked to the door, but before I could open it my father's words stopped me.

"Nadja, I forbid you from going near this Paris Duncan. If anything should happen to her you are going to have to answer to me." My father gave me a verbal slap down but instead of being cowered in a corner I was more determined than ever to rid myself of that little bitch.

Paris

51

"What's the game plan?" I asked as I stared intensely at the package between Niles's legs.

"To kill somebody," Niles dryly replied as he surveyed the care package he'd just picked up from a restaurant in Chinatown of all places. Definitely wasn't an order of dumplings, but rather one of his "kill boxes" courtesy of Nadja. That bitch was better than FedEx, but I still didn't like her.

"I thought you wanted me to learn," I reminded him.

"I do want you to learn. But by watching and observing. Not by asking questions," he retorted.

"I hope one of those is for me," I said of the two handguns he was inspecting, one a Smith & Wesson, the other a Glock 19. It brought me some relief seeing those guns. I thought he relied way too much on those stupid blades of his.

"No," he said sternly, still checking them and their clips for ammo. "You just observe. No action. Got it?"

"Look, I don't want a cut of your money; although you are going to reimburse me for my plane ticket, you stingy bastard. But I do want to be ready if shit gets real again."

"I don't need any backup . . . or help, Paris. For the last time that shit in Spain was a fluke. This one is under control. Totally."

"You gonna at least tell me about the target?" I asked.

"His name is Jonas Mercier Pitre. Some crazy-ass French man."

I bristled at the mention of the name. My family had some dealings with the Pitres before I went off to boarding school. They were the only other distribution option in this part of

Europe for us besides the Italians. I didn't push Niles for any more information, knowing how quickly relationships can turn in this game. One day you were allies and comrades . . . almost like family; the next you were going to war over turf or respect or simply greed.

A few hours later, both decked out in fashionable although slightly tacky wedding attire, we arrived at a Pentecostal church in the Saffron Hill section.

"What do you mean we're not going in together?"

"In case you haven't noticed, there aren't that many people our shade of brown. This ain't Brixton," Niles said as he checked the silencer to make sure it fit smoothly onto the Glock. "And there are some dangerous people in there. Maybe you should hang back on this one and wait for my next job."

"I'm not a baby."

"I know. I . . . I just. If something happened to you . . ."

"Awww, You care. Feeling's mutual, Brooklyn. But you got a job to do and can't be worrying about whether I can handle myself. Because I damn well can. So relax. I'm not going to be any trouble."

"Okay. Just be careful, ma," he said more like a boyfriend than a peer. It was so sweet. "Go on inside. And take the car keys. We'll meet up at the location."

So we went our separate ways: me entering the front door of the great mansion holding a wedding reception and using the one doorman Niles's instructions said would let him enter with no fuss. That didn't mean I wasn't attracting attention though in my black sequined mini dress, looking like I was ready to party.

Our rush to get here was due to the location of the reception being given out on the day of the wedding for security purposes. And then for that information to get discretely into Niles's hands. From listening to the guests' chatter in line, I was able to learn a bunch of different families from all over— New York, Asia, Mexico—were here to pay their respects to the newly married couple. I figured one of those same families wanted to take advantage of this gathering to send a message to the Pitres at the one place where they'd be vulnerable. And if Niles happened to be captured or killed, no one could trace it back to them.

I was attracting probably more attention than what Niles expected when he picked my dress out for me from the mall, so I decided to do what I was supposed to and observe. I found a good perch just beyond the railing on the second floor where I could watch the foyer and hope Niles made it inside.

But my being out of sight wasn't out of mind.

"Paris? Paris Duncan?" came from the man ascending the wrought–iron staircase with a tiny plate holding crackers and caviar in his hand. His deep charcoal suit with matching red tie and pocket square fit him like it had been tailored a size or two ago, but he didn't seem to mind. "I didn't know the Duncans were in attendance. Good to see someone from our side of the pond . . . even if from the Big Apple," the man joked as we came face to face. "Tony Lucco . . . from Buffalo," he added, obviously proud of his city. Don't know why though. The Bills ain't done shit in forever and Niagara Falls wasn't all that.

"How are you, Tony?" I responded to the portly man whom I couldn't remember with an awkward kiss to his chubby cheek.

"I'm doing excellent, sweetheart. Where is LC?" he asked, reverence present in his voice as he craned his neck around in all directions to look for my daddy. Love him or hate him, Daddy checked fools.

"Nah. It's just me. Came to pay respects to an old friend," I said, trying to maintain my cool. By conversing with this dude, I didn't know if I was fucking things up more for my family or for Niles. And if Niles overheard any of this, my cover with him would be blown too.

"Uh-huh. I see," he said, feeling safe enough to disrespect me with his eyes now that he thought I was here alone. "You're friends of the bride? *Or the groom?*" Tony asked. "Must be the groom dressed like that. Trying to show him what he'll be missing out on?"

I grinned, pretending to blush. "This isn't the place to get into that. I'm just here to congratulate the bride and groom and that is all." Hell, I didn't even know the name of the bride or the groom. Just that Jonas Pitre was somewhere among the guests and wouldn't be leaving alive. And if Tony Lucca didn't shut up, he'd be joining him.

"You met the groom when he was down in Manhattan all those years?" he asked.

"Yeah," I softly answered as I kept scanning the crowd below for any sign of Niles. I began to doubt that he'd made it inside like he'd promised.

Then started worrying about something worse happening to him. Despite the civilized nature of the blessed event, none of these people were ones to fuck with. Even if they had put on their Sunday best.

"I knew it! That boy always had a thing for chocolate!" Tony belched inappropriately as he wiped some caviar from the corner of his mouth. "Just like me. Y'know . . . this is too good to be true running into you here. I used to think about you so much when I first saw you. Of course, you were too young for me back then," he added, getting close enough for me to smell his garlic breath. Niles was wrong for putting me in this dress because not many a straight man could resist and this slob was letting his freak flag fly at full mast.

"*Used to* think about me? Awww, I'm hurt," I teased while hiding the fact that he and his monopolizing my time creeped me out. Someone was gonna remember me being here in the aftermath. Then my family might get incriminated in this mess unnecessarily. So I decided that wasn't gonna happen.

"Well, if you got a minute, you can help make the past tense present tense. I'm a big man in my part of New York," he bragged.

"Just a minute?" I squealed. "Ain't never had a so-called *big man* give me just a minute."

"Sassy. I like that."

"I got more than that for you to like, daddy," I said in a low, determined voice. It worked, too. Tony took me by the hand just as toasts to the bride and groom began just outside the doors below. Finding an empty bathroom, I took the lead and pulled him along, checking the stalls to ensure we'd have no interruptions.

Tony couldn't keep his hands off me any longer and reached for my barely covered ass as I bent forward.

"Uh, uh, uh. Get them pants down and you can touch me with something else," I seductively prodded as I reached below my tiny dress as if to get to my thong.

But my hands went somewhere else.

Before coming inside, Niles gave me his blades to hold. Some superstition of his about having them near. And despite the tight security at the reception, he knew they wouldn't check me in such a skimpy dress. Those very blades I quietly slid from my garters where they were stowed.

"What's the groom's name again, sweetie?" Tony asked as I heard him unbuckling his belt and sliding it off. I grinned to myself over the effect I was having on him.

"Ohhh, you know his name," I purred as I prepared to slit his throat then shove him into a stall. Fuck the groom's name.

But plans rarely go perfectly.

Something grazed the back of my head, but rocked me to where I saw stars. I swiftly met the bathroom's fine marble floor with a jarring thud and almost stabbing myself in the process with Niles's blades.

Tony Lucca had swung on me with his lumbering ass. Didn't know why, but maybe he was just one of those abusive types. Well, he had no idea how rough I could be even when trying to get my sexy on. As I rolled aside, in case another blow was coming, I saw him standing menacingly over me with his belt wrapped around his fist.

"Yeah. I know the groom's name. But you don't because you never met him. His name is Joseph. And he's never been to America because of his record," he revealed to me, snarling like a rabid dog. "Why you really here, bitch? I'll get it outta you one way or the other. Maybe after I get in that sweet black pussy, you'll be more cooperative."

His dick came in the way of finishing me off when he had the chance. I took advantage of that, too, opening my legs slightly to keep his focus off what I held in both hands now. As he smiled, fixated on that *sweet black pussy* he thought he was about to take, I rolled forward and popped up onto my feet, crouching in front of him before he could blink.

With great joy, I straight drove those karambit blades between the fat fuck's legs, finding their mark. Then as his sheer shock overtook him, I withdrew them from his crotch and swung upward across his throat before the howl of terror could completely escape. The color left his face, but was in abundance around the wounds I'd made.

With nothing but gurgling and hissing escaping his throat, Tony Lucca was good as dead, even if his mind hadn't realized it yet. I used that to guide his hemorrhaging, spasming body into a bathroom stall where he plopped onto the toilet.

Just so glad I was wearing black.

But those familiar crimson streaks all across the floor weren't going away.

I hurriedly grabbed a gob of napkins from the dispenser, wetting them before hastily running them over the floor. But the puddle of blood from the stall was only growing; there was nothing I could do to stop it. I immediately changed my focus.

With a quick glance in the mirror, I was lucky to catch the spot of blood on my shoulder, which I dabbed away with a wet finger. Then I rinsed off Niles's blades before hiding them again in my garter belts.

I emerged from the bathroom into a commotion, stunned voices and yelling throughout filling the air as people below rushed in the direction of the reception.

Niles

52

I assumed my job would be in an open, public place where Paris being with me wouldn't matter. But inside a wedding reception, she would've drawn too much attention to me with her stunning looks. I was sure she was pissed at me again, but I'd make it up to her.

"Get the salads together! We have to get them out to the guests now!" the head caterer yelled as he returned to the kitchen after inspecting the reception setup.

"Sir, what do you need me to do?" I said as I approached the man, figuring it best to face any challenges to my presence here head-on.

"Who the hell are you?" the tall man with the pencil moustache and slicked hair snapped. From my travels, his accent sounded more Scottish than British.

"Vince had an emergency. Baby on the way. He called me to back him up," I replied. When I snuck around back, this Vince dude was the only caterer whose clothes looked like they'd fit me. Could've killed him, but instead I gave him three times what he would've made in exchange for his uniform and his silence.

"His wife's not pregnant," a server pushing past me with a tray full of salads blurted out.

"Hey. I didn't say it was his wife," I stated with a snarky shrug. "Now do you need me or not?"

"Are you experienced with high-profile affairs such as this?" the man questioned me.

"I've got years of experience around these kinds of people," I said more truthfully than he'd ever know. "Wouldn't be here if I wasn't."

"But tuck your shirt in, button up your jacket, and draw back on the cockiness. The ladies probably love it, but that bit of rubbish won't fly with me," he conceded.

As I carried my tray of salads out, I spied Paris upstairs above the foyer. She was unmistakable in that dress I'd picked out for her, conversing with some Italian fella. At least she had my blades under that dress in case he tried something.

The band performed a poor rendition "Brown Eyed Girl" as I served the tables, looking for Jonas Pitre among the guests so I could wrap this up. My methodical search brought me near the wedding party's table, where the bridesmaids were swaying to the live music while downing way too much champagne.

"Excuse me, what's your name?" one of the bridesmaids asked, while the rest giggled over her brashness. She was bold, easy on the eyes, and looking for a night of recklessness, but I was doing my job and she didn't fit anywhere in my plans. That and knowing what Paris would do to me was enough to keep my mind on the task. I was already thinking like a man in a relationship.

"Sean," I replied as I placed my final salad onto a table.

"What are you doing later, *Sean?*" she asked with a smile I was sure she was used to getting her whatever she wanted. And if she came from one of these families in attendance, she probably did get whatever she wanted, whether legal or illegal.

"Going to my second job then home to my husband," I replied.

"Uh . . . husband?" she queried as her eyes grew larger.

"Yes. My husband," I confirmed.

"You sure about that?" she pushed, refusing to buy my lie as she looked me up and down.

"Totally," I replied. "Love those shoes by the way," I commented as I moved on beyond the howls and snickers of her girlfriends. The bridesmaid's distraction turned out to be a good thing as it slowed me down enough to recognize Jonas Pitre from his photo. He was slouched over to where I'd almost walked right by his table. The three men at the table with him were presumably some of his people by the way they ignored their food and constantly scanned the room for trouble. Even though nobody was supposed to be packing in here, those hulking men surrounding him could obviously snap a neck if it came to it. They were the ones I was going to have to distract.

Back in the kitchen, I matched Pitre's table number on the dry-erase board, looking for something to use without this turning into a bloodbath.

They wanted the job done here and I wanted to leave here alive.

And on the dry-erase board, among all the different table numbers, I thought I found the way to do it.

"Who has tables thirteen and fourteen?" the boss called out as he checked the board as well.

"I'm on it, sir!" one of the other servers shouted as he stormed ahead with the final tray of salads.

"Those are the last salads to go out. And remember . . . allergies at table thirteen. No shellfish!"

"I know, sir. I know," the server dryly acknowledged on his way out the door. I took another look at where tables thirteen and fourteen were situated in relation to Jonas Pitre's and hurriedly grabbed another tray of salads.

Except with a quick addition to them before I flew out the door.

I entered the room during toasts by the wedding party and moved to discretely overtake the other tray of salads.

"Hey. I got thirteen," I said under my breath as I nudged the other server.

"Why?" he asked, irritated with me.

"I don't ask. Just do as I'm told. Think he wants to make sure thirteen's food was kept separate from everyone else's."

"Oh. Okay," he said with a shrug as he moved on to table number fourteen.

Five people were seated at thirteen and I gave them each a salad. I wasn't sure if all five were allergic to shellfish, but I had only enough time to mix shrimp and crab into the salads of three of them.

Entrees were coming up next in the kitchen, but I returned to the reception instead to wait on the results for which I hoped. I hovered along the wall, waiting and pretending to keep myself busy. But I hadn't seen Paris anywhere around here, not even with the people milling about the foyer. *She's a big girl, she can take care of herself,* I thought. Right as one of the people at table thirteen began coughing uncontrollably.

At first, the best man ignored it and continued with his toast to the couple, both who looked to be Russian maybe. But when the choking started, he became concerned and his voice trailed off. Jonas Pitre and his boys were at the adjacent table, but did nothing to render assistance.

I milled about, pretending not to see it until someone summoned me over. It was a woman at table thirteen who succumbed to the shrimp.

"Somebody call an ambulance! This woman needs help!" I yelled out as, ironically, I did my best to clear her airway and save her life. The band and some of the banquet hall staff were the first ones to respond and gathered around while various conversations broke out at the other tables. With Jonas's view of me obstructed, I reached under my jacket and retrieved the silencer-tipped Glock from my waistband, keeping it close to me.

The moment for my shot was coming whether or not his men were distracted. I would just deal with the aftermath one way or the other.

I stayed within the ever-growing crowd surrounding the woman who was going into shock, but began maneuvering myself into position for a kill shot at the table next to us.

Just as Pitre came within view, a scream rang out near the foyer—the area where I'd last seen Paris.

I couldn't allow myself to think about that.

Just take the shot and get out.

But that scream did me more of a favor than my shrimp-in-the-salad stunt, for it was the one thing that made Pitre's men respond.

They all flew out of their seats, forming a protective wall in front of the bearded Pitre as they prepared to lead him out the building.

Other tables followed suit, all the families wary of a double cross. And in the midst of the chaos, I came up smoothly, directly behind Pitre.

Squeezing off two shots under his armpit and into his torso.

Pitre's body took a slight lurch as the two rounds entered. Not enough to alert his men, who were too focused on what was ahead. By the time he collapsed, adding to the panic, I was already heading back toward the kitchen.

Then I had to find Paris.

And hope nothing had happened to her.

Nadja

53

"It's handled," Niles's voice informed me on the other end of the phone.

"Great. We should meet and go over everything. You heading back to Valencia?"

"Nah, to the home base."

"Sounds good. We'll meet there in four hours? I have some loose ends to tie up here." I could hear the annoyance in my own voice, and why shouldn't I be upset?

"Actually I'm gonna take the week off. Let's reconvene then. I need a break," he said, sounding tired, but I knew that rest wasn't his reason for putting me off. She had everything to do with Niles's sudden need for rest, if that's what he wanted to call it.

"This is work. It comes first; or have you suddenly forgotten how you afford such a fabulous lifestyle?" I seethed into the receiver.

"No, I didn't forget, but everybody deserves some down time. This isn't slavery."

"Please. With the fees you command you can hire a harem if you like, but we need to connect and go over some things whether you want to or not."

"Fine. Call me when you arrive in the city and I will meet you." He hung up on me.

I wanted to reach through that receiver and choke him. I'd been the one to arrange to run his finances through a shell corporation so that the purchase of his home couldn't be traced back to anything illicit. How dare he treat me like his employer rather than his lover? I'd always been free to come and go and I wasn't about to take a back seat in his life. He might not have known what was good for him but I did. Men! And, speaking of the opposite sex, there was another problem that I had to handle immediately.

"Before you get upset, I did it for you." Navid stood up as I entered my office.

"Telling my father on me as if I were a child and not your boss? Is that what you consider doing me a big favor?" I glared at him.

"Nadja, you were about to ruin your father's reputation and put your own life in danger. I couldn't let you do that."

"Who the fuck appointed you my great savior? I did not need you to rescue me. I had everything under control."

"Really? Because apparently this Paris Duncan has some heavy people behind her."

"Fuck her people."

"Look, I know you're upset about Niles but you must be reasonable. We can't always get everything that we want. Life doesn't work that way."

"No, it doesn't . . . for people like you. Those that would rather let themselves be controlled, but I'm not like you. I don't lay down and just take the hand that has been dealt. If I don't like it then I change it and if there is collateral damage then oh, well. Shit happens."

"You can't mean that."

"Yes, I do, and you wanna know what else I mean? Get your shit and get the hell out of my life. You are fired."

"But, you can't."

"I can and I will. Navid, you know what your best asset was to me? Loyalty." I didn't wait for a response. I grabbed my bag and headed out to see the one person that made this all worth it.

Rio

54

"You know you don't have to do that," Eduardo said when I told him that I would be moving into my own place. Paris would be headed back to school within the week, which meant I had to prepare for my new life. "Don't waste the money. You're not a rich guy so why not just move in with me?" He kept pressing me to be his house boy or some shit.

"Nah, it's all good," I assured him but it was obvious that wasn't the answer he expected. I could tell by the veins tightening on his forehead. On second thought, it was not pretty.

"Rio, darling, let me set you up. You can have your own wing and a driver," he pressed. "Where you gonna go and meet a man to take as good care of you as I will?" As the words fell out of his mouth I came close to losing my cover. LC Duncan took damn good care of all his kids, including the prodigal son, me. I couldn't help but notice that all of my credit cards worked and there were no calls about my spending or my future.

"Eduardo, I'm not that kind of guy. I like to work for a living. I'm a free spirit and nobody is going to clip my wings. At least not yet."

"You silly boy. Do you have any idea what I'm offering you? You'll never get an opportunity like this again. Who else would take a . . . a . . . a someone like you and set them up in the lap of luxury?"

"Excuse me? Someone like me?"

"You know what I mean? Young and free." He started backpedaling.

"I learned a long time ago that just because something glitters doesn't mean that it's gold. I'm good working for you but I'm the one that made the mistake of mixing business with pleasure. It's not something that I'm comfortable with."

"Well, what if we dismiss with the work?" Old boy was not trying to let this go, but we both knew that he'd gone from invisible to on the map.

"Is that some kind of ultimatum? 'Cause I'm cool heading back to the States or even checking out the clubs in Milan, London, Paris, anywhere."

"No. Rio, I'm kidding. We're good. I'm just messing with you." He pretended to laugh but I knew that if I hadn't let him know how the hell I roll he would have steamrolled all over me.

Couldn't really do nothing cause in the space of one week I'd already helped to blow up his spot. He had two, three different magazines calling to do puff pieces on his club, and social media was giving lots of attention with celebrities posting pics from the spot. That meant lots of green for him, which was the name of the game. Last thing I wanted was for my boss to be getting all salty cause I preferred to fly solo. Made me understand why my bros insisted on never mixing business with pleasure.

"About work? What you got planned for the next few weeks?"

"It depends on the budget. I got a few DJs bring their own crowds and lots of hype. Can help keep you in the papers." Eduardo didn't hide his love of press. Hell, most people were one dream away from a reality show anyway and he wasn't any different.

"Wanna come over tonight and go over some options?" he flirted with me; but he'd already shown his over possessive side so I dodged it.

"Let's just get it done now. I'm supposed to have dinner with my sis."

"You can come by after if you like."

"I'll see," I lied.

By the time I got out of there the only thing I wanted was a shower and some rest. The life-sized present at my hotel door pleasantly surprised me.

"Hey, stranger," Navid greeted me.

"I thought you went home."

"Yeah, I did, but there is something I needed to tell you."

"So important you had to fly a thousand miles to tell me?"

"Yes."

He looked so serious I started to get nervous. *Please don't tell me this motherfucker showed up to pledge his undying love or some shit.* I had just left the Eduardo situation dodging his wanting to spend time together.

I opened my hotel door and let him in. Guess the least I could do was let him spill his guts in the privacy of our suite. Hoped this wasn't going to be one of those long-winded confessions of his love for me. Damn, a brother was fine and all but I just wished people wouldn't take the shit so seriously. Course the first words out of his mouth caught me completely off-guard.

"It's about your sister, Paris." The words spilled out of his mouth. Now he had my full attention.

"What about Paris?"

"The woman I worked for, she wanted to kill her," he confessed.

"What? The fuck you talking 'bout? My sister is in danger?"

"I handled it. I made sure that nothing was going to happen to her but it meant betraying my boss."

"That couldn't have gone well."

"Well enough so that I'm out of a job."

"What happened?"

"Let's just say your sister caught the wrong man's eye."

"So what? He's married?"

"She wishes. No, he's single, but my boss was hoping he'd choose her and instead he fell for you sister. Suffice it to say my boss is none too happy."

"So how I know this head case ain't gonna go after Paris again?"

"Because her boss wasn't having it and believe me he shut the whole thing down."

"Did you know this that day we had lunch?"

"Yes, but I handled it."

"Anything happens to my sis and there won't be a place where this bitch can hide."

Paris

55

My cab pulled up at the private airstrip where Niles told me to meet him. Of course this was after I managed to run through one of those hip boutiques and scored a cute outfit. No way you'd find me on a plane looking dressed like I was about to attend my first party ever. I made it to the airport with mere minutes to spare. I hoped to hell I'd find Niles already on board in one piece. I entered the cabin and scoped out the Cessna Citation. Luxury tan seats that swiveled, built-in television and refreshment cabinet in a deep mahogany wood that highlighted the rich carpeting. Yeah, this was right up my alley.

I spotted the jacket Niles had worn to the wedding thrown over a chair. Figured he was in the bathroom until I noticed it was unoccupied. Finally, my curiosity getting the better of me, I entered the cockpit and imagine my surprise.

"You're late," Niles barked at me from the pilot's chair. He exuded massive amounts of sex appeal with the captain's hat and flight jacket.

"Come sit with me in the cabin. I'm sure the captain would like to get his seat back," I flirted with him.

"He's already seated." He flashed his cocky half smile.

"You are not flying me. Stop playing, Niles."

"I assure you that my pilot's education from Oxford Aviation and my eight hundred hours flying more than educated me on getting this plane safely to France." He seemed slightly annoyed that I'd questioned him.

"All right, back down. I'm not used to seeing a fine-ass nigga like you flying the friendly skies. But this is something I could really get used to." I gave a couple of snaps for emphasis.

"Come in, air traffic! I will be preparing for takeoff!" As Niles spoke with air traffic control I blocked out his voice. I couldn't help but really feel like I'd hit the jackpot. Bitches back home would lose their minds if they saw Paris Duncan pull into an airstrip with this fine-ass specimen behind the wheel. *I'm getting jealous of my own damn self Niles is so off the chain; but I'm starting to think he's not just distracted by me. He's acting strange.*

"Everything okay? Is your friend gone?" I asked, of course referring to his target Pitre as I took the seat in the cockpit next to him. Niles didn't look any worse for the wear so that was a good sign.

"Of course," he answered, finally bothering to look at me. "But somehow this cat Tony Lucco joined him on his trip. Know anything about that?"

"Why would I? With those kinds of people at the reception, you think your job was the only one going down?"

"Yeah, I did, ma," he replied. "Until somebody else got merced," he whispered, glaring at me. It didn't help that we had begun to back away from the gate.

"So why I gotta have anything to do with that?" I immediately rose to the defensive.

"Because somebody used blades to send Tony Lucco on his unexpected vacation. My blades, if I had to guess," he said. "And I saw you talking to Lucco . . . when he was still alive. Paris, you freelancing on me? Trying to fuck up my life? I warned you about that shit."

"No," I answered honestly. "It was an accident, Niles. He tried to force himself on me and maybe I overreacted. It's . . . it's just that ever since the boat incident with those two assholes back in Spain, I . . . I . . ." I murmured as I attempted to manipulate him away from the truth, letting my eyes tear up as I thought about something sad . . . when Daddy first told me I had to leave the family to attend school. "I'm sorry."

"Good. Because you did me a favor . . . this time," he said, softening. "You provided me with a good distraction right when I needed one. Maybe in some kind of fucked-up way, you really are my good-luck charm, Paris."

"I love you, Niles." Suddenly a great weight lifted off me.

"I'm glad you're in my life. I love you too, Queens," he whispered softly. His words made me feel like a schoolgirl. "I can't wait to get you home." I watched as he pulled back on the throttle, pointing the nose of the plane toward the sky. The magnificence of this man coupled with flying this plane almost made me lose my concentration.

"Oh, is that where we're going?" I smiled, pleased to get more insight into this man. "And I thought you were taking me shopping in my namesake city."

"I can do that too if it's what you want. But we don't have much time before you head back to school and I want you all to myself until then. No distractions." He stared into my eyes and it grew more obvious that we wanted the same thing. Each other.

One hour and ten minutes later we arrived at a private airstrip outside of Paris. A black Town Car waited at the bottom of the stairs as we deplaned. Clearly this brother had a real James Bond thing going on and wasn't afraid to floss that shit.

Niles held my hand on the ride to his place in the 7th arrondissement. He lived on the top floor of a spectacular old-world building that had been updated to reflect modern times. Large French windows, beautiful parquet flooring, and spacious rooms all with a view. You could even see the Eiffel Tower from the bedroom. His place had been sparsely decorated in hyper masculine tones of gray, white, and black with metal, steel, and glass.

"This place could use a woman's touch. Maybe some pillow for splashes of color?"

"Oh, really?" Niles pulled me into his arms.

"I love it here." I grabbed his hand and led him to the window that showcased the architecture of the neighborhood. "Just maybe add some rugs and warm it up a bit."

"Ma, you are welcome to make yourself at home." He laughed. "Do your thing."

"Yeah, but then all them other girls are gonna notice when they come back here. A b . . ."—I stopped myself from using the word—"ho can tell when another women has made her mark."

"Yeah, it's like dogs having a pissing contest. But I wouldn't worry since you're the only woman I've ever brought here. This is my cave. Where I come to get away from things."

"Oh, so that Middle Eastern terror ain't never been here?"

"Well, yeah, but that's work."

"And what am I?

"You are everything that matters."

Yeah, he had me going all "schoolgirl" over him in this bitch.

As I looked deep into those eyes that had been mentally undressing me all day long, he proceeded to slowly undress me in reality. I reached inside his boxer briefs, stroking him to full erection as he kissed upon my shoulders and sucked on my breasts as if it were the first time he beheld them.

While swept up in his passion, he wrapped his arm around my waist and held me tightly. As I continued stroking him, he placed his hand against my thigh and slid his palm up it. He needed no guiding to blades that were no longer there. For his hand went to my weapon this time, more deadly than any gun or knife could ever be, grazing his knuckles ever so softly against my mound before nuzzling his thumb up against my clit.

I gasped at his touch, but he brought his lips to mine again, sucking harder on my tongue with me kissing him equally as hard. He pressed gradually harder against my clit, making my pulse race with the ebb and flow of his thumb. By the time he slid two fingers inside me, I was good and ready.

"D . . . don't tease me, baby," I purred as I went weak in the knees, rubbing his firm chest and licking his taut abs.

Niles swept me off my feet and carried me to the bed. Removing his boxer briefs entirely before joining me, he slid his face between my legs and tasted deeply of my love. As intoxicated as he was by my honey, I did my best to drown him each and every time I came.

"Yes, yes, yes! Oh yes!" I called out as I squirmed and kicked, wanting to escape his skilled mouth and tongue, yet, at the same damn time, unable to get enough of them. "D . . . damn, you can eat . . . eat . . . some pussy."

"You taste so good, Paris. So sweet," he gasped, daring to lift his head from my pussy. "Tasty Paris in Paris."

"I want you . . . inside me. Take me . . . now," I urged.

Smiling oh-so-perfectly, Niles rose up from between my legs like a mighty bull. I almost giggled over the way sweat glistened on his body, for homeboy was almost glowing in the light.

He slid his hardened dick inside and mounted me, muscles tensing with every movement deeper, closer. I threw my head back and pressed my body against him, clawing at his back with my fingernails and biting on his ear.

Our breathing became labored, desperate, matching then exceeding the volume of the TV. Niles rocked me good, having me almost out of breath as he pumped ferociously.

"That's it. Don't stop. Oooh, don't stop," I begged repeatedly as I pointed my feet to the sky, almost in tears from the pleasure he was forcing upon me inch by inch.

I'd been righteously fucked before, but the emotions I was experiencing made this different, took this to another level. He had me so excited that I slapped his ass, startling him.

"Ooooo," I moaned as I came yet again, biting on my finger. Even though my eyes were closed, I could feel him looking at me. Knew I had to be a damn sexy sight.

"Hhrrr," Niles grunted as his body tensed before the moment overtaking him.

It was the only bit of warning I had before he released his seed, erupting in a massive wave that made both our bodies shudder and slam together.

"Oh wow," I gasped as my chest heaved.

"Yeah," Niles succinctly responded as he waited for control to return to his body.

Both our phones rang just as he rolled off.

Both our worlds intruding on the brief bubble we'd shared.

Somehow he summoned the strength to sit up in the bed. As he looked toward the other bed, his phone continued to vibrate.

"You need to take that?" I asked.

"Yeah. It's Nadja. Has to be," he admitted, kinda dampening my mood and the high I was coming down off. Yet, my iPhone kept going off too. I was sure I dreaded my call more than his.

"My school," I offered when he looked at me.

"Go on," he suggested. "Sponsors checking on their product no doubt. You're very valuable to whoever spent the money on your training. Might not be so easy for you to 'drop out' and leave with me."

"And where would we go anyway? Where would we live?"

"I dunno. We'd be mobile, but maybe go home. Set up shop in New York or Jersey? Like a homecoming for both of us. Maybe rent ourselves out to some of them gangsters down there."

"Nah," I said. "Painful memories of New York."

"Speaking of that, where'd you grow up in Queens? Maybe we know some of the same people."

"Jamaica," I said, still basking and being stupid before I corrected myself with a lie. "But I wasn't there long. Bounced around in homes all over the five boroughs."

"Oh," was all he said. "Well . . . we'll talk about it later. I gotta take this, yo," he reminded me with a final kiss as he found the strength in his legs to walk.

Yeah. That bitch Nadja was waiting for him to pick up.

But my call wasn't from the school.

Niles

56

"Okay. I can talk now," I said as I closed the apartment door behind me, having hastily thrown on some jeans and a T-shirt.

"So when you told me the job was handled did you leave anything else out?" Nadja asked.

"No," I replied, trying to ignore Paris's complications in the matter. "You got my money, yo?" I tried to change the subject and use a little humor. Soften her up a bit.

"Hmm. Funny," she chimed.

"What?" I asked, puzzled.

"You've been around the Yank too long. She has you talking like a common street thug."

"You weren't complaining about this street thug back in the day."

"So," she huffed. "I lowered my standards . . . briefly."

"Rubbish," I said, briefly using the English accent she preferred . . . even in bed. "Now . . . I'll say it again. You got my money, yo?"

"Come downstairs; unless you want me to come up?" Nadja instructed after a pregnant pause. She didn't seem amused by my banter.

As I exited the elevator, a car horn from outside alerted me. Couldn't see inside the silver Audi R8 with its high-revving engine steady purring, but I began considering my options in case this was a double cross. Of all the bullets with my name on them, one would eventually find its mark.

But not today, if I could help it.

I reached into my waistband, resting my hand on the pistol grip of the Smith & Wesson while still holding my phone with the other hand. Last thing I wanted was for them to enter my home and hurt Paris. The window lowered and I stepped outside in my bare feet.

"Get in. And put that gun away," Nadja said from the driver's seat.

"I'm not exactly dressed to be going out," I joked as I rested my bare feet on the carpeted floor mat.

"Relax. We're not going to a wedding reception," she joked dryly as she drove the car at over 160 kilometers per hour. Nadja wore her trademark black, but with a gray hoodie on this time for extra warmth.

"How long have you been in Paris?" I asked her.

"Not long," she said, slowing to hook a hard left turn before rocketing back up over one hundred on the next straightaway. "I don't trust that Yank, Paris. Figured I'd hang back. Just in case. She is here with you, huh?"

"Stop it. You already know the answer," I replied. "Jealousy doesn't become you."

"Bloody hanger-on," she crowed. "What do you really know about her, Niles? That girl is going to be the death of you yet."

"You might be right," I said as flashes of the violence we'd participated in ran through my mind. "But she's been betta for me than worse."

"Better? Wasn't there an extra body on this job? One no one got paid for? Then there's the matter of that massacre and the extra bodies back in Spain. Y'know . . . this reflects poorly on me, Niles. People aren't going to want to do business with us if it's sloppy."

"Are you trying to give me an ultimatum, Nadja? You find the jobs. I'm the one who takes all the risks."

"You really think so? You don't know what I've risked for you, you ungrateful bastard," she hissed.

Before I could respond, she slammed on her brakes in the middle of the street.

Unlike Nadja, I wasn't seatbelted and flew against the windshield like she intended, banging my forehead. When I tumbled back into my seat, Nadja went to slap me. I barely caught her hand before it struck my face.

"Nadja, what the fuck?" I groaned as I shook off the cobwebs.

As I cleared her hand away, she was already up in my face, pressing her advantage.

But rather than stabbing or shooting, Nadja used another approach.

She kissed me.

Time melted away with the renewed contact of our lips. It was too easy for me to allow it to continue as Nadja was now climbing over into my lap. She yanked my T-shirt up and ran her hands methodically over my chest, obviously smelling Paris's essence from our lovemaking. Suddenly all my thoughts led straight back to Paris.

I pulled away.

"Niles, Niles, Niles," she sang in that lovely, intoxicating accent of hers.

No. This was wrong.

"Nadja . . ." I uttered as I pushed her size-two self away. Somebody in a truck going past yelled something about calling the cops. Just that quick, Nadja was back in the driver's seat and had us underway again. The law or even the threat of it was something she refused to deal with.

"What was that about? You gonna say something?" I asked as I wiped her lipstick from my face.

"I have a room at Hôtel de Crillon or you can keep your crude Yank bitch," she grumbled, making sure I understood what she was offering.

"No," I said as I placed a calm hand on her leg. "You said we'd never again—"

"Fuck you, Niles. Fuck you for throwing that in my face," she spat, obviously wrestling with emotions that shifted gears as fast as this car.

"Nadja. Listen. It's not that I'm not tempted but I can't," I moaned, guilty over the momentary hard-on she'd granted me. "I'm not going back to your hotel with you."

As she continued to speed along, she sent a short text on her phone and waited until a response was received. "There. Your money's in your account," she stated as she screeched to a halt outside a small park on the edge of 12th. This time I was prepared and didn't smack the windshield. "The people who hired you don't like the collateral damage, but I assured them you had nothing to do with the stabbing in the bathroom. Lucky for you they believe me."

"Thank you," I said, not making eye contact.

"Now get out."

"Huh? That's bullshit, Nadja! Take me home!" I argued.

"No. You've humiliated me enough by choosing that girl. Don't think you will humiliate me further by bringing you back . . . to her. Now . . . get out."

I slapped my hand on the dash out of frustration, but complied with no further protests, getting out minus wallet and shoes.

"What now?" I asked as she lowered the window once more.

"I'm working on a big job in the States. Sit tight and wait for details. After that, we're through."

Then she sped away.

Nadja

57

"Hey, how's it going?" I spoke over the car's Bluetooth as I sped back toward the de Crillon.

"No complaints. Course some good dick would make everything better. Wanna meet in Cabo in a couple? Help me get some anonymous vacay dick?" Gabby laughed.

"Can't. Working," I lied.

"Oh, puleeze, your ass just don't want to be too far away unless your favorite cock comes a calling." Her words hit me like a punch in the stomach.

"Has this ever happened to you? Where no matter how many other men want you it doesn't matter 'cause he's the only one that matters?"

"Damn, you're sounding like Simone. But yeah, it did. Course he was married and not tryin'a leave his family; least, not for me."

"So how the hell did you deal?"

"Me? I fucked my way over him."

"Yeah, but I can't bring myself to do that."

"Girl, you're trying compete with the seven orgasms he gave you. I suggest you play the numbers game and fuck seven men and hopefully you'll get seven orgasms and then you'll be over him. At the very least you'll meet one you like."

"But no one is like him." I couldn't get her to understand what I was talking about.

"Jamaica. Let's meet in Jamaica and you will find some big Black Jamaican cock and by the time you get back you won't even remember why you liked him in the first place. Fucking those Spaniards and white boys ain't gonna compete with the Black D."

"Must you be so crass? It's not just his dick."

"But you have nothing to compare it to and it's not like he's been treating you so damn great. Let's hit the beach and I swear I will get you some big Mandingo dick to make you forget your name. Plus, you'll have a beautiful tan."

"I'm not going to bother asking if you've slept with a black man."

"Black, Dominican, Jamaican, Haitian, Moroccan, Ethiopian, half caste. I'm an equal opportunity fucker." Gabriel laughed. "Come on, we'll invite Simone."

"Let me think about it."

By the time I got off the phone I was feeling a whole lot better about things. Course it also made me rethink my plan. One thing I felt certain of was making this Paris bitch pay. Niles pushing me away both emotionally and now physically had been the final fucking thing. As badly as it hurt I still wanted him, to have it be only the two of us again. Since childhood patience had always been my strong point, I knew how to wait and bide my time in order to get what I wanted. It's how I got to go abroad for boarding school and also the reason my father finally caved and hired me. But this new problem had put a gigantic crook in my plans and I intended to eliminate it once and for all.

My mother had once explained to me that she and my father had an arranged marriage and in the beginning he was resentful that she had been chosen for him. See, he had wanted to marry another woman, but her family wasn't considered a part of the upper class and therefore it had been forbidden. Eventually he admitted to my mother that he was pleased to be married to her. That he hadn't known what was best for him. That's exactly what I knew about Niles. One day he would thank me for saving him from this classless whore and helping him to take his rightful place, next to me. I knew my parents would freak out but once I convinced Niles to elope with me they would have no choice but to accept him as my husband. And being a part of our family would insure that Niles had the kind of social currency you could only get through blood or marriage. And I knew he would make a great father when the time came. He was the only man I could see myself being with and obeying in the way my culture insisted women submit to their men. Yes, I would clean his feet and his cock with my tongue for life. Now, first things first.

Paris

58

"What, Orlando?" I yelled into the phone as soon as Niles stepped outside to take his call. "This isn't a good time. I already said I'm about to go back."

"Hello, Paris," the deep voice on the other end said.

"Daddy!" I gasped, almost dropping the phone. I immediately glanced at the front door. Fearing I'd been too loud, I took a few catlike steps toward it and paused. Waited for some kind of reaction, but Niles didn't storm back in.

"Paris, are you there? I know you can hear me. Don't play games with me, girl," LC grumbled.

"I'm here, Daddy. And I'm not playing games," I replied as I swiftly moved to the bathroom and turned on the shower to cover my voice. "How are you?"

"Since I had to make this call, that means I'm not happy. We told you to stay in Valencia until further notice. However, Orlando reluctantly told me you're not even in Spain, but London. Explain yourself. Now," he demanded with a growl that made me appreciate I wasn't standing before him. LC had a glare that could make the hardest man shit in his pants.

"Daddy, like I already told Orlando, I'm just out here shopping," I said in the sweetest voice I could muster. I was happy he didn't know I was in Paris at the moment.

"And like Orlando, I don't believe you. Paris, you know I don't suffer liars or fools. Especially those in my close circle like the rest of your siblings. So you need to decide whether you really want to be a part of this family business. Because I've invested too much in you and won't tolerate disobedience such as this any longer. Do you understand me?"

"Yes, sir. I understand," I acknowledged with a shudder. Daddy sometimes used this tone with his employees. And they weren't given second chances.

"Good. Because the next time you hear from me, it might be very unfortunate for you. Listen to your brother and get your ass back to Spain. Now!"

"Y . . . yes, Daddy," I agreed, mainly just to make him go away.

"Paris?" Orlando said, taking his phone back from our daddy, who probably was rushing off to handle whatever pressing business was on his plate. Wish I knew how bad things truly were back home, but they were keeping me on the outside.

"What!" I replied, irritated as fuck. But if I hung up on Orlando, Daddy might call me back. And I ain't stupid.

"Don't get pissed at me," Orlando argued. "I tried to keep LC outta this. But somebody had to be a hardhead and wouldn't listen, so—"

"Yeah, yeah. I got it," I chirped, cutting him off. "I'll be a good little girl. Happy?"

"Totally," he replied, hanging up.

I put the toilet cover down, took a seat, and reached over to turn off the shower before the steam messed up my hair. Topless with just my thong on, I placed my face in my hands and let out a deep sigh.

If Niles were to walk in right now, what would I say to him? And would he believe it?

Rather than hurling my phone against the wall like I wanted to, I instead used it to pull up a travel app. I looked for flights out of Paris to Spain where I would lay low like the good little girl I promised to be. I guessed more shopping could help me forget. Or a couple of obedient boy toys with no baggage, who weren't killers.

Nah.

Niles wasn't somebody I could just delete from my system with mindless distractions such as those, especially after our confessions tonight. I loved him.

"Damn you, Niles," I muttered as tears flowed down my face, which I tried to ignore. "And damn me."

I left the bathroom while wiping my eyes. It was going to be brutal telling Niles of my decision, but he still hadn't come back inside. I took it as a blessing as I checked my face in the mirror and removed the black streaks around my eyes.

But when I peeked out the curtains, Niles was nowhere to be seen. *No need to get nervous, Paris. He's a grown-ass man,* I thought. I sat down on the bed and forked a little bit of the cold rice and sausage mix into my mouth. Unusually good stuff, but I wasn't about to become one of them chicks who ate when stressed. Dumping it in the trash, I picked up the remote and thumbed through the channels. Niles had left his karambit blades on the bed, so he really must've just stepped out for his call.

Unless . . .

That word kept coming into my head as I stopped channel surfing at an episode of *The Sopranos*. Funny-ass Jersey Italians, I tell ya. If we weren't so subtle with our shit, Daddy would've fucked someone like Tony Soprano's neurotic ass up and dared him to go to war.

Unless . . .

Unless something happened to Niles.

I snatched up his blades again, which I was becoming too comfortable handling, and decided to go outside for a look-see. If I interrupted his business call, I would just apologize and keep it moving. But I needed to talk to him and it couldn't wait.

After throwing on some warm-ups, I cautiously opened the door and carefully poked my head into the night air. I let my nose smell and ears hear first if anything was wrong before my eyes adjusted to the dimly lit parking lot. "Survival is about your senses," that crazy Israeli drilled into our heads at the school I would be returning to shortly. And God bless him, everything he'd drilled into my thick skull was responsible for me still being alive.

I walked out to the street and, absent any clues, returned to the apartment. Feeling helpless, I watched the clock, checking out the window every ten minutes or so while panic gave way to fear then sadness.

I wasn't familiar with despair, but it was having no time cozying up to me as I restlessly paced back and forth under the clock's slow, grinding gaze.

Every random noise set me on alert, preparing for joy or pain. But they were just that—simple random noises. Then a depressing thought invaded my mind.

Maybe Niles was testing me in London and I failed him by not following orders. And this was his way of washing his hands of me. Bye-bye to the liability from Queens with no drama. I had to face it. I had a track record now. Couldn't listen to my family and couldn't listen to Niles. Maybe that's why my own family had abandoned me in Spain rather than wanting me in the trenches with 'em. Maybe I really was some kind of fuckup.

But Niles wouldn't have been here waiting for me after London. He could've cut his losses there and I would've never found him. And he certainly would not have brought me back to his home if I were just some jump-off. Even he wasn't cold enough to just want a final fuck. And like he said, he never killed me when he had the chance. No. We had something. Something real.

And I couldn't be apart from him.

So that brought me back to my first conclusion. Something happened to him.

So was this it? Was he dying somewhere while I stood around hopeless and helpless? I didn't have any resources to find him. Nah. Fuck that. I did have resources. I was a Duncan, dammit.

Hang on baby! Help is on the way, I thought as I considered my next move. But my happy tune was halted right as I opened the door to a shadow quickly converging on me. I dropped everything I carried and delivered a vicious palm thrust where their nose ought to be. We startled one another, but they were a tick faster and sidestepped my first move. I'd already spun around, ready to engage and unleash my frustrations when my eyes recognized the figure.

It was easy. Because it was the same person who'd left me in the room in the first place.

"Easy! Easy!" Niles called out, waving his hands to calm me. And other than looking a little weary there wasn't a mark on him. "What are you doing?" he asked.

"I . . . I thought something had happened to you. You . . . you were gone," I gasped as my adrenaline faded just as quickly as it had climbed. "I thought you were dead," I admitted, feeling foolish.

"Nah. I'm good, ma," he said as he cradled me in his arms to comfort me. "It's okay," he cooed in my ear as I felt his heartbeat next to mine. On his shirt, I smelled a familiar scent beyond his sweat.

Perfume.

A fragrance I recalled from Valencia.

"Niles, where the fuck were you? Where'd you go?" I asked as I stepped back, seeing he was still barefoot and couldn't have traveled that far like this.

As his eyes widened, my fists clenched.

Panic, fear, and sadness had left on a fast train out of here.

Leaving me with more familiar emotions of anger, and more anger, which I knew how to deal with instead.

Niles

59

"I . . . I was with Nadja. Something came up. Then we had car trouble," I offered feebly, knowing that excuse sounded weak. "More like trouble in the car . . . then she put me out. When I couldn't find anyone nice enough to stop for me, I walked over a mile barefoot. That was when I flashed and flexed some muscles for a car of party girls who were more than willing to give me a ride after dropping a sob story on them about car trouble. On my suggestion, they took me to a hotel for some fun, but I promptly stole their keys and ditched the car several blocks from here."

A lot of shady shit for an evening, but the longer I stayed away, the more I knew Paris would react just like she did. While I stood there on my sore, dirty dogs, somewhere Nadja was smiling.

"Dammit!" Paris yelled, barely relaxing her fighting stance. "Why is it always about Nadja? What? She wasn't the person who called you?"

"Well . . . yeah," I admitted. "But she was here when she called. Outside."

"Damn, I hate her ass," she cursed, her beautiful face marred by a scowl as she turned and retreated into the next room.

"She hates you just as much," I inappropriately volunteered as I followed, closing the room door behind us. *"What is it with the two of you anyway?"* I threw out there, pushing the dial even further up the ignorance meter.

"You, Niles! You're *what it is* with the two of us! Dumbass," she muttered as she hurled a pillow at me. "And to think I was having second thoughts."

"Second thoughts about what?" I asked, almost missing her comment as I caught the pillow. "What's going on here, Paris? Is this about the call you got?"

"Look," she commented with a sigh as she gathered her things. "I'm leaving. Going back to school. I got duties to fulfill. And don't need this bullshit."

"No!" I shouted. "We already talked about this. Me and you together. Remember?"

"Yeah. Before I got all worked up thinking you were in trouble. But instead you were doing who the fuck knows what with Nadja."

"I work with Nadja, Paris. And I've never tried to hide that from you," I exclaimed, passing on sharing the details of my encounter with her. "What do you expect? Huh?"

"That's just it. Maybe I expected too much from you," she said as she slapped my outstretched hand away. "I smell her perfume on you. Doesn't smell like car trouble to me. Did she get my sloppy seconds, Brooklyn? Did you fuck her?"

"No. I didn't fuck her," I said as I stood there frustrated and getting heated.

"You should have," she spat out as she walked out the door.

I waited for hours in the dark, daylight, and the birds announcing it was a new day. Hoped I'd hear our special knock at the door, signaling Paris's change of heart after some time alone.

No knock came.

Nor a ring on the phone whose number I'd shared with her.

So, having not been so utterly alone in a long time, I decided to be the one to act.

All it took was a lazy drag of my thumb across the smooth glass surface of my phone.

So simple. Yet so hard.

By the third ring, just when I thought she wasn't going to answer, she picked up.

Silence on her part greeted me. I was the one who called after all.

"I apologize," I uttered.

"And?" she said.

"What?"

"What about Paris?" Nadja asked.

"She's gone," I murmured. "I want to keep working with you. Just you and I, like always."

"So you can go back to being dependable? And lucrative?"

"What do you think?"

"Ignoring my lapse last night, I might be agreeable to it," she said coolly.

"Then bring on the work. Feed the beast," I joked.

Rio

60

Paris and I had been playing phone tag since my little talk with Navid. Each message left me more relieved than the last but I still needed to actually hear her voice live. The shit he spilled made me hella nervous. Fuckin' *Fatal Attraction* chick tripping behind Niles choosing my sis was straight-up lethal. I couldn't tell Paris the truth without worrying that she would seek revenge on this trick. My twin had no ability to let bygones be bygones and if I mentioned the aborted hit put on her she'd track this bitch down and end it . . . for good.

I was just leaving the hotel for work when my phone finally rang.

"How's life out of the closet?" She laughed, which immediately put me at ease.

"More swinging dicks than I know what to do with. Damn boss acting all sprung out and shit."

"'Cause your ass didn't follow Vegas's rule number one," Paris jokingly admonished me.

"Don't shit where you eat." We spoke the words in unison.

"Duncans are lethal. I know niggas get up in the cut and never want to leave. Remember all those chicks sobbing over Vegas?" Paris laughed.

"And moms always had to sit them down and tell them that if they were her daughter she'd want more for them." I groaned remembering the line of women: young, old, black, white, Asian, Latino, educated, hood-rats. "Vegas loved women and women loved our brother as much and as often as he'd let them," I added. "Shit is seriously in the genes. But, Paris, where the hell you been?"

"Don't matter. I'm on my way to de Gaulle. Getting the hell out of here!"

"Wait, you're rushing to leave Paris? Land of shopping? Food? Sophistication? Your mother ship?"

"Yeah, muthafucker think he can tell me anything. I'm ghost."

"Oh, so, Niles isn't coming back with you?"

"I don't give a fuck what he does," Paris said, really fuming.

"Wait. Wait. What the fuck? You were all about him two days ago."

"And now I'm all about me."

"I saw the way you looked at him and you ain't never looked at a man that way. I didn't even recognize you."

"Yeah, well, I got to get up out of here. Like I'm supposed to believe everything he says."

"Sis, Niles had it for you as badly as you got it for him. Is he really lying to you?"

"I don't know. Probably not but that's today. They all lie eventually."

"That means you're just gonna run away from someone you care about?" I tried to give her my two-minute-older big brother speech.

"Look, I'm not used to feeling like this and I'm done."

"Oh, it happened to you."

"What the fuck you talking 'bout, Rio?"

"You got bit. Never thought I'd see that love bug get your ass."

"Did not," she huffed, refusing to acknowledge the truth; but I knew her and I also knew that I was right.

"You think this shit happens every day? Why you running away?"

"I ain't running nowhere. I gotta get back to school."

"You scurrrred. Girl, your nose is going to grow like Pinocchio you lying so hard. Just admit that you have fallen on your ass for this man. At least you picked one hot as hell. Shit, you'd have to be superhuman not to want what he was serving."

"Rio, all this feeling stuff? Not in my plans," she swore. It felt kind of sweet to hear my tough-as-nails sister wrestling with real human emotions.

"How does he feel?"

"I don't give a fuck what he says. You don't leave me waiting in your apartment alone for hours."

"He took you to his home?"

"Yes." She reluctantly admitted this.

"So he loves you too?"

"Yes. But it can't work."

"You just gonna walk away from all that fineness. And you said he had a big dick?"

"Stop! I gotta go. I'm hopping a plane. I'll see you later."

"I'll be at the club."

Paris hung up the phone but I could tell some shit had gone down. To have her nose all swollen over a man. Wow. This was serious.

I stepped out of the hotel only to see Eduardo had sent his driver to pick me up. Normally this would be real cool except I knew it was his way of keeping tabs on me and I didn't like it at all. Shit was getting real creepy and I was gonna have to put an end to it. Made me rethink this whole thing about living in Spain, although I had become convinced that I'd found my calling in the nightclub business. Sure that would never fly with my pops, but there had to be some other option aside from Eduardo or law school, and I wasn't about to settle, so I had better find it and quick.

Paris

61

The announcement in both English and French warned us to be careful trusting our bags to strangers and not to leave our shit unattended.

Duh.

The cab had dropped me off at Charles de Gaulle International Airport. And I wasn't doing it as no damn "Paris Wimberly." I'd burned that ID and passport in a garbage can before coming here. I didn't care who knew it was me, Paris Duncan. A first-class trip of *fabulousity* to enjoy my last free days lay ahead.

But no, not in Valencia.

My Spanish experience was maxed out with too many searing memories of Niles, not to mention too many pro bono kills beside him. It was time to let my party-girl flag fly and I felt like taking in a fashion show, so I was headed to Milan. Far away from Niles.

Yeah. A little retail therapy with all the latest couture a sister could dream of were a match made in heaven. Besides, unless they subscribed to *Vogue Italia* or were freshly out the closet, I doubted any of my family's enemies would be gunning for me there.

"I hope I'm seated next to you. But if not I'm willing to bribe someone," a tall, lean brother in an olive sweater, jeans, and a pair of sandals said as we stood in line for the X-ray machine and body search.

"Used to getting your way with a few flattering words?" I asked, not the least bit interested in his answer.

"You tell me, lovely lady. I'm Randy. It's a pleasure." He used his best smooth daddy voice as he put out his hand.

"Look . . . I'm flattered. And I admire your confidence," I admitted. "But I've entered into a man-free phase."

"And this is your way of telling me you're not interested and I have zero chance with you. Is that the game you're playing?"

"Wow, you're a smart one," I said sarcastically, as I began digging in my purse for my ID. Unfortunately he wasn't done.

"Brothas like me are hard to find, in the States, let alone Europe. Truth is, we're damn near extinct. For every five hot women there is one suitable mate so I wouldn't be so hasty to walk away."

"Wow, and modest. My father always says that if you have to tell someone how great you are then it usually means you're hiding some real insecurities. Excuse me but I need to go."

"Running?" he asked, leaning in way too close.

"Excuse you?" I said.

"That outfit is hella attention grabbing. I saw you before you saw me. Most of the men in here did. So quit playing hard to get and maybe I will take you to dinner in Milan."

"I know you're not used to dealing with rejection 'n' all, Randy, but I have really high standards and, well, you don't meet them." I threw up my fingers, deuces to him, and I was out, stepping into the first-class line, which moved swiftly. This dude Randy had distracted me too long, so I was still fumbling for my ID as I walked up.

"Ma'am, I need to see your identification or passport," the Indian man requested impatiently as he held my boarding pass.

"I know, I know," I replied. "Just a second."

But my hand brushed up against something metallic inside my purse.

No, I gasped internally.

Stupid. Stupid. Stupid.

I still had Niles's blades. Blades that had been used in a recent murder in London.

The X-rays machines and metal detectors were up next. And I was a foreigner.

This could go so bad right about now.

"Ma'am, your passport," he repeated as he signaled for the people behind me to remain patient a moment longer.

I hesitated, visions of my parents visiting me in prison right before my eyes.

I was too pretty for prison, but of course that wasn't the thing that scared me the most. What scared me more was getting on the plane and leaving Paris. Rio's words kept ringing in my ears. Damn, I hated anybody knowing me that well.

Niles

62

"There is a big job coming your way. That's why I need you to step up your conditioning and training," she said as I maneuvered the Audi down the beltway, exiting the city.

"So you're thinking Paris threw me off my game?"

"No, I know that she did." Nadja glared at me.

I wanted to cuss her out but the last thing I needed was one more altercation with an angry female. I seemed to be on a streak and needed to ice it. So I decided to squash this topic of conversation. "We are not going to talk about her."

"She can be dead as far as I'm concerned. A non-issue. I don't know what you saw in her anyway."

"Do not go there."

"You just need to understand that I will never tolerate you putting anything or anyone else before our business. You want to get messy and undependable you are going to do it on your own and not risk my reputation."

"Whatever, Nadja. You're trippin' on me. I handle my work."

"Yeah, and since that girl there were extra collateral damages that were not as easy to explain away."

"So what is this? A ride so you can smash things in my face? You want me to get all apologetic and beg your forgiveness for living my life? Then I should let you know it's not going to happen."

"No, of course not, Niles. I only want your assurance that you won't fuck up the next job just because you finally like fucking somebody more than once."

"It's like that? And so we're clear. I've never fucked up on a job. Shit happens. This ain't some legit situation where everything is gonna be all smooth. So just back up. I'm asking you."

"Fine. Anyway we'd like you to stay at the compound. Under the radar for a few days while you brush up on your target shooting and regroup," she said, trying to act professional, but we both knew that what she wanted was me as far away from Queens as she could get me.

"Tell me about this job." I pressed her to spill the details.

"Not yet. I'm getting all the particulars worked out first. Lots of other offers are circling so I'm going to see what's landing on our plate. But this job will be a big one. Double your normal commission and possibly set you up with more jobs in the States."

My head almost snapped back when she said that. Nadja knew I'd avoided going back home but she also sensed that it was personal and that I had some unfinished business back there to handle.

"I just want to get back to work. It'll be nice to be at the complex." I smiled, showing her lots of teeth and forgiveness. She wasn't wrong. I needed to get back to the task of handling my business. As much as I hated to admit it I could use a few days at the complex to recharge my batteries and get my head right. "But I need you to do me a favor."

"What?" She stared at me.

I probably shouldn't have asked but she had access that I needed. "I need you to find out everything you can about Paris. If that's her real name. She says she's from Queens. You know everything else that I do."

"I thought you were going to forget about her."

"Yes, I am, but I need to make sure she wasn't some plant or that I'm not actually in danger."

"Just let it go, Niles."

"I can't. You want me to get my head back into the game? Then I need you to do this for me."

"Fine. But after this I don't ever want to hear her name again."

"Done," I finished. Whatever this was with Paris I needed to know that my instincts weren't that off. That I wasn't part of some bullshit game she played on me. It didn't escape me that in my line of work not having good instincts amounted to a one-way trip to the cemetery.

We pulled up to the complex, which was an exclusive gated community of massive private estates. All the properties combined were about 1,000 acres, where God knows what the hell went on. For a former inner-city kid growing up in a concrete jungle this place could be mistaken for paradise, but even I didn't notice it today. The guard at the gate nodded to both Nadja and I then hit a button to let us inside. I'd been there enough times for him to be familiar with me.

We pulled up to the house and got out. Nadja had already had the caretaker buy all my favorite foods and drinks. *Presumptuous ass,* I thought as I unloaded my bag and case of weapons. She thought she knew me that well and I wasn't that comfortable knowing she had played me.

No sooner had Nadja driven off than I felt my phone vibrating in my left pocket.

Well, one of my phones.

One I'd kept on me despite my better judgment because I'd given the number to only one person.

I'd been checking it periodically for calls since leaving my apartment.

I answered it, but said nothing.

Didn't need to.

"Want your blades back, Brooklyn?" Paris asked.

Paris

63

I followed Niles's instructions all the way to a long, un-marked road in the hilly countryside of southern France. I was near the picturesque town of Marly-le-Roi, worried I was heading in the wrong direction.

The storybook look of this part of France made me think of the first time I'd been to this part of the world. My father took me on my first tour of southern France for my thirteenth birthday. Damn! Just thinking of him brought me back to Orlando and our next phone call which wasn't gonna be nuthin' nice.

After driving about a mile, I arrived at a guard gate with a massive NO TRESPASSING sign displayed in French and English. I was familiar with this kind of life. Rich folk with little getaway properties they had for absolute privacy. We had a place similar to this in upstate New York. Course I'd heard about people having orgies and wife-swapping weekend parties at these places, too. I pulled up to the guard gate and gave him my name. Niles had instructed him to give me access. With a metallic, ringing click, the gate swung open, allowing me to continue.

Another mile later, I came upon the address. The gate that had been left open for me. I wound my way past scenic rolling hills until I arrived at a picturesque farmhouse with a tan Camry out front.

"Finally," I muttered to myself with relief.

I approached cautiously, turning down my radio while looking for any signs of trouble. Assuming I was at the right place, I parked down the road and walked cautiously the rest of the way up.

Just as I stepped onto the porch, gunshots rang out from around back.

I immediately scampered for cover, noticing a pallet on the porch's edge loaded with enough ammo canisters and explosives to make a Michigan militiaman have an orgasm. I scrambled, hoping to find a gun or something lying around, but I came up empty. When I was certain the shots weren't coming my way, I put my back to the wall and slowly, carefully inched my way around back with nothing but Niles's blades on hand.

At the end of my slinking about, I came upon Niles.

The man I admitted I loved only a day earlier was all alone and engaging in some target practice. From behind a pair of clear goggles, he rapidly switched from silhouettes to cans to bottles, the muscles in his bare arm flexing with each shot he took. And from my observation, he didn't miss.

As a glass jug along the fence cracked and splintered, I called out his name, but he didn't hear me over all the noise or with the headphones he wore like some kind of instructor.

Feeling devilish, I picked up a loose piece of wood from off the ground and tossed it underhand toward him. Catching it out the corner of his eye, Niles swiveled and blasted it with a single shot from his matte black nine mil. His motion was fluid and free of distraction.

When he noticed me clapping, he yanked his headphones off.

"How long you been there, Queens?" he asked as he slipped the safety on and lowered his smoking weapon. On a table by the back deck were three more handguns of different calibers, an assault rifle, and a couple of throwing knives. And was that a grenade I saw?

"Just got here, GI Joe," I answered. "What the fuck is all this?"

"A toy box," he replied, grinning like a schoolboy in his camouflaged pants and black sleeveless T-shirt. Pretty boy looked sexy and rugged fo sho, but was absent the semi-casual vibe to which I was accustomed. Maybe I was to blame.

"You on some shit now?" I joked, hoping to lighten the mood.

"Got a new job coming up and not sure what I'm gonna use to do it. Just making sure I'm on my A-game," he said as he came close.

I tingled all over like none of the fucked-up shit had happened, but stood my ground. I told my family I would go along with the program from here on out and that meant giving him his shit and getting my ass on a plane back to Spain.

And yet . . .

"Here," I said as I held out his karambit blades. "Sorry about accidentally taking them with me."

"Where'd you go when you left?" he asked, still not taking them.

"Airport. Until I remembered what I had in my purse," I remarked embarrassingly. "Knew you'd miss them."

Niles hesitated a moment longer, perhaps trying to find hidden meaning in my words.

"That the only reason you came all the way out here?" he said as he took them from me, carefully surveying them. He didn't wait for me to answer, probably giving me some food for thought. "Thanks," he said finally.

He had me hold his recently discharged nine, a Springfield XD, while he tested his precious babies. Doing moves I had yet to learn, he stabbed, jabbed, parried, and spun around at an imaginary target.

He was totally ramped up; not lying about wanting to be on his A-game.

While Niles engaged in his ceremonial dance of death, I decided to let off some steam of my own. From off his table, I switched out clips in the *nina* and proceeded to unload, hitting all but one of my targets. Guess I wasn't used to the gun's weight.

"Why'd you come back?" he asked again and this time I knew he expected me to answer. "You could've left my blades somewhere for me to pick them up."

"Respect for a colleague," I weakly offered as I placed the nine onto the table and walked away. "Wouldn't want you alone in a cold, cold world without your good-luck charms."

"Which good-luck charms would those be? My blades . . . or you?" Niles pressed, warming to me again and getting all up in my personal space to make his point. He tried to hug me; his musk was intoxicating. Made me want to bury my face in him. And maybe other parts even, but I couldn't.

"Easy. I didn't come here for that," I tried telling him, hoping I'd convinced myself. "I have to go."

"You have to be tired after the drive from the airport. Why can't you stay?"

"I just can't," I replied. "I have obligations, same as you."

Every step away I took was equally liberating and infuriating. I couldn't remember ever wanting the opposite of my impulses as badly as I did at this moment.

"What's the real deal with you, Paris?" Niles called out. "Did you just come back to fuck with me? To show me that I'm nothing to you?"

"What you see is what you get," I said as I quickened my pace. But Niles followed, refusing to let me go.

"Oh really?" he said with a slight chuckle, taunting me. "Is Paris even your real name? Bet you never lived in Queens a day in your life. Would explain why you were unable to tell me about your life back there."

"You don't want to go there with me," I threatened. "You're playing 'fish 'n' chips' with folk, you big fraud."

"What? You got some sugar daddy fronting your lifestyle? Some old-ass playa in the game who you belong to and I'm just a temporary distraction? Fine, don't tell me. I'll know all about you soon enough," he threatened back, ignoring my barb.

"How? Ooooh, that's right. Nadja," I said, stopping long enough to roll my eyes at him. "Your little work whore."

"Well . . . actually, yeah," he boldly admitted. Something in the pit of my stomach said to kill him right then and there, but other parts of me were confused as fuck.

"Fuck you. And fuck her," I commented instead as I threw up double middle fingers behind me.

"Paris . . . wait!" he called out. "I'm sorry about that. When I'm hurt I lash out. You can appreciate that, can't you?"

"Nah, nigga. I'm out. For good," I said as I stomped down the road to my rental.

"Stop!" His voice took on a more intense tone but I kept moving.

As I walked to my car, a shot zipped past my head, startling the fuck outta me and eliciting a mild shriek. Niles had another handgun hidden underneath his shirt. But rather than trying to shoot me, he'd taken aim at my car.

The hissing sound from the punctured tire was unmistakable.

"I said 'stop,'" Niles grunted like he'd found his nuts. "You ain't goin' anywhere."

Now, as I turned to face him standing on the porch of the cabin, all parts of me were in agreement about killing him.

Nadja

64

"Madame, it is Jeremy at the compound gate. Mr. Boateng had a guest arrive."

"And is this guest a woman?"

"Yes, a black woman named Paris."

"Thank you, Jeremy." I hung up the phone and flung it across my hotel room. How dare this bitch keep showing up like some bad penny? And Niles didn't seem to know how to keep away from her. I would have to take care of Paris once and for all. My father's words rang out in my ears. Disobeying him would cost me everything I valued, the most important thing being his respect. I couldn't actually kill the bitch, even though that would be the quickest way to end this problem. The one person that could help me figure out a plan had actually agreed with my father on this very issue.

"Hello, it's your boss."

"My ex-boss. You fired me, remember?" Navid sounded smug, like he actually thought talking to me like that was an option.

"Yes, and I've decided to give you another chance." I used my kind voice on him.

"Nadja, working with you didn't end well, and actually I'd like to use my powers for good. We hurt too many people and that's not the life I want anymore," he informed me, using one of our favorite phrases.

"Yeah, well, we can't always get what we want in this life."

"What is that supposed to mean?"

"It means that, Navid, I own you. All of the years you worked for me. Those secrets you shared with me about your sexual peccadilloes that your family would disown you if they knew? Well, unless you do exactly as I tell you then expect me to have a nice conversation with your family."

"Nadja, please, my family would die of shame and heart-break."

"Well, I wouldn't be the one breaking their hearts."

"But I do not agree with you. And you were right. I betrayed your loyalty."

"That's my fault, Navid. I didn't fully explain to you that loyalty can be bought and exchanged or gotten through blackmail. Either way, I expect you to help me on my next assignment."

"I am afraid to ask what that may be." He sounded all broken but I couldn't say that I cared. I needed him to come through for me. To help me destroy Paris Duncan.

"I need you to help me find a way to destroy that bitch!" I screamed into the receiver.

"But your father? You cannot go against him."

"Oh, I'm not going to kill her but I am going to ruin her life and you are going to help me come up with a plan."

"No. I will not help you. It is wrong. We love who we love and nothing you do will change how Niles feels about her." He tried to warn me but his words brought everything into sharper focus for me.

"You're right. I cannot change how he feels about her but I can change how she feels about him." And as soon as the words left my mouth I knew I had gotten that much closer to a plan.

"Nadja, please," Navid begged. "You are better than this. You deserve a man that loves and chooses you. Not chasing some man who doesn't really see you."

"No, I'm not better than this, and at least I'm being honest about it. And yes, there are many men that would love to be with me but I want the man I want. And I intend to have him. Nothing you or my father says is going to change that. So unless you can internally alter how I feel in my heart, then I suggest you shut the hell up and get on board. And I mean quick unless you want me to tell your parents everything . . . and I mean every single detail."

"This doesn't make any sense."

"Then you have never been in love! It doesn't need to make sense."

Niles

65

"You ain't goin' anywhere," I crowed, either too dumb or stubborn to finish my statement and say all that I was thinking. *Because I can't bear to have you walk out of my life again,* was what I left unsaid.

Maybe if I'd spoken up, Paris would've understood.

Maybe.

Paris rushed toward me in a full-on Olympic sprint. I didn't think Paris cared one lick for her safety, either. She screamed something, but I was fixated on the snarl on her face. My natural reaction would've been to raise my gun up, but I couldn't. Not against her.

I'd pointed a gun in the face of the girl I loved way too many times.

Paris took a single step onto the porch before launching into a flying sidekick meant to take my head off and she almost succeeded. My forearms deflected some of the force, but the impact sent me tumbling backward onto my ass.

I let my momentum carry me into a back roll so I could get back to my feet, but I crashed into the pallet of ammo. Paris had no such problems, instead landing on her feet like a cat. I was up to one knee when she caught me with a solid right hook to the jaw as if she were Laila Ali. I'm not going to lie, for I was straight-up seeing stars. It took that to give me a real appreciation for how good she really was in hand-to-hand. Whoever she was, Paris had to be much further along in her schooling than I'd given her credit for. I was right wobbly but got to my feet in time to block the overhand knife edge chop she delivered with her left hand. Switching martial arts styles in mid-flow, Paris flew upward and drove a vicious knee into my rib cage, which elicited a wince.

"Stop!"

She was caught off-guard as I caught her and wrapped her in a bear hug. When I didn't let go, she went to bite me, but caught a head butt for her trouble.

"Ow!" she cried out.

While I had the enraged hellcat stunned, I head-butted her again, then swept her off her feet. She tried to block my move with her legs, but I slammed her onto the porch anyway, placing my full weight atop her.

"Ugh . . . get off me!" she groaned as I barely gave her room to breathe, let alone move or wiggle free.

"No!" I yelled back as I scrambled atop her before she could reach my gun or some other weapon. "Not until you calm down."

"You shot my tire then you . . . you head-butted me! Twice!"

"I only shot your tire to stop you from leaving. And you attacked me first!"

Her scowl faded, surprising me as I thought it a ruse to get me to drop my guard. "How'd I do?" she asked as she slipped into a big, cozy smile, her anger turned off like some switch.

She was certifiable.

And sexy.

I was in love.

And maybe . . . certifiable too.

"Incredible. You are incredible, Paris," I admitted, so proud of her despite my achy jaw and ribs. In their place, an ache of another sort began to blossom and grow in intensity. "How'd I do?" I asked back.

"You weren't too bad," she replied with a smug grin.

"Gee. Thanks," I groaned. "I was defending myself. Didn't want to hurt you."

"Oooh. Sometimes a little hurtin' can . . . be . . . good," she uttered, acknowledging my growing *presence* pressing up against her.

"So if I let you go, you promise you'll behave?" I asked.

Paris grasped my ass and pulled me even closer onto her, our bodies assuming a familiar rhythmic tempo of lust. "How's this for behaving?" she teased. "You know what I want," Paris moaned.

"Yeah. I do," I replied. "But let's take it inside. Don't want a *spark* setting off the ammo."

I worried Nadja might return from her dealings and have an unimpeded, deluxe view before I could explain why Paris was suddenly back in my life.

I slung her over my shoulder, eliciting a yelp as I stormed off the porch, kicked the door open, then went inside with my woman.

My woman.

For a serial womanizer like me my sudden need for ownership felt oddly right.

The farmhouse, while looking basic from the outside, was a testament to modern amenities and privacy; something the original owners saw fit to do before Nadja paid them for their discretion and purchased it for some "big-time hunters." I touched a keypad near the wall, scanning through streaming audio selections until Jamiroquai's "Corner of the Earth" played softly throughout the place. The button beside it activated the fireplace for which it wasn't cold enough, but mirrored my burning desire for her.

As I carried Paris toward the oversized bed, I worked her skimpy little pants until they came down, exposing nothing but a nice derriere and thong. I bit at one of her golden delicious ass cheeks then gave her bottom a smack. She giggled in response, singing, "Oooo. Get nasty, daddy!"

I dropped her onto the furs adorning the foot of the bed and watched her slide. She removed her blouse then as she unfastened her bra and slowly exposed each breast.

"Your shirt first. And make it hot," she instructed as she rubbed on her clit through her thong. Her moans made it hard to concentrate, but I obliged. My black shirt reeked of spent gun powder, so I was happy to remove it, going extra sexy like I was her private toy.

"Damn, boy. I love your hardness," she cooed while she crawled over to the edge of the bed and lazily licked every crease of my abs with her tongue as if ice cream were running down them and she didn't want to miss a drop.

When she touched my tender ribs, I flinched a little. Barely noticeable, but with her lips against me it was easy to detect.

She looked up apologetically. "I'm sorry," she whispered. "Let me kiss it and make it better."

When I dropped my pants, she slid her hand into my boxer briefs and gently cradled my balls.

"Damn," I moaned as I felt hot breath tantalizing my penis.

"Boy, you don't know how bad I want to suck you right now," Paris growled, sending my hard-on to almost painful levels. "Can I . . . suck it?" she teased, her voice doing things to me.

"Yes," I gasped, unsure of how long I could stand before her like this.

"Like this?" she asked, her voice raising an octave. "Mmm. You taste good, daddy. Want to taste my pussy, too?"

"Yes," I said, almost grunting as I licked my lips. "I'd like that so much."

Paris obliged, turning onto her back while she continued sucking me off. She grasped the back of my knees to steady herself on the mattress then amazingly kicked her body up into a headstand.

I appreciated her presentation, showing her just how much as I reached for her waist to steady her and drilled my tongue deep within her folds alternating between that and gently munching on that clit to drive her crazy. Still upside down, she cried out while sucking me, never backing off while I plunged my dick in and out of her beautiful sloppy mouth.

Before she passed out, I flipped her upright by her waist then entered her while she wrapped her arms around my neck.

"Uh-huh. Mmm hmm," she moaned with her eyes closed as I penetrated her.

"Look at me," I whispered.

Uncharacteristically quiet, she complied, slowly lifting her head to gaze into my eyes.

"I love you, Paris," I gushed, getting equally lost in her seductive light brown pools.

I pumped harder, building in intensity as I refused to let her look away.

"I . . . I . . ." she stuttered as another orgasm consumed her, her sweet honey flowing down more and more by the minute. I took one of her legs and raised it to me, going deeper inside if such a thing is possible. "Oh! Oh! Oh, Niles!" she rambled, giving in to her sweet, sweaty body as she worked to give it all to me. Her surrender was a beautiful thing as she screamed out like someone having a vision, "I love you! I love you! Yes! Yes! Yes!"

I dropped her leg and took her with me onto the bed, both of us crashing rudely onto the expensive fur throw as a crash of my own lay ahead.

Paris cackled as she dug many a nail into my ass, prodding me with, "Give me your love, baby. Let me feel it. You gonna let me feel it?"

Grunting, I redoubled my efforts, coiling and releasing like a snake as I fucked her vigorously toward the magnificent end to this stanza. Paris wrapped her legs around me, meeting the challenge as we rolled about. For we fucked like we fought; and fought like we fucked.

A shudder followed by a rush from deep within signaled the moment Paris had demanded of me was close at hand. She smiled, feeling my body's message as she surrendered another orgasm of her own to me. "Ooooh," she sang wonderfully.

"Paris, I . . ."

She clutched my head to her chest and held tightly. With a tickle of her tongue in my ear, her ragged breath begged for me to join her.

And I did, my body trembling and shaking with a final hopeless attempt at keeping the monster at bay.

In an explosion of ecstasy, I gave it up to Paris. Surrendered my seed as my body shorted out from the intensity of our lovemakin'.

I'd known passion before, but in reflecting on it later, a component was always missing.

Atop the stripped bed, we cuddled tenderly with my arms around her waist, our fingers intertwined. And as our hearts slowed, sleep was our reward for survival.

But sleep doesn't always grant us escape from the demands of the waking world.

Something I would learn shortly.

Rio

66

One of the major tenets my parents drilled into all of us kids was to always have a backup plan when it came to business and dealing with people.

"People are not always reliable and trust that often they come with their own agenda that has nothing to do with you or even what they promised," LC told us a million times. "You can never truly depend on anyone other than family, so as long as you were dealing with civilians make sure they know your value." As tired as I had gotten from these talks being drilled into our heads I had to admit they were now saving my ass. Eduardo's threats, joking or not, made me realize that I couldn't afford to get comfortable in my position at his club. He wasn't used to Black-Amex-having niggas that didn't need his dollars to live the high life. If Lando hadn't insisted on me using an alias I would have flossed the Duncan pedigree quick. Let him know there were some rich-ass young black men who lived the five-star life without any help from trick-ass wannabe pimps like his ass. I knew women that dealt with this sugar-daddy shit all the time and maybe it worked for them but he'd be six feet under if he tried to "buy" me again.

"Hey, Rio," the bartender greeted me as I entered the bar area. "Trying out a new specialty cocktail. I need to get your opinion." He slid a green-colored drink toward me.

I took a sip. "Nice." I stepped away to check on the new uniforms I'd ordered for the cocktail waitresses. They were sexy without being overt. I figured that would discourage the female customers from having drama when their boyfriends leered at the waitresses. Eduardo joined me in the office as the girls modeled the outfits.

"Much better!"

"Might save us some lawsuits," I laughed.

"Too much cleavage, a few husband left on stretchers," he added, throwing up his hands in the drama sign. "That DJ you hired for the weekend. Is he as good as the last one?"

"Nobody can rival DJ PLUS 1NE but everybody's calling Dr. Zeus the Second Coming and he's never played out of the States so there's a real buzz on him. The VIP section is booked with a waiting list a mile long so I think people are up on his talent."

"You really came through. You give people chances and you never know how it's going to turn out but in your case you were more than just a pretty face."

"'Scuse me?"

"Rio, you told me yourself you never finished university so who knows what you are capable of? You came with no track record and I gave you a chance."

"University? Have you ever heard of Harvard Law School?" I asked his bitch ass.

"Yes, of course."

"Well, I'm here because I got accepted into that school and it's not what I want to do. When I set my mind to something I'm all about succeeding at the highest level. I don't just talk about it . . . I be about it," I schooled him.

"If you say so but I am fine. It's working well."

"So I'm going to get my paper on Monday?" I reminded him but he just looked at me like we were talking different languages. I was 'bout to close that language barrier quick since he didn't seem to get it. "My paycheck?"

"It's only been a week. I like to pay people on a monthly basis. Makes it easier."

"For who? Shit I like to see my money once a week." It wasn't even that I needed that little bit of paper to survive or nothing, but the principle. Who the fuck gets paid once a month? "Yeah, that's not working for me."

"Fine. Got it. So I assume you have your work papers? Your permit that says you're legally able to make a living in this country?" He smiled, even though his words weren't measuring up to his tone at all.

"Yeah, I'm gonna get them this week."

"Well, soon as you get them let me know and I will cut you a check."

"No problem." I got up and left the room. See this wasn't the kind of shit I'd ever had to deal with back home. Folks wouldn't try to stiff me or fuck with my money. Made me want to pick up the phone and call Vegas, but I knew something was going down with him at home and the last thing he needed was to rescue his baby brother being taken advantage of, especially when I could handle it myself. I marched up to the DJ booth and caught Dr. Zeus unloading his MacBook.

"Wassup, Rio!" We bumped fists. I'd only met him once but we ran in the same places, and when it came to real club life even a city like New York got small.

"Look, I got a hookup for a gig in Paris this week. I can put you down. Three nights, better pay, and, well, it's Paris. You got to see the Eiffel Tower."

"I'm with that."

"But it's not looking like this is gonna pan out. You can keep the advance and I'll get you set up in France by tomorrow."

"Sweet. Looks like I'm on vacay." DJ Dr. Zeus lifted up his computer and placed it back in his bag. As I turned to walk DJ out we were stopped by Eduardo hurrying over to us.

"Everything all right?" He offered a warm smile as if shit hadn't just turned rotten as hell and left a sour smell in the air.

"Yeah, nice meeting you." Dr. Zeus nodded as he headed out the door.

"Where is he going?" Eduardo asked, confused as fuck.

"Yeah, this isn't going to work," I let him know.

"Excuse me?" He was now more than confused. I could see the sparks of anger jumping off of him.

"See, I needed to make sure that you weren't going to try to fuck me when you realized that I was never going to fuck you again."

"Why you talk like that?" He tried to pull the innocent act but I couldn't buy that.

"See, Eduardo, you don't know me, because if you did you'd understand that I will never need anyone like you. Your work ethics are fucked and I ain't got time for that. So I took a job at a well-known club in Paris. And the owner is not going to try and bully me. She's not that type."

"But I was just kidding." He gave an award-winning try.

"And you will pay me for this week . . . in cash. Unless you want everything I've done this last week to be erased. I'm able to hire every one of your staff to come and work for me for better consistency."

"I will not pay you one dime until you produce papers." He got up in my face threateningly but I had something for his ass.

"In one week I learned everything that I need to about the way you do business. That watered-down alcohol. The underage girls you allow to drink here, and the fact that you're cleaning money for some very dangerous men. Want me to keep my mouth closed then pay me now . . . and in cash."

"You have no idea who I am," he threatened.

"No, Eduardo, you are the one that has no idea who I am. You attempt to fuck with me and I will make sure that you are destroyed."

"You couldn't."

"Do you know the Santa Maria di Gesu family?" I almost smiled at the undisguised shock on his face as he nodded yes. "Well, they owe someone very close to me a favor. Do you understand what I'm saying? So instead of me collecting on that favor you should probably just pay me. Now, motherfucker!" I growled as he quickly pulled the wad of cash out of his pocket and peeled off $1,000. "I'm thinking my work deserved a little more compensation."

He gave me another thousand dollars before getting the hell away from me.

"I hope to never see you again!" he yelled as I sauntered out the door ready for a new adventure. This time I had promised myself to follow Vegas's rule number one.

Niles

67

I awoke to the soft light of the crackling fireplace, the rest of the cabin bathed in darkness except for the random glow from electronic displays.

One of those displays was blinking and emitted a sound barely noticeable over the Chris Botti streaming through the speakers in the cabin.

We had company.

I looked around, regaining my bearings and adjusting to the darkness. An empty bottle of wine lay on the floor beside the bed and the essence of lovemaking hung in the air. Paris was snoring after what had been our third session of letting bygones be bygones. But when I stirred, she sat up.

"Huh? Whazzat?" she mumbled, not sure what she was saying, but trying to sound alert.

I smiled fondly and hugged her before kissing her on her cheek. "Nothing," I said calmly. "Just remembered I left the guns outside. Go back to sleep."

"Word? All right," she clowned, eyes already half closed as she plummeted back onto the mattress, free to dream whatever.

I threw on some clothes, grabbed my phone then stepped onto the porch, warily taking in the still of the night. Nothing unusual was nearby except Paris's rented Volvo, reminding me I had a flat to change come morning. Checking my phone, I saw I'd missed several calls in the last hour. I picked up my gun I'd left on the porch during my struggle with Paris and chambered a round, taking the safety off. The weapons on the table out back could wait a little longer. I looked up the road past Paris's car in the direction of the gate before leaping off the porch. Charting my path off-road, I broke into a sprint toward it, unsure of what awaited me.

Minutes later, I arrived at my destination, remaining cloaked in darkness while I made sure this wasn't an ambush. A truck sat parked at the gate with its engine running as I slipped up on it, my gun aimed at where I thought a person would be inside the cab.

Upon making myself visible and that I was armed, the truck door opened and someone stepped out, their hands above their head.

"What took you so long?" Nadja asked as I trudged up to the gate, her headlights blinding me.

"Sorry. Was sleeping," I growled in response as I punched in the code to disarm the alarm and open the gate. "Anyone in the truck with you?" I asked casually, pretending her answer would be no big deal either way while keeping my finger on the trigger. I was prepared to squeeze off two quick rounds into the passenger seat if it came to it.

"No. Of course not," she answered.

"Then turn off those fuckin' high beams," I groused, finally slipping on the gun's safety. I followed Nadja over to the truck where she nixed the headlights.

"Why'd you change the gate code?" Nadja asked as expected. Well, so much for putting things off.

"Just a precaution. Can never be too careful," I replied as I went around to the passenger side of the truck. On its door was a magnetic sign that read PIERRE'S WILD GAME & SMOKED MEATS. *Cute.* "What if you didn't come back and somebody else decided to pay me a visit?" I proposed, nervously feeling I needed to say more. Actually, I only changed the code after Paris showed up. To protect her.

As Nadja began to put her ride in gear, I placed my hand up, signaling her to stop.

"No. Let's go over it here," I said cautiously.

"Why? You're saying I can't go back to the cabin? That's a bunch of rubbish!" she howled.

"I have company, s'all," I said, looking away.

"Paris, or whatever her real name is, is back, huh? After what you told me, too? You bastard. You bloody bastard."

"Hey, this was totally unexpected. But I am happy about it. That should count for something, right?"

"What about your promise? To get back into work. No distractions?"

"Okay. So that's how it's gonna be, right? Well, whatcha got for me?" I asked, extending my hand. "Might as well get this over with. We're still professionals, right?"

She handed over the folder as I turned on the interior light with a punch of the overhead button. The file was thicker than usual, possibly symbolizing the level of difficulty of the job.

"First. Let me make this clear. This is a solo hit, not some team thing. You do not involve that woman in any capacity. You do not share any of the intel with that woman. Or so help me, I'll blow the whole thing up. Got it?" she threatened.

"Totally," I replied just wanting to finish this convo and get back to bed.

"The customer is a bloke by the name of Salvatore Dash. He wants a business rival forcibly retired, but doesn't want to go through proper channels within his organization. And he wants a brown face to do it, but he fears the locals might have some misguided sense of loyalty to this bloke and either botch the job or alert him," Nadja recited as if reading a dating profile instead. I almost waited for Salvatore's turnoffs and turn-ons.

"What kind of business? Mob stuff? Turf war?" I questioned as I analyzed the data.

"Yes. All of that apparently," she replied. "Despite their noble public personas, these are major drug merchants, these people."

"Well, one less of those couldn't hurt," I said smartly, stifling a yawn as I pored over the photos of a finely dressed older black man and some of the people in his organization. "LC Duncan," I recited aloud as if presenting the man with an award. "Hmm. Sounds important. And two of the other men from the photos looked like they could be his sons."

"That's because he is and they are," Nadja confirmed. "As connected and powerful as they come. Someone worthy of the big price tag."

Something else in the photos caught my eye. "Is this job in New York?" I asked, recognizing some of the East Coast features. Hadn't been in the States in forever. Too many bad memories that sent me chasing better ones elsewhere.

"New York, New Jersey . . . wherever you can pull it off," she answered. "No stipulations. But, yes, he resides in New York. Jamaica Queens, to be exact."

"Queens . . ." I mumbled with a wry smile and thoughts of Paris back in the bed. "Queens" had become something of a pet name for her after our wild adventures. Funny thing was that she probably wasn't really from that borough. Nadja was so close to finding out the full deal on her, but I couldn't ask it of her any longer. I bore enough guilt for putting her on the case while lying about my true feelings and motives. I would get the answers myself.

"Something funny?"

"No. Not at all. I'll do this job, we'll make major bank . . . then I guess this is it for us," I said with a long sigh.

"Only because it's your choice," Nadja said, rubbing her eye. "So . . . you need a ride back to the cabin?" she asked as she cleared her throat.

"No. I think I'll walk. The night air is so fresh here. Good for my senses. Can I have a day or so before I mobilize?"

"Yes. You can rendezvous with me in Manhattan for any last-minute instructions or changes to the job. Think I'll take in a Broadway play. Maybe meet a hot Yank of my own."

"*On Broadway?* I highly doubt it. At least not a straight one," I joked.

Nadja actually laughed. "Go on. Get out," she urged, turning back on the headlights.

Paris
68

"I don't see why 'that woman' can't bring this shit to you during the daytime," I complained while lying naked across the bed. Niles thought I didn't realize how long he was gone last night—that his dick and the excellent bottle of Pinot Noir took my mind off of reality. But no, I'm a little harder than that. LC Duncan didn't raise any punks. I even noticed the envelope he'd tossed onto the dresser.

Not long after Niles left me to "check on weapons," I carried my exhausted, tipsy ass on a little mission of my own. I had left my phone in the car, so I went to see how badly I'd fucked up.

And judging by the missed calls, there would be hell to pay, but nobody said when I had to pay it.

I stowed my phone again and scurried back inside. I'd have to deal with the Duncan men soon enough.

But I was a big girl now, making big-girl moves.

Just not the moves my family had ordered me to make.

Still couldn't believe that I was the one they didn't trust on the frontlines. Wasn't like Harris, London, Orlando, or even Chippy had my shooting skills. Shit pop off and I would actually be an asset. At least Niles appreciated me and what I had to offer. Couldn't believe that I had fallen off the cliff and so deeply in love. Never ever expected it to happen and certainly not this quickly.

"We don't keep regular office hours. You should know that," Niles reminded me as he shoved his stuff in a bag. With his other hand, he finished off the last piece of bacon from the breakfast he'd cooked for us.

He was a man custom made for me: he served me breakfast in bed in the scenic wilderness of France and could shoot a gun.

Some of these big-girl moves were paying off kinda nicely.

"All right. And my temper is under control. Nadja won't get under my skin this time. See?" I said, smiling all gleefully 'n' shit. "So what's our job?"

"*Our?*" He frowned.

"Yeah. I thought we were gonna be a team," I reminded him as I walked over. His eyes locked on that damn mission folder of his rather than my sexiness, letting me know he didn't want me anywhere near it.

"We might. But that's something to discuss after I get back from this job."

"She making you exclude me?" I asked, already knowing the answer. Her Tweety Bird head had to have exploded when Niles told her I was back.

"Nah. The job is making me exclude you. *It beez that way sometimes,*" he said, flashing that smile of his to make me turn all mushy. It only confirmed Nadja was making him exclude me. "And besides, until I know that you're all in, I can't risk a repeat of London. It reflects poorly on my work. And my reputation is all I have, babe."

"Well, how about Valencia when I saved your ass?" I shot back.

"Please. I already thanked you for that, but I need you to see where I'm coming from. I love you, Paris. No doubt about it," Niles said as he stood up from the table and stretched. "But we each got some real blanks to fill for the other. I need to know if that phone you stashed in your car rings you won't feel tortured or the need to run out of here and back to that school. It makes sense that we take some time to figure this out. And know that if we do move forward then I'm ride or die to the end."

"Y'know . . . speaking of my school," I started as I rubbed his sore arms. "What if my sponsors were looking for more than one person to employ? Maybe somebody already established?" I had no way of knowing if my family would hire Niles, especially after he'd *led me astray*. But dad did hire Harris after London married him. Maybe I could find a win-win in this situation for both of us.

"Babe, I appreciate your trying to help, but I don't need it," he said, more sweet than dismissive, as he leaned over and gave me a kiss. "Especially after this job. Besides, gotta maintain some of my independence. This dog doesn't like a leash."

"Yeah, yeah. Gotcha. Just trying to contribute to . . . us," I mumbled as I ran my hands through his hair and gazed into his eyes.

"And you'll have plenty of time. Right now, I gotta focus," he said as he did his best to resist me. "But I do have a question for you."

"*Yeah?*" I asked, my hopes of maybe something more relaxing than weapons maintenance ignited again.

"How would you know if your sponsors are hiring? Most sponsors are semi anonymous as far as my understanding goes. Unless you've got a special relationship with your folk," he said as he cut his eyes at me without actually cutting them.

"Me? Nah," I scoffed. "I'm just trying to think outside the box."

"Well, you're doing that. But, y'know what?" he said, suddenly pulling those damn blades of his from out of nowhere and playing with them. "I have a confession to make. I was gonna wait 'til I got back, but figured I'd come clean now. I had Nadja looking into you."

"What?" I blurted out, taken aback by his news. Did he know about me?

"After you left me in Paris. Thought I wouldn't ever see you again. I . . . I kinda used her. Figured I'd never stoop so low, but I was desperate. Knew she could maybe find you with her talents. I just wasn't ready to let you go."

"And now?"

"I called her off," he replied with a nervous shrug. "Because now I can hear it directly from your mouth. Well . . . after I come back. If you decide you're all in."

"Uh . . . where are you going anyway?" I asked 'cause maybe he would let me tag along.

"It probably won't hurt to tell you that," he said, genuine warmth and boy-like mischievousness flooding back into his eyes. "New York."

"Where in New York?" I asked, suddenly nervous. Probably paranoid because New York was a big city with lots of work.

"Uh-uh, Paris. No more details. I may be gone less than a week, but I'll check in. I promise," he said, kissing me on the lips. "And I'll change your flat before I leave. This spot is safe, so feel free to chill and enjoy the amenities. Maybe get some practice in if you want. I'm gonna put my bag in the car."

"Hey!" I yelled out.

"Yeah, Queens?" he asked while peeking his head from out the trunk.

"I broke my phone. The one you know about in my car? Smashed it. To bits," I admitted, feeling a wave of nausea over admitting it. However, Niles's smile and nod soothed me.

Yeah. Real big-girl things, turning your back on your . . .

Your family.

I inhaled deeply, fighting off baby tears.

I was about to cop a seat on the porch, but Niles had other plans. "Baby, could you get my file for me?"

"Sure," I said, glad to feel somewhat useful. Popping back up onto my feet, I went inside, sauntered over to the table where that damn folder had lain.

When I emerged from the cabin, my feet were unsteady. In the back of my throat, bile was threatening to come up. As I handed it to him, I clutched my stomach, grimacing.

"Thanks," he said with a quick smile over his shoulder. I was gingerly making my way back to my seat when he called out again. "Paris?"

"Yeah, baby?"

"You look ill. Is something wrong?"

"Yeah. Feeling a little sick. Probably the bacon. I usually avoid the swine," I offered, shaking a fist his way.

"Aww. Wanna go back inside and rest? I can finish this on my own."

"I think that's probably a good idea. Got any Sprite?" I asked.

"Yeah. There are some cans in the fridge. When I'm done, I'll run you a nice bath."

I nodded then headed back indoors, passing a small open crate of explosives on the porch.

"Oh. One other thing," Niles added, stopping me when I was halfway in the door. "You didn't look at the file, did you?"

"Of course not," I replied with the sweetest smile I could muster. I smiled while my stomach lurched, churned, and cramped.

I smiled to keep from crying.

I smiled to hold back the pain.

But bacon be damned . . .

Of course I looked at the fuckin' file.

Niles . . .

The man I loved.

His big job was to kill my daddy.

Rio

69

Even though I'd requested a "do not disturb" message on my phone the incessant ringing woke me up. I tried to block it out with one of those cushy hotel pillows but she kept going. I thought cutting my phone off would have given me some peace. Had to be Paris since she's the only one who'd really want to talk to me. Then a knocking on the door got really old super quick.

"What?" I yelled at whoever was at the door.

"Rio, I need to talk to you," Navid hollered from the other side. *Fuck he want at this hour?* I thought after glancing at the clock. I got up, stormed to the door, and swung it open. Didn't bother putting anything on, just going full frontal on his ass.

"I am so glad you answered."

"Fuck, Navid, you calling and pounding on my door and shit. Not cool."

"No, I didn't call you. I just got here. It's Nadja, she's gone crazy."

I allowed him to step inside as I grabbed my jeans and got dressed. "What the hell? You said her father forbade her from messing with Paris."

"I know. But I've been checking her e-mails and phone correspondence to make sure your sister was safe and I just noticed something that worried me."

"Is she going after my sister?"

"I'm not sure but she's contracted a job in New York and I'm not certain this isn't about your sister. Something's not right. The person demanded a black hit person because the target is black."

"And does that mean it's Paris or not?"

"No, but there is something she said to me. She wants to make sure that Paris hates Niles."

"You're talking in riddles."

"I know, but there is something that makes me believe that someone close to your sister is the target."

"Me? You think that it's me?" I had to say that I felt shocked at this.

"It has to be. Who else? You're twins," he said, wringing his hands.

I grabbed my phone and turned it on. Forty-six missed calls. All from the same number. I hit redial. "Hey, we have a problem."

"Where the hell have you been, Rio? I've been calling you all night," Orlando screamed into the phone. "Shit is out of hand. Where is Paris? And don't lie to me."

"She was supposed to come back here last night but I think she's still in France."

"Yes, I know that, but she's not answering her phone."

"I think she's in trouble, Lando. Or I am." I told him everything that Navid had shared with me.

"Just sit tight. You're gonna be okay. And don't move. I'll be there soon."

Hanging up the phone I turned to Navid. "Thank you. My brother is handling it. But I am going to kill that bitch."

"I understand."

"Why did you go back to work for her?"

"I didn't have a choice. She threatened to tell my parents everything."

"Well, she's going to tell them now."

"I know," he replied.

I shook my head as Navid left. Sorry his life had gotten fucked in the process of helping me. I checked my phone and found several messages from both Mom and Pops. Apparently my new life remained anything but secret to them.

"Rio, it's your mom, wanted to tell you that if you want to come home and run a club somebody has offered to buy one for you."

"Rio, it's Pop. Needed to make sure that you're okay and to remind you that in this life family is all that we have." I was going through the messages when my phone rang. Clicked over to the other side.

"Yeah?"

"Hustle to the roof. I'm waiting for you," Orlando barked in my ear. I didn't know how he'd gotten there so quickly but I threw on a shirt and hit the door.

Nadja

70

It was one of the most beautiful mornings I'd had in a long time. Paris in the springtime just like in some sappy fifties movie. I called room service to deliver me all of my favorite breakfast foods: eggs Benedict, waffles, bacon, and even a fresh scone with clotted cream. Usually I skipped the first meal of the day but today I'd felt like treating myself. After all, today marked the start of my new life. I'd probably go to the Louvre and then shopping. Buy something overtly sexy for the next time I saw Niles in New York. Just thinking about him brought a delicious smile to my lips.

I lay back on my bed, slipping my fingers in my mouth to wet them first. Then I expertly manipulated the folds of my vagina to expose the tiny round button at the top. Funny that a man had taught me the value of touching myself. Of knowing firsthand how I wanted my body to be touched. That it was not only acceptable to bring myself to pleasure but that he expected it and I should. Imagining that my hands belonged to Niles caused me to moan in ecstasy and brought me to a swift conclusion.

"Niles, Niles, Niles," I whispered and my hips rose off the bed as I came to a body-shaking orgasm, my juices dripping wet all over my fingers. "Damn I miss you." Now that was the way to start the morning.

After breakfast I checked my messages. Nothing from Navid. I'd really have to whip him into shape. This time I refused to fill him in on my master plan. Couldn't risk him running and crying to my daddy as if I were some child having a tantrum and not some grown-ass woman fighting for what was rightfully mine. Total luck that I had located information about the hit placed on Paris's father. It figures that any man that powerful would have to have equally powerful enemies, or at least those that needed him out of the way in order to become powerful. When maneuvering in the underworld at the level we did there were usually only one or two degrees of separation. I'd hit the jackpot and there would be no way my father could trace the hit back to me. Now I would just sit and wait for the next call.

I'd gotten the guard at the compound to phone me as soon as Niles left. Thought maybe I'd surprise him at the airport for a good-bye and also to make sure that bitch didn't manipulate him into letting her tag along. That would ruin my plan and it wasn't going to happen.

I picked up the phone to call Navid. I'd made a list of the things I wanted him to handle in preparation for my trip to New York. I'd pretend to be just as shocked as Niles would be when he found out that the mark he killed, LC Duncan, was Paris's father. He'd really need my loving comfort and I intended to give it to him.

"Hey, I need you to come to my suite. I forgot to give you that list."

"I can come this afternoon," he said but I detected something in his voice.

Discomfort?

Nerves?

"Where are you?" I growled into the mouthpiece. "And do not lie to me."

"I'm in Valencia," he admitted.

"What the hell are you doing there?"

"I just needed to see Rio. Nadja, I really like him."

"Fine. As long as you weren't making any bedroom confessions." I pretended to be lighthearted but inside I was seething with rage. If he'd betrayed me again there would be a hell to pay like no hell he had ever known.

"No, I just wanted to see him."

"And where is he?"

"Uh, he had to go to the lobby." His voice took on a desperate tone and I could tell that he was lying. Even though I hadn't actually shared my plan with him, Navid was smart. I only hoped not sharp enough to figure out my intention. I'd worked all the angles and knew that this was the quickest way to destroy this growing relationship. Niles had actually told me that she made him happy. Well, if he liked dark pussy that much then I would get a tan and show him that mine was superior and it would always come to life under his expertise.

"Navid, I need you to get your ass back here," I raged at that damn Judas.

"No."

"Excuse me? What did you say to me?"

"I can't come back and work with you. You're not a good person."

"How dare you judge me? And what do you think your parents will say?" I threatened.

"I don't know. I'm going home to tell them myself. I won't let you hurt anyone anymore."

"Oh, grow the fuck up. This is real life and in real life people get hurt. Deal with it."

"No. Not this time."

"What did you say?" I growled, the wheels turning in my head.

"Nothing. Forget it," Navid mumbled.

I slammed down the phone. I needed to check that nothing was getting in the way of my plan. Something did not sound right.

Paris

71

I rolled off of Niles, butt naked and thoroughly satisfied. This man knew my body as if we had always been together. God, I loved him.

"Where are you going?" Niles asked as I rose and started dressing.

"With you."

"Paris . . ." he said cautiously.

Wiping my tears, I stifled a laugh. "No . . . no, no, no," I said, sniffling. "I'm going to drive you to the airport. I think I deserve a sappy good-bye," I lied. "Besides, I need to get my ass out of here and back to Spain. Left all my shit there."

"Is this some ploy so you can go along?" He got up, revealing all the reasons I should just throw him back on the bed.

"If you were going to any other city, but I'm not tryin'a show up in New York."

"Yeah, I get it. I'm gonna go jump in the shower. I would ask you to join me but we'll never get out." He laughed, grabbing me around the waist and planting a deep, wet kiss on me.

"I'm not showering. I want to smell you on me all day. Maybe I won't shower at all until you come back."

"That is so fuckin' nasty and hot. You dirty girl," he joked as he headed to the shower.

"Hey, since you fixed my tire we'll take my car. I'll transfer all your stuff into it," I said.

He turned around and smiled at me, all teeth and cocky as hell. "See, this is why I'm keeping you. You're like a sexy ninja girl scout."

"Go! I don't want you blaming me for being late." I pointed him to the bathroom. As soon as I heard the shower turn on I got to work gathering everything I would need. Twenty minutes later we were headed out of the compound.

"You gonna turn on your phone?" Niles motioned to the phone I thought I had hidden so well.

"I'm not going to see you for a week. I'll deal with it later."

"Somebody likes living on the edge."

"Well, somebody wouldn't be with you if they didn't."

"So we're together?" Niles's voice took on a serious tone as his eyes bore into me.

"Yes, we are." I wanted to turn and face him but I had to keep my eyes on the road so I pulled over to the side.

"Why you stopping?" He placed his hand on top of mine.

"What if you don't come back?" I proposed.

"Then I will reflect on the wonderful moments that I've shared with you in way too short a time," he said softly, caressing my face. "But the main thing I'm gonna do is my job. And do it effectively so we don't have to worry about such things."

As much as I needed to change his mind I knew that I couldn't. The job was what he did and he would no more walk away from unfinished business than I could.

I grabbed his arm and held it tight, begging him with my eyes. I wanted to tell him the truth. But I just couldn't bring myself to speak.

"Hey. I've got something for you," he interrupted my thoughts. He reached into his waistband then extended his hand. One of his karambit blades rested in it. "It's for you . . . until they're reunited."

"What . . . why?" I babbled before taking the blade from him.

"Tell you what," he started. "When I get back. We'll lay it all on the line, me and you, and see how things go. Paris, you make me nervous like a little schoolboy and I'm not used to feeling all open and shit. But I do believe fate brought us together back in Spain. I love you with all my heart, you crazy, sexy woman. And I'm ready to commit to you."

I was stunned. On top of my frayed emotions, this left me speechless.

"Just something I needed to get off my chest . . . on the off chance that something does happen to me and I don't return. Tomorrow's never promised, but I need you to know that my love for you is . . ."

Niles kissed me tenderly. As he pivoted, I locked my grip on the single blade. Mad at myself for enjoying the kiss. When we finished neither of us spoke. I drove away from the side and let him direct me back to the private airstrip. I pulled my car up to the plane and let him out. God, I didn't want to. I wanted him to stay here with me. He unloaded his bags and I watched him walk toward the plane. Then I pulled out my cell.

"Paris?" he answered, surprised by the suddenness of my call. He hadn't even made it to the first step. He turned to look at me sitting in the car.

I hesitated at first, biting my lip. "You . . . you told me to tell you when I made my decision," I mumbled.

"I recall saying that," he said with a chuckle.

"Well . . . I did."

"And? Are you all in, Paris?"

"Yeah. I am," I solemnly said.

"Good. Because I know you looked inside the folder," he stated, startling me. "Just wanted to show that I trust you with my business . . . no matter who says I shouldn't. No secrets. I love you, ma," he said, oblivious to who I really was.

Who I really am.

A Duncan.

The daughter of the man he was going to merc.

"I love you too," I replied. "Always."

"Then we're the same." Walking back over he gave me a quick kiss on the lips, holding me around the waist. As his hands fell away and he began to move away I grabbed his arm holding it firmly. At first he looked confused because my grip had intensity but when his eyes met mine they were soft, smiling.

"Do you trust me?" I fought back tears.

"Yes, and that's not something that comes naturally to me," he said, holding my gaze for a full minute.

"Then believe me when I say you can't go. Call it a hunch or a feeling or a premonition but you have to walk away from this job." I heard my voice catch from the emotional hell swirling deep down at the core of my heart.

"Bae, it's gonna be all right. I'm not leaving you. Plus, I need to finish this job so that I can walk away from Nadja."

"I don't care. Do another job for her. I need you to stay with me." I knew the begging wasn't sexy but I couldn't just let him go. He reached out and swooped me up in his arms and held me close. But by the time he put me down I knew he'd made his decision and nothing I said would deter him. I watched as he walked toward the plane and stepped up the ladder, disappearing into the G5. And just like that he was gone.

My hands trembling, I donned a pair of gloves I'd hastily stowed in my pocket in anticipation of this moment. From the opposite pocket, I produced a wireless transmitter and removed the safety with a flick of my thumb. I waited until the plane had taken off. I imagined him there in the cockpit, thinking about me the way that I was here thinking about him.

Taking a deep breath, I closed my eyes and counted to three as I fought back tears.

But in the end, the outcome was predetermined from the moment I looked in that file.

Back in a cheap motel in Valencia, Niles once taught me a valuable lesson about having to make hard choices. When he wanted me to prove I was *about this life*.

Well, I am.

I opened my eyes . . .

And pressed the trigger.

And all I could say, "I love you, Niles."

Only when the sky erupted in a blaze of light was I convinced of my success.

Success was synonymous with misery right now as the transmitter fell from my open hand.

I screamed at the top of my lungs, but there was no one there to hear it. My chest heaving, I screamed again. But none of it diminished the hurt.

***

I drove out of the airstrip, the flames of the airplane lighting the sky and falling into pieces everywhere. As my car sped down the road, tears streaming down my face almost blinded me but I didn't care. I couldn't. The thought of crashing violently into something—a tree, another car, a brick wall—and turning my emotional pain physical filled me with relief. Or something resembling that but at the moment I wasn't close to feeling okay. Especially when I could still smell him on me, and imagine him pressed against my body alive, his arms encircling me, him breathing, loving me. What choice did I have? I gripped the steering wheel, wrapping my free arm around my belly trying to alleviate my pain and regret. Just then I passed another car emerging from the opposite road. My body went cold as a blinding rage washed over me. It took everything I had left not to whip my car around and follow. She had done this.

Nadja. Her face a mask of hatred and shock as she rushed toward the aiport. Too late.

She stopped the car and got out. In my rearview mirror I saw her falling to the ground in grief. Seeing her mourning the man I loved, who loved me, the one she had sent to his death forced me to place both hands on the steering wheel as I slowed down to a mere crawl.

Why should she be able to live? Why shouldn't she meet her demise with the pistol I'd placed in the glove compartment earlier? The more I thought about the devastation she had set in motion the angrier and more determined I became to avenge Niles's death. She deserved to be shot down like the manipulative dirty dog she had shown herself to be. Maybe I wouldn't need to use my gun. This car had the power to mow her down without me getting my hands dirty.

"Fuck it!" I started to U-turn just as I noticed another car speeding toward the airport. I quickly whipped a U and sped toward the airport. Within seconds the car behind me gunned its engine and sped past me, spinning around in the middle of the road and stopping. Pressing down on the brake I stopped a couple of car lengths from this new barrier. I had no idea who had come after me but they had picked the wrong day. There was nothing more dangerous than a person with nothing to lose and I had lost everything. Once I got rid of them I planned to place one bullet between Nadja's eyes.

I grabbed my piece and exited the car. Slipping around to the rear for a better shot I raised the gun ready to put this motherfucker six feet under.

As a black man exited out the passenger side, I dropped to a knee and lined him up in my sights, ready for whatever. Wearing a suit and dark sunglasses, he moved in my direction.

I picked up on the familiar gait and body language, having seen that pompous-ass swagger one too many times.

"*Orlando?*" I gasped in disbelief as I moved my eye away from the sight. It was hard to believe, but true.

"Orlando!" I yelled as I stood up, dropping my gun and sprinting toward him. I knew for a fact that I was never happier to see that asshole in my life. Then the other car door opened and Rio jumped out, running to join us.

I ran into his arms and collapsed, nothing left to give.

"Easy. Easy," he said, reminding me of Niles's steady assurance so many times over the past week.

"I . . . I killed him, Orlando," I said wearily as my brother just held me. "He was going to kill Daddy."

"It's all right. We know, sis," he assured me. "We've known where you are every step of the way. When you broke your phone, we lost the signal. Thought something had happened to you, so I got here as fast as I could. We just radioed LC that we found you."

"What . . . what do you mean? You knew about Niles?" I asked as I pushed away so as to look my brother in the eye. Rio rushed over to my car and grabbed all my stuff and stowed it in the trunk.

"That's his name?" Orlando asked, flashing a smile as he watched the black smoke still rising from up the road. "Yeah. We got word about the Italians' move and that a hit man outta Europe was gonna come gunning for LC, but weren't sure about his identity. A lot of the info was sketchy. Why do you think we put you up at the hotel in Spain?"

"Are you serious?" I threw out, to which he smiled and nodded.

"And with the way you look, no one would see you coming. Of course, when you started bopping around all over the place, we became worried that maybe our intel was bad. But that hit in London we heard about told us you were probably with him, so we backed off to see how this was gonna play out. My calls nagging you were just my way of checking in. If your boy Niles had made it to the NYC, we had something waiting. But you took care of things, sis. Damn proud of you. Now let's get you outta here before somebody comes nosing around."

"*No!* I have one more thing to do!" I fumed. Nadja had to go down for her part in this tragedy. I walked over and got my gun. Orlando came after me.

"You can't." He opened his palm for me to relinquish my piece but he must have been insane if he thought I would walk away this easily.

"You don't understand. I have to do this." I felt the tears starting to form again.

"Paris, you can't."

"You can't stop me, O. She can't live."

"She's protected. If you kill Nadja there will be an international war and it's one we are not in a position to win. Not yet."

Orlando took the gun from me. He opened the door, exposing one of our bodyguards wielding a rifle. He moved aside to allow me to enter. As they belted me in, I sat there numb and processing what had just been revealed to me. My being in the same place as Niles wasn't a fluke. I was supposed to be Niles's downfall from the moment we met.

Everybody just pieces on a chessboard.

Pawns, really.

As we drove off I turned and could see the black cloud where Niles's plane had been.

"Anything left in that Volvo?" Orlando asked me as we remained there.

"No. I don't think so," I mumbled. Niles had put the spare on this morning.

"If so, it won't be for long," my brother commented.

"You used C4?" Orlando asked, breaking me from my funk.

"Yeah. Remote detonation," I remarked as if reciting from my training.

"You a natural, sis," he commented, sounding oddly proud. Orlando never sounded proud over anything I did.

"Y'all sending me back to school now," I wearily accepted, finally speaking. I was numbed by it all and perhaps welcoming Headmistress Madame Joan Marie's discipline and her thick French accent.

"No, it's time to go home," Orlando spoke.

"Yeah, sis, we're all going home," Rio added.

"Home?" Just the word brought the avalanche of tears cascading down my face. Instead of feeling like a badass assassin I felt like a wounded five-year-old who needed her mother to hug her and assure her that it would all get better.

Rio reached over and undid the seat belt. He pulled me into his arms and let me completely empty out my emotional well all over his shirt. Then something hit me. I leaned up and stared at my twin.

"What about your job?" I couldn't believe Rio had caved.

"Pop is letting me add club ownership to the family business," he bragged, a huge smile on his face.

"Guess a few days at home will be good for me," I said, holding back tears.

"Oh, as far as school is concerned you passed your final exam. Consider yourself graduated." Orlando smiled at me. "Right now you need your family and, Paris, we need you to come home. We need you. It hasn't been the same without you. Too damn quiet and predictable. And if you ever repeat that I said this I will deny it." And suddenly through all the pain and grief I knew that he was right.

"You knew this was gonna happen?"

"I didn't. But Pops did," he finished.

"If there is one thing LC Duncan knows, it's the Family Business." Rio laughed and for the first time I felt relieved to be going home to my family . . . and the family business.